THE FIXER AND THE FUGITIVE

FUGITIVE

(IN PARADISE)

VANESSA GRAY BARTAL

DRY CREEK PRESS

PROLOGUE

She could fit anywhere. *Probably could have won Olympic Gold in gymnastics,* she thought. As if anyone would have enrolled her in that. No one had ever put her in any sort of class, outside of compulsory public school. And she'd missed so many days of that it was nothing short of miraculous she graduated. Probably the teachers had a conference and realized if they didn't pass her they'd have to keep her. Outside of school, she'd taught herself to swim, along with everything else.

Now she used her natural flexibility to shimmy between tiny spaces in the rocks, like a hungry mouse. *Six elite SEALs on standby and I'm the one they send in, only a few months out of basic. Not too shabby.*

She supposed she shouldn't be cocky, but it was becoming harder to accomplish. Basic had been a cakewalk, as had everything since. If not for all the tricky work of relating to other people, she'd probably be recommended for Officer Candidate School. That and her lack of a college degree, or desire to ever procure one. She'd had enough education to last a lifetime, thank you very much. Anything else she had to learn could be acquired the way she'd found everything else: through the school of hard knocks.

One of the SEAL guys gave her the signal, a tiny little sound that was supposed to be like the croaking of a frog. She didn't tell him she'd never heard a frog croak in real life. City kids like her didn't get a lot of nature.

She eased into the opening, darting through narrow passages only big enough for someone her size. If not for the providentially tiny openings, would the SEALs have used her? *Probably not.* She was nothing to them. She saw the way they looked at her, so superior, so dismissive, and wanted to make them pay. And she would, if they had time.

The sound of scuffling feet alerted her to someone's presence. This part of the building was supposed to be empty, but even a few months in the army had been enough time to teach her things rarely went according to plan, especially not in the middle of the desert where tech was spotty at best. Her head whipped back and forth, looking for a spot to hide. There was none. In desperation she looked up and, like a beacon of hope, saw an opening in the ceiling. With a jump worthy of a standing ovation, she leapt, her fingers barely making purchase with the ceiling's crack. And then she was through, fitting herself in the tiny little space like a centipede taking shelter from a harsh storm. All of her contorted around whatever she now shared the ceiling with. Squinting, she leaned closer and sniffed, smiling in delight at what she found. Because, without a doubt, it was exactly what the Navy brats came for. And she, lowly newbie soldier she was, had found it for them.

She was so gleeful she forgot to keep track of her allergies. A sneeze popped out before she could stop it and then a dark face loomed below her, scowling.

Stay and hide or fight it out? A little puff of laughter escaped at the idiocy of her question. When had she ever walked away from a fight? She twisted, lowering her foot onto the guy's face like a boom. He screamed and backed away, clutching his bloody, broken nose.

It was over almost before it could be fun. The SEALs had that effect, swarming the place like ants at a picnic, taking out all the targets while she stood by like, well, like a helpless female. And they were *mad.* That was the worst.

"You weren't supposed to engage," the leader said, whirling on her with a bossiness she didn't appreciate. He might outrank her, but that didn't make him better.

In lieu of an answer, she raised a finger and pointed above her, maintaining eye contact with the SEAL. He followed the line of her point, eyebrows rising interestedly at the crack.

"Is that what I think it is?" he asked, much friendlier now.

Again she refused to speak. Instead she shimmied back into the hole and began dumping all the stuff they'd come for down through it. Drugs. Guns. And information, hard drive upon hard drive of it. She shimmied back down and dusted her pants. "Will that be all, Lieutenant Ridge?"

He gave her a little nod, distracted by the bonanza on the floor. "Thank you for your help, Private. I'll put in a good word with your CO."

She swallowed her snarky reply. It would feel a little too good to give him one, but he was one of the hoity-toity elite. She could tell by the way her commanding officer practically fell all over himself trying to impress him. A little nod was the best she could manage. Her gaze slid over him and landed interestedly to the person behind him, a pretty boy who was smiling at her in a way that was familiar. He was interested. She gave him a little look. He gave her one in return. Unfortunately the Lieutenant caught it and frowned, giving his head a hard shake.

"Ethan, no. We finish this, and we're out. No distractions, no diversions."

With a sigh, Ethan returned his attention to the task at hand, summarily dismissing her. That dismissal made her enraged. It felt too much like every other dismissal in her life. Interestingly, they all came at the hands of some man.

She spun on her boot and fled, trying hard not to stomp like a pouty toddler. *I'll show them,* she thought. She could have anyone, and she would. Nelson had been giving her the eye lately. She'd held off because he was with Tina, the only other woman on this assignment. But desperate times and all that...

She returned to base, ignored everyone who tried to ply her with questions, and made a beeline for Nelson. He was just leaving the shower when she found him. Without a word, she ushered him back inside.

An hour later, Tina found her. Normally she could take Tina easily. Despite the fact that Tina was bigger, she was a better—and meaner—fighter. But Tina waited until she was asleep. It was almost a fair fight, almost. Tina said all the ugly things women always said when they learned what she'd done. Strangely they always blamed her instead of their philandering significant other. Oh, well. She'd take it. It wasn't as if she'd ever had female friends.

The MP's arrived and tried to break up the fight, but it was too far gone. And because it was her third such fight since the assignment began, she was the one they dragged to the brig. She thought she'd cool her heels for a while and they'd let her out. She should have known her life never worked out that well. But even she was shocked when they came for her and led her to the CO's tent.

She readied her defense against her CO. Rather, she readied her defensiveness. It would be hard for him to discipline her, given what she had on him. Namely their time together with him in Nelson's place. He might deny it, but she had proof, backup just in case. It wasn't her first time. She played for keeps; it was better people knew that up front.

When she entered the tent and saw The Colonel sitting still and silent, watching her, all her defensiveness fled. She'd never seen him in real life, of course. But she'd heard the rumors, the whispers. He was a legend, so much that she'd started to doubt he was real. He must be something the army told all newbies to scare and impress them. *This is what you should aim for, and this is what you should hope you never encounter.*

Tina must be related to him. That was the only explanation. The army was filled with such blatant nepotism. It made her sick. For that reason she skipped the requisite salute and slouched into the chair opposite from him, uninvited. He didn't comment, and she was strangely disappointed by that.

For a while, they stared at each other in silence. He was expressionless, so much it was eerie, like staring at a robot. She remained mutinous, arms crossed tightly over her chest. When he finally spoke, it was so unexpected she couldn't help but jump a little, then cursed herself for the show of weakness.

"Why did you join the army?"

Even his voice sounded tough, especially for an old dude.

"Army or jail," she answered, after running the list of scenarios and deciding nothing could be gained by stubborn silence.

"Why did you think the army would be better?" he asked.

No one had ever asked her that before. She looked away before she answered. "Maybe I wanted to break the family legacy." Both her parents had been in jail at one point and might be again for all she knew. It wasn't as if they'd ever been real parents, the kind who cared about her and kept in contact. Based on her memories of them, jail was a much better place than imagining them let loose on the streets to cause havoc.

"You graduated high school despite missing a hundred days your senior year."

She blinked at him, realizing for the first time she had no idea what this was. The thought made her uncomfortable. She had spent so long at the mercy of the system, she'd learned all its ways. Wrong behavior equaled punishment at the hands of the higher ups. He was the highest of the higher ups, but this didn't feel like a punishment, at least not so far. She shifted slightly and uncrossed her arms. "Yes," she said, because what else could she say? It wasn't like school had been hard. If she'd been able to attend, hadn't been shunted from home to home by the state, maybe she would have been like one of the nerds she used to torment. As it was she'd been able to show up and pass all the tests, without ever having done the reading or requisite homework.

"You were the best marksman in basic."

"Not so hard to accomplish," she said and squinted. Did his cheek flick upward with amusement, or was that her imagination?

"Not only in your unit, but out of everyone in basic that entire year," he added, and now it was her turn to flinch. No one had told her that, of course. Probably hadn't wanted to make her cocky. Rather, cockier.

The Colonel leaned back, eyes boring into her with rapid assessment. "In fact, you're a pretty good soldier."

"Thank you," she said slowly. Was he hitting on her? He was old. She was too far gone to be grossed out by that. Instead her mind went to all the ways he might help her. If she got dirt on him, with proof, it would be like gold in her pocket. She softened her expression and leaned forward, smiling a little as her hand eased closer to his on the table. "What can I do for you, Colonel?"

His expression didn't change, but somehow the air in the room became colder. He took a breath, held it, and let it out slowly, silently. "It's more a question of what I can do for you, Private."

Her smile deepened. Her hand inched closer to his, but somehow she couldn't bridge the last centimeter, couldn't make herself touch him. It was as if there was some sort of invisible force field around him, stopping her advances. It bugged her, settled next to her heart and poked in a way that made her squirmy. Why, though? She'd been with old men, powerful men, all the men she wanted, and some she didn't. This was an old game, nothing new. What felt different in this moment?

The Colonel tipped his head slightly and she had the uncomfortable feeling he could read her thoughts. She squirmed again, fighting the urge to pull back and cross her arms protectively again. It was a while before he spoke again. She had the sense he had weighed his words, sifted them so they'd be perfect.

"Sit up, Private, and put your hands in your lap. Wipe that smirk off your face. I have a wife at home and daughters your age. I do not want what you are pedaling. Let's get that clear up front so there will be no misunderstanding. Are we clear?"

"Yes, sir," she said and realized as she did so that she was now sitting at attention, hands in her lap, completely incognizant of how she'd gotten that way. Did her body obey him without her consent? She didn't like that, didn't like it at all. And yet she couldn't seem to undo it. It was as if he'd cast a spell and bound her. All she could do now was listen.

He rested his hands on the table. "You're going to leave this assignment and work for me. You'll receive special training and then further instructions. I'll send you where, I'll tell you when. But if you ever try a stunt like you tried here today, your time in the army will be over. You will find yourself buried in misery so deep, you will never recover. Clear, Private?"

"Yes, sir," she said, voice unrecognizably meek and tremulous.

He might have relaxed slightly, it was hard to tell. He took another of those deep breaths and eventually spoke again. "I'm privy to all the details of your life, even the ones you think you've kept hidden."

She blanched. The things she'd tried to keep hidden were so numerous it was difficult to pick which was the most mortifying. Her face felt red, eyes teary. When he spoke in a softer tone, it was nearly her undoing.

"This is your chance to start afresh, Private. But you need to make a clean break of it. You think you're using these men, but you have it backwards. They're using you. Enough of this. Be a better woman, soldier."

She swallowed, with difficulty, past a hard lump. Anger, hurt, or embarrassment? She didn't know. Maybe all three. She gave a little nod, it was all she could do.

The Colonel gave her what might have been a smile and, if she didn't know better, might be something like approval. He knocked on the table between them. "Pack your things. Your new life begins now."

CHAPTER 1

She stood in the rain for what might have been hours, not bothering to check her watch. Previously the watch had meant a lot to her, had meant everything. A six hundred dollar Swiss diving watch wasn't something to take lightly. But now she didn't think of it as she stood perfectly still, waiting and watching. It was raining, a fact she only vaguely registered. She was probably soaked, maybe shivering. She didn't care.

The man emerged from the building at last and she made her move, stealthy enough to be a shadow, slipping so close behind him it gave her a small thrill, even in the midst of such misery. How many people had gotten that close? Not many.

He prickled with awareness and straightened, alerting his driver who tossed her against the car, his arm at her throat.

"Drop it," the first man said in the tone of someone telling an errant puppy to let go of a stolen sock. The driver did so immediately, trained to act on orders like a seal waiting for a fishy reward. He stepped back. The two men regarded her together.

"In the car," her target said.

The driver opened the door for them both. They slid inside, waiting to speak until the driver closed the door.

The Colonel stared at her, waiting her out while she shivered and dripped all over his fancy leather seat. "I'm ready to come inside," she said, voice soft but firm.

He regarded her in that way he had, that way only he could. It was at once comforting and terrifying. "All right."

She blinked at him, trying not to reveal her shock. She'd expected to have to fight for it, to lay out all the reasons she was done. She should have known better, though. The Colonel had never acted the way she thought he would. For that she was forever grateful.

"Where are you going to go?" he asked.

She blew out a breath. "I have no idea." This was the tricky part of the plan. Some people prepped for the end, longed for it, spent all their lives living for that day. She hadn't. She had been happy to be where she was until all of a sudden she wasn't, and now what?

"I know a place," The Colonel said.

Only years of training and acquaintance kept her from the inane response. *You do?* He hated stuff like that. She sealed her lips together and waited him out.

"How do you feel about small towns and country living?" The Colonel asked. By now she recognized the hints of amusement in his tone.

"About as well as you'd expect," she said.

He chuckled and somehow the sound was more terrifying than silence. "A person in your unique situation needs somewhere unique to settle, somewhere rural with a lot of space, somewhere not on the map."

"Does such a place exist?" she asked. She'd been a lot of places, all of them on the map and teeming with people.

"You'll love it," he said in a tone that told her she'd likely hate it. His eyes almost crinkled when he spoke again. "It's Paradise."

CHAPTER 2

Tony Dalton had never made it down the street without being stopped. It happened so often he'd long ago started calculating the extra time into his route. Seemingly every time someone saw him, they needed a word about something. And because they couldn't jump right in with their own selfish requests, they started with him. *How is Elena? How is Elliot? How is Missy? How are the girls? How's the shop? How's your...mother?* Once the niceties were over, they could finally say what they needed to say. *Last year the snowplow dumped twelve feet of snow in front of my driveway. Took me three weeks to dig myself out. You ought to talk to them about that.* Or, *Now, far be it for me to gossip, but my sister in Ontario mailed me some maple cookies and they arrived half-eaten. You know Jody at the post office loves maple, can sniff it like a tracker hound. I'm not making an accusation, I'm saying it's awfully suspicious. If it happens again, I'm smelling her breath.*

He had never been elected mayor of the town. Try telling that to the town. Somehow everyone assumed he ran things. The truth? He kind of did. Mostly because he was that sort of person, the nosy sort with his finger in every pie.

So now, after making pointed small talk with every person on Main Street, he finally arrived at his destination. He opened the door to his wife's shop, smiling when the bell jangled merrily. Her business partner, and one of Tony's best friends, was also in the shop today, a pleasant two-for-one coincidence when he had juicy gossip to spill.

"Hello," Tony said, his heart doing the flippy-flop thing at the sight of his wife. No matter that they'd been together forever, first as friends, the sight of her still made him happy, still made his heart flood with love. Her return smile said she felt the same as she leaned over the counter and kissed him. "Mrs. Montgomery," he added, nodding at Maybe as she regarded him in amusement. Though they'd been married for nearly a decade now, she never got over her joy at seeing him and Elena finally together.

"'Sup," she said, tossing him a nod.

"Apparently you're not aware they recently changed the law. It's now illegal to use rapper language after you become a grandmother," Tony informed her.

"It's because I'm a grandma I'm talking like this. Kept the kids last night. So sleepy." She scrubbed a hand over her face. "I think Baird faked working cattle to go on the range somewhere and sleep. Seriously forgot how exhausting babies are."

"The memory is fresh for us," Tony said, shuddering. Their twin girls were three, young enough that they still occasionally had the rough sleepless night.

"So, what brings you?" Elena said, rubbing her hands together expectantly.

"Can't I come to see my favorite girl? And one of our favorite people?" He encompassed Maybe in his look. Both women remained staring at him, waiting. He grinned. "Someone new moved to town. You'll never guess where."

"Jones Orchard," Elena guessed.

His face fell. "How did you guess?"

"Because it's been for sale for the last fifteen years. Statistically someone had to buy it eventually."

"You're no fun," he pouted.

She leaned over the desk and whispered something in his ear, changing his frown to a smile. "Point taken, mind changed."

Maybe raised her hand. "Hi, outsider here. I have no idea what Jones Orchard is. We have an orchard here? Why is this not common knowledge? Or, wait, are you talking about that abandoned farm on the edge of town, the one with all the gnarled trees? "

"It hasn't been an orchard since we were kids. The Jones family settled here eons ago and passed it down and then sort of died out. I'm guessing most of the trees died, too. The property has to be in rough shape, along with the house," Elena said.

Maybe grimaced. "It's not another rich person from California, is it?" The wealthy from the coast had become a scourge, buying up cheap land and creating demand that made it ridiculously expensive, far out of reach for most people. Baird had become so tired of strangers showing up and offering to buy the ranch from under him that he'd put up a "Trespassers Will Be Shot" sign. Maybe wasn't certain it had actually helped deter people, but it at least alleviated a bit of Baird's annoyance.

"Look at you, talking like a local," Tony said proudly. He folded into the cushy chair across from Elena's counter, one she'd kept specifically for him the last fifteen years. He'd sat in it so often the sag in the middle conformed to his backside. "I have no idea who it is. Some woman."

They blinked at him, processing. "A woman? Alone? All the way out there? Is she some kind of trapper?" Elena asked. There were a few trappers who still lived far afield and kept to themselves, hunting mink and fox pelts to sell to foreign markets where there was still a demand. Some of them were women who were unusual, to say the least. Hale, hardy, and eccentric didn't even begin to describe. Heaven help the man who ran afoul of one of them in a temper.

Tony shrugged. "Don't think so. I've been waiting for her to come to town so I can politely ogle and discern, but so far she hasn't. No idea what's she's doing for supplies."

Maybe clapped her hands excitedly together. "Can you imagine if she gets the orchard going again? Wouldn't that be amazing? Fresh apples and cider. Apple picking, apple dumplings."

"Now you sound like a grandma," Tony said, pointing his finger at her like a gun.

She wadded a piece of paper and tossed it at him, pinging it off his temple. "Think of what it could do for the community. What an amazing draw that would be."

"We don't need any more draws. Too many city people are getting the wrong idea and trying to settle here, completely misjudging how harsh it is," Elena said with uncharacteristic disdain. "I hope she at least has some sense of what she's doing in those backwoods. Otherwise things could go very, very poorly for her."

"I'm sure she does," Tony said smoothly. "It's hard to imagine any woman who isn't capable packing up and moving to Montana, completely ignorant of our ways with no plan on how to take care of herself." He darted Maybe a conspicuous look, then faked a cough. "Oh, right. Sorry, Maybe."

"I knew what I was doing," Maybe argued.

"You knew you were ensnaring a big, strong cowboy?" Elena guessed.

Now it was her turn to be pinged by one of Maybe's rolled up papers. "I had a plan."

"To marry the neighbor?" Tony piled on.

"I hate both of you," Maybe said. Her gaze landed on the giant diamond on her ring finger. "Although I guess all's well that ends well. Hopefully the new woman will be as lucky."

"I bet she has a plan," Elena said.

"She totally knows what she's doing," Tony added.

They stared at each other a few beats in silence before Maybe spoke again. "Should we send Elliot to go check on her?"

"I already gave him her name and address," Tony said and the three friends high fived.

CHAPTER 3

She had no idea what she was doing. None whatsoever. She sat on the cold, hard ground, willing it to do something, anything other than remain dirt. Were the trees in front of her dead? She had no idea. Did she want them to be? Again, no idea. Her glance slid to the house, feeling similar dread and dismay. She'd paid a tidy sum to make it livable, had brought in a plumber and electrician to bring things up to code and make them habitable. Somehow she thought that would make the place a home. It hadn't, of course, and she had no idea what to do next.

Everything in her life she had learned by doing. First she had survived her hardscrabble childhood, no easy feat. Then basic training. Then assassin training. Then being an assassin. And now phase three. After overcoming everything else, she'd been under the mistakenly optimistic impression she'd somehow know what to do. From far away in DC while tying up the loose ends of her former life, it had seemed so easy. Buy an orchard. Fix it up. Become country, at one with the earth. What she failed to take into account was that she had never so much as owned a houseplant, let alone an entire field of trees. And the house. She'd never lived in one before, at least not one like this, with two stories and a spacious layout. The vastness made her feel strangely stifled and adrift, insecure about all the things she didn't know, all the things she lacked to fill the space. Worse, she had no one to teach her.

In basic, she'd had drill instructors. After, she'd had her CO. And then The Colonel. He'd instructed her, guided her, mentored her. Their relationship had always been professional. Even so, he was the closest thing to a father she'd ever had. And now she was on her own in the middle of Montana with no idea what to do next.

A sound alerted her to someone's imminent arrival. Palming her gun, she turned her head toward the long driveway and waited. *They found you. They're coming.* It would have to be a hostile. Who else? She knew no one here. There was no reason for a random stranger to show up uninvited. Except there was.

A massive forest green truck, the word DEPUTY painted in school bus yellow letters on the side, made the long drive slowly, as if he was as wary as she was. *Maybe he does know about you but he's not here to kill you; maybe he's here to arrest you.* Slowly, she stood and tucked her gun away, stumbling forward and working her jaw, reminding it how to speak. Soon she would need all the words she'd shelved four days ago when she arrived.

The man parked and unfolded himself from his truck, literally. He was tall, far taller than most men she'd met. He wore an eye patch, one that covered a ragged scar that somehow put her at ease. *IED. Army. Familiar. Safe.* Her shoulders relaxed as she let out a breath. He raised a hand in greeting and she followed suit.

"Good afternoon," he called.

"Hello," she said.

"My name is Elliot Runningbear. I'm what amounts to the law in these parts, I suppose."

That made her smile, if only a little. "You're not sure?"

"I'm certain I'm the law, I'm not sure there's much need for it. We like to keep it quiet out here." There was a question in the tone, one asking if she was the type who also liked to be quiet or if she planned on making trouble.

"A good policy," she answered reasonably. Once upon a time she'd hated the law, had found herself too often on the wrong side of it. Life had a funny way of making corrections.

"I didn't catch your name," he said pointedly.

"I didn't give it," she returned, but not unkindly. Her life had made her factual and no-nonsense. It was no longer in her nature to pussy-foot. Maybe it never had been; she could no longer remember. "I'm Celeste."

"What brings you to Paradise?"

"Retirement."

His brows rose, assessing her age and—rightly—thinking she looked young to be retired. She was, but assassins had their own time-line. Instead of remarking on her age, he gazed out over the orchard. "It's funny, I've lived here my whole life and never been here, even thought my parents told me a lot of stories about it." He motioned a hand toward the decrepit barn. "Any plans to bring it back to life?"

She also gazed at the barn and repressed a sigh. All of the equipment was still there; it had come with the house. "Would that I knew how."

"Ah. Well, I'm sure you'll get lots of advice around town. Whether you'll find it helpful or not is up to you."

"I'm not much of a townie," she said, an understatement. She planned on being Unabomber levels of unavailable to the local populace. It was sort of the whole point of moving here.

Elliot snickered and coughed when her glance slid questioningly back to him. "Sorry. It's just…Paradise might have other ideas about that."

"I don't think it's up to them," she said.

His smile was definitely wry this time. "If you figure out how to stop them, tell me how." He touched the brim of his cap—an actual cowboy hat—and gave her a little nod. "It was nice to meet you, Celeste. I'm sure I'll see you again sometime. Feel free to call if you need anything or have questions."

She didn't reiterate that she would neither need anything nor have questions. No need to further his amusement at her expense. When she failed to show up in town, he'd soon figure out that she wanted to be left alone. And so would the rest of the town. "Thank you," she forced herself to say. Polite manners were another thing she'd had to teach herself, in order to function in society. They were another way to blend in. People noticed abrupt rudeness much more than niceness, at least in America.

After Elliot drove away, Celeste meandered to the barn, staring around with something that felt a bit like panic. There were machines and equipment she couldn't begin to name. At first she'd been excited; it had seemed like a bonanza. But then as she tried each piece of machinery and failed to make it go, her enthusiasm dimmed. Then began to turn to a bit of despair. Should she sell it? Could she sell it when nothing worked?

She walked to each piece, attempting again to turn it on, in case some magic had happened between the last time and now. As before, nothing worked. Her last stop was the giant tractor. She climbed atop it and turned the key. It made no sound, not even the semblance of turning over. She remained sitting a few moments, imagining that it worked, that she drove it out of the barn and attempted to use it.

I am country now, she told herself, but the words wouldn't stick. They slid off her and splattered uselessly to the ground. She was not country. She was not an assassin any longer, was no longer even in the army. What was she? She was afraid to find the answer, afraid it might be the same as before The Colonel pulled her out of obscurity. Afraid she had gone back to the same nothing trash heap she started from.

CHAPTER 4

She would have to leave for supplies. There was nothing for it. While she'd hoped to have everything delivered, thereby saving her the pain of human interaction, she found it nearly impossible. Only after she ordered her fourth box of canned food—and failed to have it delivered—did she learn there were two Paradise, Montanas. One was on the map. Hers wasn't. Delivery companies scratched their heads when she gave them her location. Not even Google Maps had heard of her whereabouts.

She sat in her shiny SUV for fifteen full minutes before she could garner the courage to start the car and drive it. *I'm going to town,* she pep talked herself. *Groceries, that's all. In and out. I've gotten groceries a hundred times. No one will notice my presence. I don't have to talk to a soul.*

On the way to the town's lone market she spotted the library and, before she knew what she was going to do, pulled into a parking spot. *I am at the library. What is happening?* In Celeste's pre-assassin life, she would have beaten herself up for even considering a stop at the library. But her new role as plant ambassador left her feeling a bit desperate. Maybe they had books on trees. Maybe those books would give her some clue what she should do with them.

In any case, she was curious about the adorably tiny little building, so little it looked like a miniature library, like it should go with an adjoining dollhouse. Before she could talk herself out of it, she unbuckled and hopped from the SUV, resisting the urge to roll her shoulders and take a look around. *No competition here, no one gunning for you. You're safe.* Still, she'd feel better once she was inside and not so exposed. She opened the door, took a step toward the rows of books, and that was when she heard it.

"Psst, New Girl." Someone was whispering at her. She spun and saw one of the most handsome men she had ever encountered in real life, all six feet blond hair and blue eyes of him. He was smiling cordially. At her. He raised his hand and added a friendly wave. "I'm Tony, Elliot's dad."

She did a site-gag-double-take worthy of a Bugs Bunny cartoon. "Holy geez, you must be joking. Did you have him when you were five?" There was no way this guy had a son as old as Elliot had seemed.

"Seventeen. Stay in school, kids. Although I actually did, because I basically abandoned his mom and left her high and dry a couple of decades before I got my act together."

Celeste blinked at him.

"I'm spewing a lot of deeply personal information at you, huh?"

She nodded.

"Care to return the favor?" he asked, somewhat hopefully, she thought.

She shook her head.

"Probably a good call." He cupped his hands around his mouth and added a loudly whispered aside. "I'm the town gossip."

She continued to stare at him, uncertain how to make a safe and speedy exit.

"This is where you back away slowly," he added helpfully, fluttering his fingers at her in a "shoo" motion.

No one had to tell her twice. She back stepped a few times until she was swallowed by the stacks. And then she faced a new problem: she had no idea how to locate anything in a library. It was likely they'd tried to teach her once or twice in school, but she definitely hadn't paid attention. She stared at the tidy rows of books, tilting her head to read some of the spines. How hard would it be to find a few books about fruit?

"Oh, hi."

Repressing a sigh, she turned toward the friendly female voice to her left.

"You're the new girl. Oh, my goodness, so adorable."

The woman who spoke was fairly adorable, too, with blond hair, sparkly aqua eyes, and honest to goodness dimples. She looked older than Celeste, so homogenously older that Celeste couldn't calculate her true age. Older but well preserved in that middle-aged wealthy white woman way that spoke of serums and face oils. "I'm Maybe Montgomery."

Celeste quirked an eyebrow at her. "Maybe. You're not certain?"

"I'm definitely Maybe. It's short for Maybelle, but tell anyone and I'll kill you."

"I highly doubt that," Celeste said, making sure to keep her tone even.

"Do you like beef?"

Celeste blinked at her with no idea how to answer. It was, hands down, the first time someone had ever asked her for a meat preference.

"If not, you'd better or they'll find you."

Celeste tensed. "Who?"

"The cowboys. Oh, I'll give you a list."

"What list?" A hit list? Certainly they couldn't know her proclivities.

"A list of which ones are datable and which ones to avoid. Here's a hint." She cupped her hands around her mouth and spoke in a loudly whispered aside, exactly as Tony had done. Celeste wondered if it was a bit they'd tag-teamed. "If the teeth are black, take a step back."

Celeste blinked at her, wondering how best to make her disappear. "Beef good, black teeth bad. Got it."

She must have because Maybe beamed at her. "You're all caught up. Welcome to Paradise. If you need anything, don't hesitate to ask."

Her glance fell to the shelves of books. "Were you hoping to check something out?"

"Yes?" Celeste said, but it came out like a question.

"Did you bring mail?"

"What?" Was this woman on crack? Was the entire town insane? All signs pointed to yes so far.

"Mail," Maybe reiterated. "They won't let you get a library card without mail to confirm your identity. But, hey, use mine. Just tell them Maybe said you could."

"They won't let me get a card, but they'll let me use yours?"

"Sure, they know me." She glanced at her watch. "Oh, no. I was supposed to pick up my granddaughter from *Twinkle Toes.*"

"This town has a dance studio?" Celeste blurted.

"Lassoing school," Maybe explained. "The twinkle toes designate the lassoed calf." She raised her two hands, mimicking hooves, pawing them in the air. "Twinkle, twinkle, moo, moo, moo."

Celeste blinked at her, unable to fathom a hasty reply. "You look freakishly young to be a grandma."

"Had her mom when I was eighteen," Maybe explained.

"Is that a prerequisite in this town?"

"I'm not a local. I'm adopted, like you."

Before Celeste could contradict and say she was absolutely nothing to the town, nor would she ever be, Maybe began walking backwards, still talking. "Make sure and stop by the store. Elena can design your house, she's chomping at the bit."

And then she was gone, leaving Celeste by herself in stunned dismay. "Who is Elena?" she muttered.

"Tony's wife," someone in the next stack answered, though she had clearly been talking to herself.

Following Maybe's lead, she backstepped out of the library and bumped into a man, a cowboy, she realized when she spun to face him.

He lifted his hat and spoke politely, giving her *the look.* He wasn't bad to gaze at, and he was definitely large and well muscled. But then he spoke. "Ma'am." Celeste stared at his teeth. The four in front were blackened by tobacco juice stains. She took a step back.

He scowled and slammed his hat on his head. "Think I'll be having a word with Maybe Montgomery," he muttered and stormed off.

Celeste backed all the way to her truck, locking the door once she was safely inside.

CHAPTER 5

She arrived at the market and took a wary look around, making certain no insane local would accost her. Satisfied that she was alone, she hopped out and locked the door.

"You don't have to do that here."

Celeste closed her eyes and let out an aggrieved sigh. When she opened her eyes again, she saw yet another handsome man smiling down at her. At this point there seemed to be so many of them she was beginning to wonder if the town was some kind of experimental wasteland. Had they put things in the food and water to make men turn out this way? So handsome, debonair, and charming. First Elliot, then his father, Tony, and now this unknown man with perfectly sculpted wavy brown hair and a wide smile. Her gaze focused on the teeth, ready to back away if they were black. They weren't, though. They were almost phosphorescently pearly and white. Were they real? Her finger itched to poke them and find out. Belatedly she realized she hadn't spoken.

"What?"

"The door, you don't have to lock it. I realize it's a hard habit to break, but the only danger here is from bears in search of food. And the locks don't slow them down much. They use hangers to bypass them."

She blinked at him.

He blinked in return. "That was a joke. You can laugh."

"Ha."

He sighed and gave his head a little self-deprecating shake that did nothing to alter the state of his helmet hair. Exactly how much putty and or hairspray was this guy wearing? And why? "Okay, look, let's address the elephant in the room."

She made a show of looking around. "We're outside."

"The figurative elephant. Yes, I am considerably famous. No, I am not a snob. Yes, I will sign an autograph for your 'friend.'" He actually used air quotes when he said that.

Celeste glanced behind him to make certain no one was chasing him with a giant net. "Are you hitting on me?"

He blanched. "What? No, of course not. I'm happily married, everyone knows that. I have four kids." Here he dabbed his sleeve against his forehead.

"My condolences," Celeste replied.

He lowered his arm and scowled at her. "Don't do that."

"Do what?" she asked, genuinely puzzled. What was she doing? Nothing but searching for an escape hatch out of this conversation, out of this town.

"Don't be one of those women who pretends children are awful. Children are life's greatest blessing. I would have a million of them, if Chloe would consent."

She presumed Chloe was his wife. Her arms crossed over herself in challenge. "Apparently Chloe doesn't believe they're so great."

"She does. She loves our brood, it's just…"

"Just what?" she prodded with no idea why. How was she standing in the middle of a parking lot talking reproduction with this weird stranger?

"She says women aren't designed to be water sprinklers, spitting out a new baby every few months."

"I like her already," Celeste declared.

"You definitely would, once she warms up to you. She's shy. Also crazy busy because, you know, four children. Do you really not know me?"

Celeste pressed herself against her SUV with prickles of alarm. "Have we met?" A better question would be did *he* know her? Had The Colonel told anyone who she was or why she was here? Was this where he deposited people after he was done with them? Was the entire town populated with former assassins? That would explain a whole lot about the populace's shaky mental wellbeing.

The man in front of her stared in shock, mouth agape. "You're serious. You have no idea who I am."

"The town lunatic? When it rains, do you take off your pants and play tambourine at the airport?" she guessed.

Instead of being insulted, he stepped forward and hugged her, very briefly until she squirmed and shoved him away. "You're the one I've been searching for," he whispered.

"So creepy," she said, wrenching free of his embrace with another shove for good measure. Far from being offended, he was now beaming at her.

"This is incredible. Wait until I tell Chloe."

"Tell her what? That you hit on me, told me I should have babies, and then hugged me? Exactly how understanding is your wife?"

"She's going to love this," he muttered, ignoring everything else she said. Maybe there was no Chloe. Maybe he really was crazy, in which case she should probably feel bad for making fun of him. Once again Celeste's gaze traveled the horizon. Was this some sort of post-army wasteland? A place The Colonel used to stash all his difficult and anti-social operatives? She was really beginning to think it might be possible, especially when she looked forward again and realized the mystery guy was gone, had disappeared entirely as if he never existed. Maybe he hadn't. Maybe her imagination was already playing tricks on her after so many days isolated at her orchard.

Cautiously, she made her way into the market. People stared, but no one else accosted her. She was able to load her cart with everything she'd need for a week—maybe two, if she worked hard to make it last. She loaded the items in the truck and headed for home when her stomach began to growl. Loudly. Lately she'd been subsisting on dry cereal and coffee and it wasn't enough. She needed food, real food. And since she still had no idea how to cook, the thought of all the frozen meals she'd bought left her wanting.

Without allowing herself to overthink it, she turned and headed toward the diner she'd spotted at the edge of town. The lot was loaded with cars, so much that they overflowed into a nearby lot. Not that it meant much in a town where there was nothing else. But so many years in the army and traveling the world had taught her to care more about sustenance than taste. As long as it had calories and some redeeming nutritional value, she'd be satisfied.

Once again she parked and took a few breaths, gearing herself up to go inside and face the townspeople. It didn't seem to matter how standoffish she looked or seemed. They talked to her anyway, and about bizarre, random things. She would have to change tactics and become blasé, so boring and vanilla she failed to arouse their curiosity. Mentally she prepped a few phrases to break out, bland things that wouldn't invite further speculation. *I retired from the army and moved here from DC.* How could anyone want to know more after that? As far as Paradise was concerned, there was absolutely nothing special about her, outside the fact that she was new.

Having never lived in a small town before, she vastly underestimated how fascinating "new" was to the people who lived there.

CHAPTER 6

Every single person in the entire diner stopped what they were doing and turned their laser focus on Celeste. She wasn't shy, but she had been taught to be wary, to blend in, to try and disappear. So to be in the spotlight now was so uncomfortable she momentarily froze, one foot in the air like a startled doe.

And then it was as if someone passed the memo at the same time to resume normal activity and ignore her. Because that was what everyone did at once. Eyes dropped, forks picked up, chatter resumed.

"There's an empty booth. Feel free to take it," a disembodied voice said from somewhere inside. Celeste didn't try to figure out where. Relieved, she sank into the booth and picked up a menu, inhaling deeply. At least it smelled promising. A short time later a waitress appeared at the end of the table, tall and willowy with a baby resting on one hip.

"Hello, and welcome to Paradise. My name is Avery. Have you had time to decide what you'd like or do you need longer?"

She seemed so sweet, so utterly normal after the nonsensical morning that Celeste relaxed and even managed a smile. "Are you eighteen?" It seemed to be the town commandment to be a teenage mother.

"Yes, plus a lot." Avery hadn't seemed to find the question odd. In any case, she was still smiling.

"I thought it was in the town charter that you had to be a teenage parent. I've encountered a few of those today."

"Oh, I am a mother, and I was much past my teens, but this one's not mine. I borrowed her from the Reeds." She turned to nod at a couple in the corner and Celeste flinched. There sat the plastic-haired-pearlescent-toothed man from the grocery parking lot, along with a stunningly beautiful blond. He waved frantically at Celeste and pointed to the woman beside him mouthing, *This is Chloe!*

"Uh, huh," Celeste said. "Is he delusional?"

"Who, Fletcher?" They turned to survey him in time to see him holding his bicep aloft while his wife poked it and shook her head. "Yes."

"Right. What do you recommend, Avery?"

"Beef," Avery said. "In any form, beef will make a good first impression."

Since she was the second person to recommend beef, Celeste didn't argue. She chose the pot roast and handed Avery her menu.

"I'll grab a water and be right back," Avery said. Celeste watched as she handed the baby back to the Reeds, guessing she took it in the first place so they could free their hands to eat. After depositing the baby she walked to the counter where a ridiculously handsome man handed her a plate with a smile. She delivered the plate and brought Celeste her water.

"What is up with the men in this town?" Celeste asked her.

"What do you mean?" Avery asked.

Celeste waved her hand toward the diner, encompassing Fletcher and the man behind the counter who, if the way his eyes followed Avery was any indication, was somehow attached to her. "You don't find it unnatural how pretty they are?"

"Oh, that. You get used to it."

"Really?" Celeste asked.

"No, but it definitely helps to have something nice to look at during the long winters."

Celeste snorted a laugh, causing Avery to smile and several people to turn their heads and gawk again. She smoothed her expression and picked up her straw wrapper as Avery wandered away, retrieving dirty dishes from the table next door.

She finished her meal in surprising silence. No one accosted her and, if her senses were to be believed, no one gawked at her. Avery stopped by a few times to check on her and refill her water. She was friendly, but not in a prying way. Celeste left her a good tip and began the long drive home.

It would be easy to zone out here, to become too comfortable with the long silent drive. Celeste smacked her cheek a couple of times to stay with it, to remain alert. In her previous line of work, complacency ended in disaster and often death. Situational awareness was something she could never lose touch with, even here in the middle of nowhere. Safety was an illusion. It was something her childhood taught her early and her career confirmed again and again. Nowhere was ever completely safe. She had to remain alert and on guard, even here in the boonies.

To help with brain fatigue she turned on the radio, grimacing when a country song blared. So far the only music she'd been able to find was country. It wasn't that Celeste had particular tastes in music. Maybe she enjoyed country, she had no idea. She'd never been in one place long enough to listen to any one thing. But so far the twang grated on her nerves. She knew enough about the genre to understand not everyone who sang it hailed from Nashville, nor even the south. Wasn't it sort of hypocritical to sing about the woes of rural American life when you were from Australia? Nonetheless it was country or nothing so she left it on, using it as a diversion against brain fog.

She arrived home, took out her gun, and swept the house. Everything felt normal when she opened the door, but she had learned not to ignore her routine in favor of her gut. Her life worked best when the two things went together, a balance between training and instinct. Things might feel okay, but she couldn't be certain until she performed her nightly inspection, checking each room and closet for intruders.

Once that was completed, she sat on the couch and picked up her pen. So far the evenings had been the biggest source of angst in her new life. She had never watched television. When she was a child, it had belonged to whichever grownup was currently in charge. She had found other things to do in order to avoid said grownup. As an adult, she'd been too busy traveling the world, doing her job, to indulge in mindless entertainment. She had never been a reader, either. She'd actually tried, the first week of her retirement. She went to a store and bought an assortment of fiction books from the recommended display. She got as far as the first three pages with each. For some reason her brain wouldn't calm down and engage. She'd found her mind wandering to places it didn't want it to go. Somehow, in an effort to avoid all the things she didn't want to remember, she had decided to consciously make herself remember. And so she started to journal.

At first she'd felt like an idiot, like one of those self-involved twenty somethings on social media who believed the entire world should be treated to their untested grand insights. The difference in this case was that she knew for certain she had zero grand insights. And she would rather die than have anyone read what she wrote. This was, to her, a way to try to understand all the ways her life had gone wrong, from the very beginning. Though only a few months in, she was already nearing the end of her third journal. Coincidentally she had reached third grade. She paused, pen held aloft.

Third grade was the year she met Sasha. They sat across from each other at the lunch table on day one. Celeste prepared to eat whatever free meal the school provided for kids like her. Up to that moment she believed everyone ate the same thing. And then Sasha opened her Minnie Mouse lunch box, removed a little metal tin, and began unearthing an assortment of the most beautiful food Celeste had ever seen. Fruit cut into the shape of stars. Cheese cut into little crescents. Homemade crackers cut into circles. On top of the food was a note. *I love you to the moon and stars! Mom.* Celeste knew what the note said because she stole it, stuffed it into her pocket, and took it out that night when she went to bed. She had stared at the note seemingly for hours, pondering. Had Sasha's mother really made her that food? Was that a thing mothers did? She found no answers that night, but she tucked the note under her pillow, feeling a strange mix of yearning and anger. She wanted what Sasha had and felt angry over the lack.

That was the first inkling Celeste had that she was different from other kids. And it was the first time she began to resent them for the difference. In the beginning she and Sasha were friends. The girl was a source of fascination for Celeste in all the ways, from the clean, good smelling, and matching clothes to her hair that was always properly combed and arranged into some interesting updo. Heart braids for Valentine's Day. Shamrock braids for St. Patrick's. Their friendship was a glimpse into another world, one that felt like a fantasy. Sasha had her over a few times and Celeste couldn't get over her awe. They ate supper together at a kitchen table. And her mother *cooked*. The family held hands and prayed before the meal began. Sasha had her own room with her own toys. Her clothes were in her closet. She had sheets on a bed with no bugs. Trash went into the trashcan. Their car didn't make a rumbling noise, had no apparent rust. It always felt a bit like she'd stumbled onto the set of some movie and was merely paid to stand in the background and observe.

The friendship lasted until fifth grade. By that time anger had overtaken the awe. Celeste started her period when she was nine and enjoyed her status as the first of her friends to do so. She held it over them, she who had so little to uphold. That was around the time when boys began to take notice of her. She began to tease Sasha for her flat chest, for her continued love of playing baby dolls, for the fact that boys didn't notice her at all. These encounters usually ended with Sasha in tears and Celeste in the hallway getting a lecture from the teacher. She remained smug, however, because smugness was all she had.

Eventually Sasha stopped eating lunch with her, stopped talking to her entirely. And then Celeste's ninth grade "boyfriend" found out she'd been telling people about him and beat her up, insisting he would never have a girlfriend in fifth grade, that he'd been merely using her because she "put out." All in all it had been a confusing time. But instead of seeking help, she leaned into the confusion, found another boyfriend, learned more ways to torment the other girls with her newfound notoriety.

Celeste stared into space a long time, pen aloft, thinking. Laying it all out this way made her see key moments where her life flew off the tracks. She saw all the ways someone might have intervened and saved her. What if a grownup had stepped in to protect her that summer before fifth grade? What if someone kept predatory boys away, informed Celeste that ten was way too soon to lose her virginity? Would she have listened? Would it have altered the course of her life in better ways? Or was she already too far gone at that point, too long without care, affection, and direction?

As ever when she finished writing, she was exhausted. Weary now, she tucked the pen and book back on the shelf, climbed the stairs, and fell into bed.

CHAPTER 7

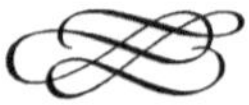

The best part about the painful process of journaling her meager life was that it helped her sleep. Each night when she was finished, she practically fell into a coma, drained of all energy and thoughts. She slept hard, barely moving until morning when she woke feeling, if not optimistic, at least refreshed. The drawback was that she often woke disoriented with no idea where she was or whether it was day or night.

She did so on the night she wrote about third grade, woke with heart thumping, palms sweating, head pounding.

You are in Montana, she coached herself. *It's the middle of the night. Everything is fine.*

Usually the reassurances were enough to make her take a few deep breaths and calm down. Sometimes, if she verified it was the middle of the night, she went back to sleep. But this time something was different. In Celeste's world, different was always bad.

Cautiously, silently, she reached to the nightstand for her gun, palming it as she closed her eyes and attuned her senses to the house around her. Something was off but she couldn't yet discern what.

Squeak.

There. That. It was faint, but there was a tiny squeak downstairs. If she had a cat, she could easily attribute it to that. But since she was still too frightened to take on the responsibility of trying to nurture another life—especially when she was failing to nurture her own—it was definitely not an animal. Unless a bear broke in. When she started researching her future home, she read that bears sometimes broke into buildings or cars in search of food. A bear would make a lot of noise, wouldn't it? They would scratch, paw, snort, sniff, growl, and stomp. Not faintly squeak, as if trying not to make any noise.

Satisfied that the noise went beyond mere paranoia, Celeste slipped out of bed and headed for the stairs, pausing every ten feet or so to reassess. The first thing she did when she moved in was walk up and down the stairs a few times to memorize which boards made noise. She avoided those now, tiptoeing her way down the stairs. Once at the base she paused again, cocking her head to listen. Someone was breathing. The sound should have been alarming because absolutely no one should be breathing inside her house. But it was instead reassuring. No professional would allow themselves to breathe so loud or noticeably. Maybe it was a wayward local who had a bit too much to drink and decided to allow curiosity to over-come common sense in their quest to glimpse the "new girl" as everyone in town called her. It had been so long since anyone referred to her as a girl, she decided to let it stand, secretly delighting in the fact that they clearly thought she was younger than she was. Ever since she turned thirty a few years ago, she'd started to feel her age a bit more. *I'm still young,* she assured herself, gripping her gun to her chest. Young enough to take on an intruder and win, for certain.

"You might as well show yourself. I know you're here," she announced, trying to sound stern in case it was a teenage local. That should be enough to flush them out or make them run away.

Instead nothing happened. The breathing remained in the same spot, not increasing or decreasing. No feet shuffled. No one leapt at her or fled in panic. And now she was getting annoyed. Journaling helped her fall asleep, but if she woke up like this, all hope was lost for regaining her rest. She would be awake all night, and then she'd be a grumpy mess tomorrow. And it was the intruder's fault. Time to make them pay.

"You have about five seconds to make an appearance before I put a bullet in your brain," she said, each word firing out of her like the threatened weapon.

"Don't shoot," a male voice said. It was at once smooth and mellow and raspy and that pinged on her radar for reasons she couldn't yet discern.

"Give me one good reason," she demanded.

He stepped into her line of view then, hands aloft in surrender. "Because I've already been shot," he said, and then dropped into an unconscious heap on her floor.

"Well, that was unexpected," she said. To no one, apparently, since the man seemed to be sincere in his faint. Or at least he appeared so.

Now what? Part of her wanted to kill him and have done with it. She so didn't need this headache now, in her new town, in her new life. She had left trouble behind forever, or so she hoped. *I'm country now.* Country people didn't kill intruders in the middle of the night. Did they? She sighed, annoyed as she thought through the ramifications of taking him out. She couldn't, obviously. In the army she had lived her life by one rule: *I don't need to know the why, but I have to know the who.* They had sent her to take out various people in various places over the years. She never asked why, never, not once. But she never, ever took out a target without verifying his identity. The de-sensitivity training had worked wonders on her. Her conscience remained untroubled as she did her job. Someone told her where to go and she trusted they had a good reason; she didn't feel the need to know it. But she always, always, *always* verified her target's identity. If she had any anxiety or remorse over her job, it was that she would inadvertently take out the wrong person, deprive some child of a mother or father incorrectly.

And that was why she couldn't eliminate the man on her floor. It didn't matter why he was there, only who he was. Without knowing his identity, she couldn't assure herself he was on the wrong side. So she remained frozen a cautious thirty seconds, gun trained on his inert form, before carefully inching forward. Once she was close enough, she toed him a few times, giving him a couple of light kicks that received no response.

When it became clear it wasn't some ruse to spring at her and attack, she let her gun go slack as she crouched and frisked him. He wore a holster, with a gun—American made—and it was loaded. She took it, along with a wicked looking knife from a sheath attached to his ankle. Only after he was safely disarmed did she make an inspection of his body. And then she sucked a breath and gripped her gun again, bringing it to his temple.

He was Middle Eastern. And that was why his voice had pinged on her radar. He had the precise accent of someone who had learned English as a second language, and not from television. Someone had taught him and taught him well. In her—admittedly slanted—experience, terrorists were the ones who did that. And she'd killed more than her fair share of them. Was this man coming for retribution? They had long memories and liked to hold grudges, not resting until the debt had been repaid: a life for a life. Celeste figured she had more than one bounty on her head, a head which would likely be displayed on a pike if they ever got hold of it. The misogyny of the culture had worked in her favor. The men she'd killed had believed her to be an idiotically naïve tourist, someone with a fledgling social media following who wandered into hot spots while taking selfies. Few of them ever realized how vastly they'd underestimated her, and by then it was too late. Thankfully no one had ever learned her true identity, thanks to The Colonel's many layers of camouflage. But it was a fear she'd live with for the rest of her life, the certainty that someone out there would find her, would finally come to collect a long-held debt and avenge whichever friend or family member she'd killed.

With the new knowledge in mind, she searched him again, this time looking for better clues. He had a wallet, but it was clean. No ID, no money, nothing. He smelled like sweat and dirt but not the particular spices she'd come to associate with the culture. If he'd left his tribe in pursuit of her, it hadn't been recently. He was either rogue or had been working alone for a while.

She was making her final pass when she felt something taped over his heart. With her own heart thumping, she retrieved it, giving a yank to unstick the tape stuck to his hairy chest. *Good thing you're asleep, pal, because that would have hurt,* she thought. The card was blank on one side, but when she flipped it her heart stopped completely because she saw something she recognized, something she'd carried for as long as she'd worked as an assassin, a sort of SOS that could be used in any country at any time to contact one man and one man only.

She inspected the guy's face again, her own clouding with puzzlement. Whoever this guy was and for what reason he was there, one thing was certain: he'd been sent by The Colonel.

CHAPTER 8

Celeste scrambled back a few paces and fell over, landing hard on her bum. Such was her faith in the man that she didn't believe for a second The Colonel was trying to have her killed. If he wanted it done, he'd be more likely to do it himself, realizing correctly that he was one of the only people who could successfully carry out such a mission. But hard as she tried, she couldn't come up with a reason for this man's presence in her new life. When her brain failed to provide an answer, she decided to find one.

He answered before it even rang. How did he do that? No one knew.

"Did you get my package?"

"Yes, but it arrived damaged," she said, almost smiling when that gave him pause. It was always a thrill to stymy a man who'd seen in all.

"In what way?"

"Shoulder shot."

"Will he live?"

"Unless I kill him for kicks," she said, which earned one of those rusty laughs. She wanted to ask if the guy was all right, if he was trustworthy. But she refrained because The Colonel wouldn't have sent him otherwise. *Blind trust.* He'd earned that much and then some over the years, first by mentoring her and then by occasionally rescuing her from some scrapes, once personally in Morocco. The sight of the downed man sent shivers of remembrance through her, though. Most of the targets she'd taken out over her career had looked an awful lot like the person now lying unconscious on her floor. "What am I supposed to do with him after he wakes up?" *If* he wakes up. How badly was he injured? Maybe he would die on his own, which would be both a relief and a worry because then she'd have to deal with the cleanup and no one wanted that sort of headache.

"Babysit him until I figure out where to stash him next. He's stirred up a hornet's nest, so eyes out. Someone might come looking."

She wriggled a little. Every time The Colonel bestowed faith in her, it had the same effect. If he thought she was good enough to babysit this guy and handle anyone who came looking for him, then who was she to doubt herself or her abilities? "Can he handle himself?"

"A bit. Not as well as you. You're in charge here, don't let him tell you different when he comes to."

"I won't," she said so deadpan he gave another rusty laugh before disconnecting without a goodbye. "Let's see how bad you're banged up," she said to the guy, rolling him onto his back so she could make her inspection. As he'd said, he'd been shot. A clean hole through his upper right shirt, which had become so saturated it was hard to tell much else about it. Had this happened nearby or far away?

With that thought came the next pressing need: if someone was after him, she'd better make certain they hadn't already found him. She secured her weapon and stood, staring down at the unconscious man. "I have to do a perimeter sweep. Don't move." He didn't, of course. She smiled at her dumb joke, then winced. *Don't lose it when you've made it this far. A few weeks off the job and you're already talking to a guy in a coma. Pull it together, woman.*

Stealthily, she eased out of the house and made her way around the building, sweeping outward in concentric circles toward the barn. Everything was calm, settled, undisturbed. The animals in the nearby wilderness made their usual nighttime noises. No alarmed cawing of birds, no startled scrambling of paws or hooves. No tracks around the house, no sounds of a car or ATV nearby. Everything was still and silent as it should be, as she had come to expect in a shockingly short amount of time. She paused, absorbing that thought. For a lifelong city dweller, she'd come to accept the peace of her new rural life with relative ease. In fact, it soothed her. No engines roaring, cars honking, metal clanging, people yelling. It was…nice.

Shaking off the introspection, she went back in the house, gripping her weapon in case her houseguest awakened and had ideas.

He hadn't, though. He lay in the same place she'd left him. Still, she crept close and frisked him again. Being careful was the only way she'd survived to the ripe age of thirty three. She wanted to make it to fifty at least, which might be some sort of record for assassins, The Colonel being the exception to every rule. No one knew exactly how old he was but people took bets on the possibility that he was part of some experiment that brought him forward in time from some warrior age and only modern science kept him living. During those occasions when she'd been holed up with special ops teams, they'd had a bit of time to ponder. Perhaps too much, based on the insane theories they'd come up with.

"All right, let's get you patched up. Don't make me kill you later because I don't like having to undo work I've already done," she groused as she cut off the man's ruined shirt and peeled it away. He had hair on his chest, a pleasant smattering shaped like a T. She stared at it, wondering if she should shave the portion around his wound. Would that trap bacteria or keep it away? *Nature put it there, who am I to disagree?* Plus it felt weird and creepy to shave someone while he was unconscious. A bit too serial killer for her tastes.

With that decided she readied a bowl of warm water and soap, along with a clean dish towel, the only makeshift sort of bandage she had on hand. In her line of work, she should really have a first aid kit available. She added it to the list of things she needed, which so far consisted of a first aid kit because she had no idea what she needed in order to survive, let alone keep house. *Cleaning supplies, probably.* Not being a total slob, she would need to give everything a good scrub at some point. The only items in the house had expired long ago. *More food.* She would soon run out of what she'd bought from town, for certain now that she had an extra mouth to feed. What else? She had no idea and that frustrated her because it pointed like a beacon to her abnormality. Other people, people who had grown up in a family with parents who taught them things, probably knew exactly what they needed to function, to make a house a home. Celeste was as clueless about it as she was about everything but taking orders and killing people.

"What a spectacular resume I've developed," she whispered as she worked over the guy. Her glance fell to his face. He was handsome, she supposed. If you liked that type. If you hadn't spent the last fifteen years killing that type. "You're dull company. I've had better conversation with corpses." She had, actually. So much of her career had been solitary that she'd developed the habit of talking to her victims, post mortem. Her way of finding closure, she supposed. She had never gone so far as to apologize, but she had assured them their bodies would be retrieved and taken care of properly, wouldn't be left for their enemies to abuse or parade. It wasn't much, but it was something. Respect, The Colonel had taught her, meant a lot, both in life and in death. Under his tutelage she'd learned to respect herself and others, something she certainly hadn't learned during her chaotic childhood.

She finished cleaning him, pressing a clean towel beneath the wound and on top. It wasn't bleeding too much anymore. But it had clearly bled a lot. Loss of blood was likely what had led him to lose consciousness, but he also didn't appear to have lost enough to send his body into shock. "You're being kind of a baby about this, actually. You got off lucky. I've seen worse. I've dealt worse," she told her visitor as she knelt next to him and wondered what to do next.

When he woke, he would probably do so in a panic, not knowing if he was her prisoner, if she still intended to kill him. That was how she would feel, at least, if she woke up gunshot on a stranger's floor. She would have to leave him a message to assure him he was safe and she wasn't hostile. What, though? She dared not write something. He had spoken English, but what if he couldn't read it?

With a sigh, she retrieved a blanket and draped it over him, being careful not to disturb the wound. Then she poured him a glass of water and set it beside his head. Lost blood took an enormous amount of fluid intake to replace. She turned toward the stairs and then, on second thought, retrieved an apple and set it beside the water. *An apple a day keeps the assassin away.*

Maybe he had some hidden injury that would kill him, but as far as she knew she'd done the best she could to fix him. The rest was up to him. As for her, she was going back to bed.

With renewed exhaustion, she climbed the stairs and fell into her bed in her own unconscious heap.

CHAPTER 9

The next morning Celeste woke with a stretch and a yawn, feeling strangely at ease for someone who may or may not have a dead terrorist in her kitchen. Such was her life that she was calmer over the thought that he might have expired than that he might still be alive. If he was dead, a lot of her problems would solve themselves before they could begin.

She went to the bathroom, brushed her teeth, smoothed her hair, then scowled at herself in the mirror. *It's not a date; it's a custody arrangement.* She was on babysitting duty until The Colonel figured out what to do with the guy. If The Colonel was out of options, things must really be a mess. The man knew people all over the world. If Paradise, Montana was his last resort, it was truly his last resort.

Rounding away from the mirror, she went down the stairs, pausing momentarily when the spot on the kitchen floor was empty. She'd brought her gun because, again, one could never be too careful, especially with an unknown man in the house.

"I'm positive you won't have to use that," a quiet, polite voice said. She eased farther into the room and saw him sitting on the floor, his back propped against the outside wall of the kitchen. Beside him, the glass of water was empty, the apple core tucked neatly inside it.

"Thank you for the food and water and, I assume, the cleanup." He motioned lethargically to his shoulder.

"You're welcome." In contrast to his surprisingly gentle tone, hers sounded rough and forced, which it was. She was used to bawdy conversations with fellow soldiers, the more ridiculous, the better. Civil discourse escaped her. They stared at each other a few beats. Celeste had the idea she should probably do something, but she had no idea what. She had never taken care of anything or anyone before, not a plant, not a pet, and certainly not a person. Five minutes in and she was already failing.

More water, her brain told her. He must be thirsty and probably hungry. She edged forward, keeping a wary eye on him, as she bent over and picked up the water, carrying it to the sink. She retrieved a clean glass, filled it, and set it on the floor beside him.

"Thank you," he said. He had watched her actions as intently as she watched his, each not a hundred percent certain they trusted the other but left with no other option than to do so, at least for the moment.

"Food?" she asked.

"If you'd be so kind," he said.

Kind had never been a word people used in reference to her. "I only have cereal," she warned, wincing inwardly when she felt the need to add, "It's pretty much all I know how to make."

"Cereal would be fine though, I must confess, anything would be fine at this point."

She prepared a bowl of cereal and milk for each of them and dallied, not certain where to put his. "Do you want me to help you to the table?"

"It seemed to take all of my energy to crawl to this spot, so I think I'll remain for now. Perhaps after I eat things will look brighter."

With a nod, she sat at the table and ate, trying to ignore the stranger in the room who watched her between bites. He finished his cereal and set the bowl aside.

"You must have questions," he declared.

"Only one," she said.

One side of his mouth quirked. "Only one? Miraculous. Please," he motioned feebly for her to proceed.

"What's your name?"

"Sam," he said.

She blinked at him, waiting for more.

His mouth ticked again. "You don't think I look like a Sam? Do you think it's a nickname for some unpronounceable foreign name?"

She said nothing.

He gave a tiny shrug and winced with remembered regret. "It's Din Chatti. I prefer Sam. And what shall I call you?"

A thousand saucy replies ran through her mind. She disregarded them all. "Celeste."

"How very heavenly," he said.

"You have no idea," she replied. She carried both their bowls to the sink and returned to him, hands on hips. "Let's get you set up on the couch. It came with the house, but I think it will be a lot more comfortable than the floor." When he didn't argue, she came along his good side, levered him up, and took as much of his weight as she could on the short journey to the living room. Still, the trip exhausted them both. Celeste dabbed her forearm on her sweaty head. "You're heavier than you look."

"You're stronger than you look," he replied.

"Next time I'll sweep you into my arms, pull out all the stops," she promised.

He snorted a laugh that ended on a wince. Celeste regarded him, out of ideas on what to do next. The day stretched endlessly before her, awkward in the extreme with this stranger invading what she had come to think of as her own private oasis. "I should probably go to town for more supplies." There was no need to tell him she had just gone to town yesterday and vowed not to do so again for a long, long time. Plus with him eating her meager stores, she actually did need more food.

He gave a curt nod in reply. The beads of sweat on his upper lip told her he was probably in a fare amount of pain.

"What can I get you? Besides pain reliever, of course." How did she not have any on hand? *Because I didn't think of it.* She wasn't even good at taking care of herself, let alone others.

"Nothing comes to mind," he said between gritted teeth.

"Unfortunately I haven't had a landline put in and I'll be taking my cell with me. I don't suppose you have a phone."

"It didn't survive the journey," he said.

Journey from where? She wanted to ask but didn't. The less she knew, the better. Soon enough he would be on his way. She didn't want to have to wonder about him when he was gone. Not that she was in danger of becoming attached. It seemed to be one more thing that was deficient about her, the inability to form lasting relationships with others, save The Colonel who had more than earned her trust and loyalty.

"I'll be fine," he added, making her realize she was staring at him as she thought about her dismal life.

Without a word, she spun, grabbed her keys, and headed to her truck. Unlike yesterday, going to town now felt like a reprieve. Maybe today would be better. Maybe yesterday they had all gotten their fill of staring at the new girl like she was a freak. Whatever the case, she absolutely could not let on that she now had a houseguest. That was a way to get them both killed. Word would get out and then every assassin in the known universe would come calling. Celeste really didn't want to have to spend the beginning of her retirement dispatching unwanted annoyances and dodging their bullets in return.

Then again, it would be a handy way to fill days that were already long and empty, a good way to distract a mind that wanted to do anything but heal.

Pushing away thoughts and feelings again, she focused on the looming town, on Paradise.

CHAPTER 10

"Back again? That's quick."

The speaker this time was Minnie, the pint-size woman who ran the gas station. Celeste usually liked her for her plainspoken, no-nonsense demeanor. Except, it seemed, when her insights applied to Celeste herself.

"Needed some things, things I forgot," Celeste said.

Minnie eyed her with x-ray vision. Celeste tried not to squirm. Did she know about Sam? Had word already gotten around? Exactly how fast was the gossip mill in this place?

"For the storm?" Minnie asked.

Celeste blinked at her. "Storm?"

Minnie tsk'd, so fast Celeste almost missed it. A lot was said in that tsk. *Newbies, outsiders, young people. Fools, all of them.* "There's a storm coming."

"But it's perfectly dry and warm and almost March." Celeste had heard about Montana's notorious winters, of course. But so far her time there had been sunny and dry. She assured herself, with a lot of false hope, that it had all been hype. *Maybe the winters aren't as bad as people say.*

"First of all, it's still winter in Montana. Don't ever forget, and don't ever let yourself be unprepared. Second, the weather can turn on a dime." She snapped her fingers for emphasis. Celeste resisted the urge to shudder, but she did look out the window. *It's completely clear out there,* was what she longed to say, mostly because she didn't want to face a storm. *There's a metaphor for my life in there somewhere.*

With a sigh, Minnie reached beneath the counter and handed Celeste a sheet of paper. "We came up with this when Maybe moved to town and have tweaked it a bit since."

Celeste glanced down and saw a list marked "Winter Provisions." "Thank you." She turned to go, but Minnie hailed her back with another sigh, a stern one this time.

"Those aren't a suggestion, little miss. Start here with kerosene."

Celeste began to wonder if perhaps the counter was magical because now Minnie produced a yellow plastic fuel container and handed it over.

"All right," Celeste agreed. She took the canister, went outside, and filled it with kerosene. For once she was thankful for the tab she'd opened with Minnie, the one that meant she didn't have to go back inside to pay. Not being the sort of person who did well under authority, she wasn't certain how much more of Minnie's overbearing condescension she could take in a day.

She capped the fuel and stashed it in the back of her SUV before hopping inside and glancing at the list again. It was immense. Without permission, her gaze turned toward the sparkling blue sky. Not a cloud and the temperature was moderate. She hadn't even grabbed a coat before she left home. "Do I really need to do this today?" she asked herself.

Eyes bored into hers. A quick peek showed Minnie staring at her through the gas station window, lids lowered like a vigilant hen.

"I guess so," she muttered. At the very least it would provide a distraction from her houseguest.

She started the vehicle and drove to the grocery, loading her cart with all manner of things she otherwise wouldn't have thought to get: peanut butter, crackers, beef stew, soup, canned fruit, jerky, fruit leather and every other emergency convenience food the town thought she might need to survive a big storm. For good measure she also picked up extra milk and more cereal. Her guest wasn't a tiny fellow. He could probably out eat her and then some.

"Prepping for the storm?" someone said, peering into her cart.

"Yes," Celeste said, avoiding the urge to place both hands over her groceries. What was it with this town and their inability to mind their business?

"I'd put in some hot cocoa, tea, chocolate candy bars, and cookies, if I were you," the interloper said.

"Thank you," Celeste said tightly. She had no intention of complying but then it was as if the power of suggestion began to work against her. Soon she found herself tossing tea, cocoa, candy, and cookies into the cart, along with instant coffee that could be prepared if the power went out.

The bill was enormous, but that didn't concern her. The Colonel would provide a stipend for her houseguest, probably one worth more than he used in food or utilities. An overly eager bag boy helped her carry her groceries to the SUV, loading them into the back despite her protests. She tried to tip him but, blushing, he refused, saying they weren't allowed and it was, "All part of a day's work, ma'am." When he touched his finger to his head, it was all too easy to picture him wearing one of the ubiquitous cowboy hats she saw everywhere. Despite the fact that she felt old and useless, standing by as a teenager loaded her food, there was something pleasant about his nice manners and schoolboy stammers.

I would have destroyed a boy like him, back in the day, she thought, then quickly pushed the thought aside. No chance to recriminate herself over her shady past when she still had to go to the... She picked up Minnie's list, groaning when she realized where she'd need to go next. "Not the hardware store," she whispered.

It was *the* hangout in town, the place where all the retired cowboys gathered, and the young ones, too, when they weren't at work. There was an actual checkerboard, but mostly they sat or stood around, gossiping and speculating on life. She'd stopped by during her first week in town, out of curiosity, and quickly backed out again when she realized what it was. *A man nest.* The place was crawling with them. Not that she hated men, she didn't. But over the last fifteen years, her relationship to the male of the species had become very…fraught. *It's complicated,* she told herself as she took a deep breath and opened the door.

As expected, all activity came to a halt as all the men paused what they were doing and stared at her. Squaring her shoulders, she headed toward one of the aisles, hoping to become invisible as soon as she was hidden.

"Hey, it's our most famous, and coincidentally only, new girl," Tony said, appearing beside her as if by magic.

She mustered a smile that had to have looked strained.

"What can I help you find?"

It seemed unlikely that a man such as he was following her around for the sole purpose of trying to gain insight into her life. Therefore she came to the next obvious conclusion. "This is your place?"

"This is my place," he said, patting a display of mousetraps and then straightening them when he realized they were askew.

"Minnie gave me a list," she said, holding it aloft.

"The list! Haven't seen that since Maybe came to town." He took it now, letting his eyes roam over it. "Wow, this thing has really grown. I see every business owner in town has had a hand in adding something. I'll leave it to your interpretation whether you actually need one of Sheila's homemade huckleberry pies, but the rest looks pretty good. Let's see how efficiently we can take care of things on our end." He handed the list back to her and began heading toward a display. He was taking charge, and she should probably be annoyed. She had worked hard to be as independent and capable as possible, mostly because she had no one else to rely on. But there was some relief in following mindlessly behind someone who knew exactly where he was going and what he was doing. It was the same feeling she got with The Colonel, a feeling of weightlessness as she was finally able to let go and unburden, if only for a moment. She took a deep breath, one that went all the way in and out for once.

"For the car," Tony announced, stopping in front of a display with a flourish. "We made these for the tourists, but it turns out the locals like them, too. It saves the trouble of having to remember what to pack or put together. Here we have an emergency car kit that has some power bars, some water, a couple of space blankets, a basic first aid kit, and some flares." He picked one up and held it out to her, pausing as he delivered a warning. "If you get stuck in the snow at any point, make certain you keep your exhaust pipe clean. About once every handful of years someone dies from carbon monoxide buildup from that very thing. And if the snow is too deep, the flares will melt right through and be useless."

She took the kit, nodding, trying to add the new information to her already overcrowded brain. *Carbon monoxide. Flares. Death. Got it.* At least the car was prepared now. That was one worry off her mind. Of course she hadn't even had the worry when she walked in the door, but she was still relieved to have added it and then removed it so quickly.

"We're going to need extra hands here," Tony said. He put his hand in the air and it must have been some kind of signal because soon a teenage boy appeared and began gathering all the things Tony listed. "Flashlight, extra batteries, lantern, candles, a couple of cans of Sterno." He paused and regarded Celeste. "How are you on blankets?"

She froze, deer like.

Tony turned to his sidekick without waiting for an answer. "A couple of blankets and a bottle of iodine, in case you have to use water from your creek."

She nodded, trying to process that deluge. *Blankets. Lanterns. What is Sterno? Water from my creek? Why not water from my faucet? Iodine?*

She must have looked as overwhelmed as she felt because Tony plucked the list from her and scanned it again. "On second thought, you should probably get the pie."

*C*eleste felt as if she had put in a full day of work. As before at the grocery store, the helpful teenage clerk loaded the SUV for her, doffed his imaginary cap, and called her ma'am. She was so tired she minded less this time. Or maybe she was starting to become used to the people and their strangely friendly, helpful, and intrusive ways. Whatever the reason, she wished for the teenagers again as she arrived home and made trip after trip unloading everything.

Though she hadn't seen him, she sensed that Sam was still in the living room, on the couch. When she finally ran out of tasks, she popped her head in to check on him. He lay on his good side, staring at her with a baleful expression.

"Sounds like you've been busy," he said.

She gave a small nod in reply.

"Sorry I couldn't help you unload."

"I'm not used to having help," she said, then wished she could take the words back. Though they were supposed to be a display of rugged independence, they came out sounding sad and needy. She cleared her throat. "How are you feeling?"

"About the same."

"Oh, I bought pain reliever. And food. And pie."

His brows rose. "Pie?"

"It was on the list." She disappeared before he could ask which list, if he had ever intended to. She returned with the pain reliever and a glass of water. He popped the pills and guzzled the water, draining it in about three gulps. She refilled it, and he drained it again. Next she searched the cupboards until she found a large pitcher. She filled that and set it beside the couch.

"Thank you," he said, sounding exhausted.

"Replacing lost blood is a lot of work," she commented.

"Sounds like you have experience," he said.

She tipped her head in acknowledgement, but otherwise didn't respond.

He let out a sigh and closed his eyes. He was fading, but all of a sudden his eyes popped open. "Oh, I forgot I need to tell you something."

She braced herself, not certain why. Something in his tone told her she wasn't going to like what he was about to say. "Did someone come looking for you while I was gone? The person who shot you?"

"No, but that's what I needed to tell you. The person who shot me, it had nothing to do with me."

"How do you know?" she asked.

"Because the person who shot me is a local."

CHAPTER 11

Elliot was perplexed. He liked being perplexed, actually. It was a nice change of pace from his other job making pizzas. There he only had to repeat the same rituals over and over: make the dough, form the dough, bake the pizzas. But during his job as a deputy, the one he was now performing, he had to use his brain a surprising amount. That was what he liked about being a cop. No day was ever the same, especially in Paradise where he might help rescue a calf from a freezing pond one minute and break up a fight between husband and wife over whose fault it was the calf got stuck the next. But this was a new one on him.

"So you shot the guy," he reiterated, staring at a patch of trampled grass. It was starting to snow, but he could still see blood spatter among the dried blades of grass.

"Of course I did," Edward Jonas said around his chew of tobacco. He spit a stream out the side of his mouth. Far from being disgusted, Elliot felt the familiar pull of addiction. He had given up first smoking and then chewing when he and Missy got together, but he never lost his love of the stuff. Instead his love for Missy was greater, great enough that he wanted to cut his risk of mouth and lung cancer significantly, if only for her sake. In an effort to distract himself, he reached into his pocket and popped a piece of gum. Mint gum, thoughtfully purchased and given to him by Missy, who knew he still struggled, despite his protests to the contrary.

"Why, though?" Elliot asked, trying not to sound as longsuffering as he felt. He had grown up in Paradise. He knew everyone, understood exactly how they thought and felt and acted. And yet he still felt baffled more often than not.

Edward blinked at him as if Elliot was the one who didn't make sense. "Why? Because he was on my property."

"What if he had a valid reason to be here?"

Edward's eyes narrowed farther. "Valid? Valid like stealing cattle or tractors or 4-wheelers?"

"But he didn't do any of those things, right?"

"Right. Cause I shot him."

"How do you know it was a man?" Elliot tried.

Edward rolled his eyes and spit again. "When's the last time you heard of a woman rustling or thieving?"

Last week, actually, but Elliot didn't say so. No need to spread more gossip than necessary. "But you don't know that he was rustling. And he arrived here on foot. How was he planning to make off with cows or equipment?"

That stumped Edward, but only for a moment. "He was the scout," he said with a decisive nod.

Elliot pinched the bridge of his nose, thinking. It was highly likely a man who showed up alone at night in the middle of nowhere on foot was up to no good. But what if he wasn't? Or, worse, what if it wasn't a man? What if it was the person who lived closest? The woman who wouldn't yet know that everyone here lived by the code "shoot first and ask questions later, if they're still alive?"

"No one has showed up at the vet's office, asking to be patched up," Elliot said.

"Of course they wouldn't. Everyone would know they'd been shot by me. I was at the hardware store today. Everybody already knows to keep a look out."

Elliot sighed again. The only reason he was here was because his father, who owned the hardware store, called him when he heard Edward shot a man, a fact Edward hadn't felt the need to pass along. Technically, *technically,* Elliot could arrest him. He had admitted to shooting a man unprovoked on his lawn, not in the act of breaking into his house, not in the act of holding a weapon on him or making a threat. He'd shot a man in cold blood because he had the audacity to step foot on his property uninvited. It was illegal any way you looked at it. But it was also Montana, where the unwritten law often superseded the written one. Plus he had no victim. The man was either well enough to go somewhere and get treatment or he was so injured he crawled away somewhere to die. Maybe they'd find his corpse in the spring thaw. If so, he'd deal with any charges then. In the meantime, all he could do was check on the one person he knew who might be in danger, the one person unknown enough to show up unannounced in the middle of the night at a neighbor's house.

He squinted his good eye toward the west and glanced at the falling snow, trying to estimate how much time he had before the roads became too bad to drive for the day. With a nod to Edward, one which left everything unsaid—*you shouldn't have shot an unknown man, this might not be over, I'm going to see what more I can find out*—he hopped into his truck and headed away.

*H*e sat in his truck a minute, inspecting the house. It was quiet, but that was to be expected. She was one lone woman. The tracks behind her SUV were fresh but fading, quickly replaced by snow. No curtains ruffled, no lights came on. If he wasn't parked behind her vehicle, he might believe no one was home.

Eventually he stepped out of the truck and made his way to the door. He expected a lag after he knock, but she opened promptly. *Was she waiting on me?*

"Elliot," she said.

"Celeste," he returned, trying not to be obvious as he peered behind her.

"Is everything okay?"

"A storm's coming, thought I'd stop in and check on you while I was out this way on a call, see if there was anything you needed."

"Oh, I was in town this morning working toward that very thing. In fact your dad helped me finance a new wing of his house by loading me up with every possible contraption I might need from his store. Good news, though. I finally figured out what Sterno is."

He chuckled, which was unusual. He didn't normally do well with strangers, and especially not women. He found them too fluttery for his tastes. Really, he mostly only liked Missy and his parents and a select handful of family friends. She motioned behind her to the large stack of items on the floor.

"Is there anything I can help you with?" he asked.

"No," she said eagerly and gripped the door. His gaze rested on those fingers. Was she tense or was it his imagination?

"Are you sure?"

Her grip tightened a few beats before she let out a breath and relented. "Actually, yes. I didn't want to mention it, didn't want to put you out. But among my list of necessity items was a kerosene heater. It turns out I already have one, but it's massive. I have no idea how to get it upstairs."

He blinked at her, assessing. Was that really all this was? She needed help and didn't want to ask for it? "Well, sure," he agreed, taking a step inside and doffing his hat as soon as she moved aside. He used the motion to make a sweeping glance around. Everything looked like a lone woman lived there, a woman who had recently been to town and had no idea how to decorate. He'd seen military bunkers with more personality, but then he had become spoiled by his mom's cozy tastes, first in the home where he grew up, and now in the home he shared with Missy.

She led the way to the rickety stairs of the dark basement, walking in front of him. He lingered a step behind her, taking a full look around. Nothing was out of place, nothing was unusual, minus the antiseptic and unused feel of the house.

She flicked on the basement light, a lone bulb that swung

ominously back and forth. The stairs shook as they made their descent. They both gripped the banister for balance, and Elliot had to duck when they reached the bottom. She led him to an ancient kerosene heater, a metal one that looked like it fell out of the Korean War.

"I can go backwards up the stairs," she offered.

Elliot couldn't help it; he laughed again as he handed her his hat. "It's fine." She looked dubious so he bent and lifted the metal contraption, carrying it easily up the stairs. "Where do you want it?" He was glad he didn't sound winded. The thing actually was particularly heavy. But as long as she didn't want it on the second floor or dither needlessly, he'd be okay.

"The kitchen," she said, going ahead of him again.

He deposited the heater in the middle of the oversized farm kitchen. She handed him his hat, staring at the heater.

"Something wrong?" he asked.

"Do you think this is an okay place for it? I was trying to pick somewhere central."

"Most people put them in the kitchen or living room. Depends on where you spend the most time."

She frowned and bit her lip as if uncertain of where she spent the most time. Something about her reminded Elliot of himself right after he came home from the war. Injured and missing an eye, the worst part had been the uncertainty of what to do next, of his place in the world. If not for his family and Missy, he would have fallen to pieces. Who would make certain the same didn't happen to Celeste?

"Thank you," she said, motioning toward the heater.

"No problem. Do you know how to light it?"

She opened her mouth, probably to assure him she'd be fine, but hesitated a beat. "I'm sure I can figure it out."

"Let me save you the trouble. It's easy once you get the hang of it. Do you have kerosene?"

Now her expression turned wry. "Do you think Minnie would have let me leave town without it?" She left before he could answer and returned a moment later with a full can, peering over Elliot's shoulder as he crouched, unscrewed the cap on the heater, and poured in the fuel. When that was done, he adjusted the wick, talking out loud as he did so, and then pushed the button to light the heater.

Nothing happened.

"Sometimes it's a little stubborn," he said, trying again.

"Aren't we all," she muttered, still watching intently.

On the third try the flame sprang to life, giving off an instant glow of heat. It was so cheerful and inviting, Celeste was tempted to leave it. But it was probably better to conserve, so she didn't object when Elliot turned it off and stood, brushing his hands together.

"Thank you so much," Celeste said, hating that she had to. In the army, everyone had been equal. Some might say Celeste had the advantage because the places she went viewed her as non-threatening, usually to their regret. Misogyny had given her an advantage. But now that advantage was gone. She had returned to a time when brute strength counted for more. Her plan to get the kerosene heater upstairs had been to locate a dolly and tie the heater to it. And at that it would have been a painstaking process, bumping up each step one at a time. Sam was certainly incapable of helping her. And now Elliot, almost seven feet of him, had done in two minutes what it would have taken her half a day to accomplish. And she couldn't resent him because he'd helped her so much. What did country people do to show appreciation? Send baby hogs? Bake pies? She had no idea. In her defense, she also had no idea what city people did to show appreciation. Really, she had no idea how normal humans functioned in day-to-day society. All she knew was taking orders and killing people, two skills that wouldn't help her survive her new life at all.

"It was no problem," Elliot said and probably meant it. All the things he took for granted—brute strength, survival skills, country living—were completely foreign to her. "Take care with this storm. I'm thankful you got supplies in time. That's one worry off all our minds."

Whose minds? His and his father's? The entire town of Paradise? It was unfathomable to Celeste that strangers should care about her wellbeing. Perhaps it was something country people said. If only there were a translation guide for this sort of thing. A State Department manual on safely dealing with rubes and ranchers.

She walked him to the door and that was when he dropped the bomb. He turned and, with forced casualness, asked, "By the way, have you seen anyone suspicious?"

Without missing a beat she replied, "I'm from the city. Absolutely everyone I've met so far in Paradise seems suspicious," and was rewarded when he laughed out loud.

Tipping his hat to her, he laughed all the way to his truck.

Celeste waited until he was gone, leaning on the door, heart pounding. "You can come out now."

When no one emerged, she went to the closet where she'd stashed Sam and opened it up. He lay curled on his side, staring dazedly out. "Is he gone?" His voice sounded weak, a thready wheeze.

"Yes, are you?"

"I'm in fighting form," he assured her, groaning a little as he tipped forward onto his hands and knees and began crawling toward the couch.

"Come on," Celeste encouraged, patting her leg as she walked slowly beside him.

"I feel suddenly like your kitten," Sam said.

"I wouldn't know; I've never had one."

"Never?" He reached the couch and paused, taking a bracing breath before slowly climbing aboard.

"Nope."

"Dog?"

"No."

"Hamster."

"Nada."

"Goldfish?"

"Does it count if they come in a bag from Pepperidge Farm?" she asked. He shook his head. "Then no."

"Do you hate animals?"

"No, I'm ambivalent toward animals," she said, but the truth was a bit more complex. Pets had always been something for other people.

People with families and life skills. Every time Celeste considered a pet, she talked herself out of it, certain she would kill it by either neglect or ignorance. And though she had killed more people than she cared to number, somehow it felt worse to accidentally kill a living being who depended on her for survival. It was a level of failure she wasn't willing to risk. Speaking of dependence on her... "Are you hungry? I bought food when I was in town."

Was it her imagination or did he perk slightly? "What sort of food?"

"Some cans of soup and some cans of stew and some frozen lasagna and mac and cheese."

"Oh," he said, sitting back. Was it her imagination again or did he sound disappointed. If so, why?

"What kinds of things do you like to eat?"

"I'm not picky," he said, but his tone suggested otherwise. It was definitely lethargic now and that made her feel bad, but why? For some reason she felt like she'd let him down with her food selection. Not enough vegetables? Maybe he was a health fanatic.

"Also pie," she added, hating the plaintive note she heard in her tone. He was practically her captive; there was no need to impress him with her shopping prowess. But then his eyes lit again and he squiggled.

"Pie?"

"Yes, pie. A lady in town makes them."

"What kind of pie?" he asked.

"Huckleberry."

Now his eyes were blinking rapidly but not in disappointment, more as if he were processing the new input. "I've never had huckleberry before. Is it good?"

"I have no idea, but it must be because everything here is made from it. I swear if I see huckleberry kitty litter somewhere I'm moving back to sanity."

He laughed and, in that weird way, it felt like a victory. But not really. Celeste didn't want to be tied to him, not in any way, not in the slightest, simplest manner. She had survived her entire adult life with no attachments. Now was not the time to form one, not with someone temporary, someone untrustworthy, someone who looked a bit too like men she'd spent the better portion of her career hunting and eliminating.

When she gave herself a mental shake, Sam was staring at her in that way that was becoming familiar, as if he were assessing her the way she was trying to asses him. He definitely had questions about her. So far he'd kept them to himself, but she couldn't hold him off forever, especially not if he stayed for any length of time. But of course he wouldn't stay for any length of time. She forced a bit of sternness into her expression, hard to do when he was staring at her with his cow eyes, big and brown and fringed with long lashes. *Kind eyes,* she thought and banished it. She had no idea if he was kind, but she doubted it. Being in The Colonel's world meant you'd done enough and seen enough to eschew kindness from your life, possibly forever. When you saw so much bad, it became hard to find the good.

"Tell me again how you got shot," she commanded. All he'd had time to say before Elliot arrived was that someone local shot him when he was trying to find her house.

"I paid a coyote to bring me over the border from Canada, but it's not the sort of service that extends door to door. He dropped me at the end of the road. Nothing is marked here, however. The Colonel gave me a description of your car, along with your license plate."

Celeste hadn't informed The Colonel that she'd gotten a new car, and she certainly hadn't told him what it looked like. One of his hackers must have found out. She fought a shudder. It was no fun to be spied on, even if it was for a good cause. No matter where she went, even here in the middle of nowhere, she wasn't far enough to avoid detection.

"I was creeping toward what I thought was the house, intent on looking for a vehicle, when a man stepped onto his porch and shot me."

She blinked at him. "Just like that?"

"Just like that."

"No warning?"

"No warning. One moment I was looking for a car, the next I was shot and scrambling for my life."

"That's insane. This isn't Afghanistan. We're not in a war zone. You can't shoot someone without asking who they are or why they're there."

"There we agree. However, I do not think this is a place like any other. The land is remote, self-sufficiency a necessity. Perhaps he's been robbed before."

"Are…are you defending the man who shot you?"

His answering smile was wry. "I'm afraid I have the terrible habit of always seeing both side of an issue. It's my fatal flaw."

"Literally," she said. Unconsciously she tapped the spot above his wound and then yanked her hand back. *No touching,* she reminded herself. It was much easier to keep herself in check if she followed all her rules. No touching was definitely at the tippy top.

Sam seemed not to have noticed the touch, nor her hasty retreat. "And what about you? What brings you to this wild and unsettled realm?"

She stared at her hands as she answered. "I recently retired. Thought I would try country living for a change."

"A city dweller, are you?"

She gave a slight nod.

"Which city?"

"Most of them."

His lips tugged upward again, amused at her vague avoidance. "And how are you enjoying retirement and country life?"

She opened her mouth to answer and closed it again. "I suppose it wouldn't be fair to say yet. I've barely gotten started with either."

"And here I am, intruding. My apologies."

She gave a slight shrug. "Not your fault The Colonel had to stash you."

"Except I think perhaps it is," Sam replied. He let out a breath and closed his eyes.

"Are you allowed to tell me?" she asked. Celeste had grown comfortable with classified information. Long ago she quashed whatever part of her remained curious. Most of her life in the army had existed on a need-to-know basis. Eventually she came to prefer it that way. The less she knew, the better. And while she had no desire to trample security clearance or Sam's privacy, she thought it was best to know anything that might keep them both safe and alive.

He gave her the smile again, the wry one. "Celeste, I may do anything I want. I'm a free agent."

CHAPTER 12

Celeste's gut pitched before drawing level again. *He wasn't hitting on you. He didn't mean it like that,* she assured herself. He meant it literally, she knew. Unlike her, he wasn't part of the army, didn't exist under The Colonel's command. Except it seemed he did. But how did a private citizen fall under The Colonel's jurisdiction?

"I'm confused," she said.

Sam chuckled. "Welcome to my world." He swiped a hand over his face. "A few years ago I ran afoul of the law in the worst possible way. Your Colonel gave me the option of prison or working for him. Clearly I chose the latter."

Celeste studied him hard. "Why would he do that?" Why had he done it for her? What did the man see in them that made him take the risk? Because when Celeste looked in the mirror, she didn't see it. All she saw was a messed up kid, unloved and unwanted by everyone in her life, unable to perform even the most basic actions in order to thrive. Was that what drew The Colonel to her all those years ago? Because she was a throwaway kid who wouldn't be missed by anyone when she inevitably died? She had expected to be killed on one of her many missions for that purpose, because she thought it was what The

Colonel expected. But instead she'd beaten the odds and survived every one, and now what?

"For a couple of reasons, I suppose." His accent was pleasant and she found herself relaxing as he spoke, almost as if he was telling her a bedtime story. "I was uniquely positioned to provide a treasure trove of intel. I'm tri-lingual. I had already been trained in all the ways that mattered and, finally, The Colonel and I have a common ally, one he was likely certain I wouldn't betray."

Celeste bit her lip, holding back her frustration. That explained why Sam had been useful, but not her. From the sounds of it, Sam had everything to offer in exchange for clemency. She, meanwhile, had had nothing besides the drive and ambition to prove that she wasn't a waste of oxygen, to herself and others. Had she accomplished that? She supposed it depended on who made the definition and who did the judging. The Colonel had always seemed happy with her work, and that had meant everything to her back in the day. All she had wanted was to be his protégé, to make him proud. And now that her work was done? Whose opinion mattered? What counted as success? Because by every metric she could think of, she was failing completely.

"And how did you wind up here?" She motioned around them at the sterile, dumpy farmhouse, as if unable to believe it herself that they were both in this position, even though she'd arrived by choice.

He took another breath and pressed his thumb between his eyes. The gesture was familiar to Celeste, of trying to push back thoughts she'd rather not remember. "In my capacity as double agent, if you will, I had to walk a fine line. In order to convince those on the other side that I was still theirs, I had to perform some…illegal and unsavory actions. I suppose I set myself up as a sort of Robin Hood or vigilante, only choosing to harm those I was certain had done wrong."

She gave a little nod, understanding completely. Even though Celeste had always been following orders, she had comforted herself that the people she exterminated always had it coming, even if she had no idea why.

"It was a system that worked well for a surprisingly long period of time. Until one day it didn't." He stared into space. Celeste didn't interrupt his remembrance, or attempt not to. She waited, giving him space to work through whatever it was. Finally he gave himself a little shake and faced her. "I specialized in procuring hard-to-find weapons. Through The Colonel, I was able to pass along genuine weapons, setting up situations that brought down whichever targets needed to be removed, all while making myself look guiltless. After all, if suspects were apprehended after my portion of things was over, what had that to do with me?"

He made it sound easy, but Celeste had been in the game long enough to know it hadn't been. He must have walked a fine and exhausting line, never able to let down his guard, never knowing who he could trust, if every moment might be his last. Armed with the new information, she wondered if he was so exhausted because of his wound or because he was finally able to let go and set down the heavy burden he'd been carrying for far too many years. At the same time, a prickle of apprehension remained. He was an admitted double agent who'd lied for years. What if he was still lying? What if he was playing her right now? What if as soon as he recovered he turned on her? Her name and location would go for a high price. She could never tell him what she'd done for The Colonel, ever. He could use it against her in the worst possible way.

"For the sake of national security, I must leave a lot of details unsaid. Suffice it to say in my most recent encounter a child stood in harm's way. Try as I might, I couldn't see a way to mitigate the situation to either side's satisfaction. In the end I..." he paused, staring into the middle distance again. Celeste realized her hands were clenched, awaiting whatever he might say next. Obviously she knew he might have chosen to go ahead and destroy the child. And could she blame him? She'd been in the field, knew how often gray areas arose. Some people purposed to use children as shields. The fact that they were sometimes collateral damage was on the people who made them so, not the people in charge of protecting the greater good. But she also knew how that could weigh on a man's head and heart, could burn a hole from the inside out. He let out another heavy sigh. "In the end I saved the child, but I burned bridges I can never recover. I fled for my life, destroying everything I've worked toward for years. My home, I can never go back."

Celeste didn't offer platitudes. She'd never had a home and had no idea how it would feel to lose it. But she did understand the complexities of the sort of job he'd done. "Sometimes there are no easy solutions," she offered at last.

He gave her a sympathetic smile. "Sounds like you speak from experience."

"Maybe we have a few things in common," she said, giving him a little smile of her own. She wondered what the smile looked like because he reached out a hand, letting it hover near her cheek without ever finding resolution.

"Anyway, supper," Celeste announced, standing quickly and taking a few steps away from the couch. She spun and headed toward the kitchen, plopping a can of beef stew into a bowl before starting the microwave.

As she stood at the microwave and watched it spin, she could no longer resist the urge to press her own hand to her cheek, wondering if her own anemic touch felt better or worse than Sam's might have. One thing she knew for certain: at least her touch was safe.

She sat beside him on the couch as they ate their lackluster meal of canned stew and lukewarm water. It wasn't a smart thing to do when she was trying to find some distance, but eating by herself in the kitchen had felt too odd, too standoffish, even for her. Instead of attempting to watch television, they stared out the window, watching it snow. Celeste thought maybe it was the most beautiful thing she had ever seen. Obviously it had snowed when she was a kid, but she didn't remember enjoying it as she was now, from the safety of a warm house, filling her belly with food. Snow had always represented extra cold, extra hunger, extra discomfort. She'd never had boots, or if she had they hadn't fit right, coming as a hand me down from some foster sibling or charity bin. Coats had been a luxury, too. Sometimes teachers noticed she didn't have one and provided. Other years she went without.

The houses she'd lived in had never seemed warm. Wind had whistled through windowpanes. Blankets had been light and scratchy or completely non-existent. Pajamas were often the wrong size from the wrong season.

I should get a pair of pajamas. Since becoming an adult and buying for herself, she had always worn a castoff t-shirt to sleep. But there was nothing stopping her from buying a cozy set of matching pajamas, the more ridiculous, the better. Something with horses or cats on it, like people on TV were always wearing, fake people who somehow woke up better and more refreshed than they went to bed. Was that how other people slept? Real people? Did everyone have pajamas but her?

"It's very beautiful," Sam said, sounding as awed as she felt.

Celeste didn't reply because doing so felt extraneous. Plus her mind was still on pajamas and wondering what other people wore to sleep. All the other foster kids she knew had been like her, wearing mismatched hand me downs, often from the wrong season. Was that what everyone did or was it particular to those who relied on the state for every necessity? *I have no frame of reference for anything,* she thought, and not for the first time. All she had ever known were fellow fosters and soldiers. Both had relied on the government for everything. And she could say for certain the army did it better. At least everyone was the same and everyone was standardized. Fosters' status changed depending on how involved their social workers and foster parents felt at any particular moment. And, given the mass amount of change and upheaval they faced, they could be switched again as soon as they began to feel settled and cared for. Celeste had lived with a couple people who made a modicum effort of providing for her. But she'd been shuttled out of those homes before she could feel the effects. At least in the army they gave her a list of what should be standard issue, allowing her to check off anything she was missing. Maybe she should do that for her own life. Maybe she should create a checklist of necessities. The problem was that she had no idea what those necessities should be, nor how to find out.

"Too bad I'm out of commission or we could play outside," Sam said.

Celeste's head swiveled slowly in his direction.

"What?" he added.

"You would play outside?"

"Wouldn't you?"

"I'm a grown human adult," she replied.

He snorted a laugh. "A redundant one, apparently. Didn't you love to play outside in the snow when you were a kid?"

She faced forward and stared at the snow, trying desperately to remember a time when she had ever played in it, happy and carefree. "Not that I remember." Now it was his turn to stare at her. "What?"

He faced forward. "Nothing. Finish your meal, grown human adult."

She pushed it away, suddenly not hungry. "Maybe pie will help." She hadn't meant to say the words out loud, but Sam laughed again.

"Celeste, pie always helps."

She was inclined to agree, so it was with some sense of excitement that she unboxed the pretty pie, sliced it, and returned with a generous serving for each of them. As they ate their pie in oddly comfortable silence, staring at the snow, Celeste felt a feeling so unfamiliar it took her a while to identify it. When she did, she couldn't understand it. Why did she feel *content* in this moment in this house with this man, eating this pie? Was it the moment? The house? The man? The pie?

"Why are you staring at the pie? Does it not taste good?" Sam asked as he watched her deconstruct a bite of pie, turning it over with her fork.

"It's perfect," Celeste said and even she could hear the slight melancholy in her tone. "How do you think someone makes something so perfect?" To her the act of making a pie was as foreign as the act of building a nuclear reactor. In fact with as much time as she'd spent with the bomb demo guys, she'd probably have better success with a reactor. How did ingredients—fruit and such—turn into a masterpiece like this?

"Probably like everything, lots of practice," Sam mused. He didn't stare at his pie; he demolished it in four bites and stared hungrily toward the kitchen. Celeste didn't offer to refill his pie, her mind was still on its maker. Had the woman's mother taught her to bake? Was it yet another life skill she lacked because she was, for all intents and purposes, an orphan? How much different would her life have been if someone had taken the time to invest in her, to teach her how to make pie, apply makeup, curl her hair, wash her clothes, cook food, place her napkin in her lap, and all the other things she'd missed out on by being a ward of the state? Some of the foster parents had tried. One taught her to make her bed and do the laundry. Another taught her to wait for others to begin eating and place her napkin in her lap. Those were little things, but she had used them proudly, glad for some training in a foreign world. The other kids as school, kids with parents, had seemed to know instinctively how to behave, what not to do in order to resist drawing unwanted attention or trouble. Celeste had been like a bull in a china shop, too loud, unable to chew with her mouth closed, always a mess of crumbs and dirt. Even as a kid she had felt less than, looked down on by the other kids and teachers who realized how sorely lacking in training she was. Her perpetual frustration in life, she later realized, was that she was aware of her lack and had no idea how to fill the void. Basic training had taught her how to be a soldier. Further training had taught her how to be an assassin. But there was no manual or training for real life. And every day in Paradise was a reminder of her inability to function as a grown human adult.

Unbidden, her eyes strayed to her journal, itching to unwind her deep thoughts. She no longer wanted to carry them around inside her. Too much of her life had been spent stumbling under the weight of them. Writing them in her journal allowed her to release a bit of the pent up rage, grief, and resentment. Each time she wrote about something, it felt like releasing a long-held and stale breath, allowing her to draw a much-needed fresh one. Could she write with Sam here? It felt odd to have him in her space, filling it with his warm eyes and thoughtful, studying glances. But his blinks were already growing heavy. Soon he would sleep, and then she would write.

CHAPTER 13

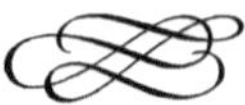

After Sam finally conked out, Celeste reached for her journal with some urgency. She could hear him snoring softly on the couch, but she darted him a glance in case, reassuring herself he was fully asleep. She could have taken the journal to her room, but she didn't want to. The bedroom was for sleep; the living room was for writing. By keeping the two spaces separate, she allowed herself to reserve the bedroom for rest and sleep, two things she desperately needed after unburdening so much of her emotional baggage.

She picked up her pen and, as ever, the words began to flow, hateful, desolate words filled with bitter remembrance from her unhappy, chaotic childhood. In her haste to unscramble what flew out of her, she tried hard to think of one happy snow-filled memory, just one to add to the growing horror. Instead she could only remember the time she'd been locked out after arriving too far past curfew. Those caregivers had been strict and harsh, believing the children in their care had been too long without proper boundaries. Celeste had gotten caught up at a construction site, fascinated by all the concrete tunnels and towers she'd been able to commandeer. When she arrived home and found the door locked, she prepared herself for a long night of no supper. *I've been hungry before,* she reminded herself. But as the temperature dropped rapidly and the wind picked up, she realized she was about to face something new: hunger in the snow.

It began to fall fast and hard and Celeste banged on the door, certain they would let her inside when they realized how cold it was, how much it was snowing. No one came, however. The door remained steadfast, a reminder of her punishment.

I'm going to die, she thought, her too-thin body wracked with shivers.

No I'm not, she argued, stumbling through the yard to find whatever she could assemble as a shelter. The family doghouse was empty, and celeste was small enough to fit. She dragged a piece of cardboard inside with her, using it to block the wind from the entrance. While not exactly warm, it provided some small measure of protection from the wind and snow. Celeste wasn't comfortable, but she probably wouldn't die. That night a new realization began to take place inside her. She couldn't count on the grownups anymore. Until that moment she'd harbored a small amount of hope that someday someone would come along and save her. But no one was coming. She would have to care for herself and, inspecting her makeshift shelter, she could. And she would. *I'm going to take care of me,* she vowed. *No matter how, no matter what.*

With the vow came a small measure of security. From now on she would be okay because she would make certain she would be okay. But there was a strange loss of something she couldn't pin down, a little piece of her heart that closed up and sealed itself away.

Celeste paused and stared into space, pen held aloft, trying to find the proper word to identify what she couldn't back then. What had she lost that night, when she gained her independence? *Hope.* She had tucked it away, replaced it with cynicism. Was it gone completely or, like her child self that night, was it simply weathering the storm, hoping for morning and a rescue?

There was an anemic little flutter in her chest, and she wondered if it was that long ago hope, locked away and trying to break free. But to what end? What if she found her hope again? What would she do with it? Could she safely bring it here, to this strange town and this sterile house where each day felt like fresh failure? What would she tell it? *I survived my horrific childhood and had a great career.* What would it say? *Great, and now what?*

Once again her life came full circle because she had no answer for any hope that might still be living in her. Her career had filled a fifteen year span of time, had spackled over a lot of fear and insecurity from her youth. Thanks to the government's recognition that killing people for a living should be properly compensated, she had no financial worries any longer. As long as she lived reasonably and within her means, she never needed to work again. But did she want to? She was thirty three years old. Reasonably she might live another fifty years, unless her past caught up with her and someone decided to take a life for a life. For a moment she almost hoped that would happen because otherwise those five decades stretched before her like a gaping chasm. What could she possibly do to fill fifty years of time?

One thing she knew for certain, she couldn't allow them to be worse than the first thirty. A dream presented itself before her, a functioning orchard with her at the helm, greeting customers and children who came to pick apples, retiring each night to sleep in this house, transformed to a cozy habitat instead of its current sterile wasteland.

She blinked once and the gossamer vision dissolved. *Ridiculous.* She'd never even had a houseplant. How did she purpose to revitalize a hundred year old—probably dead—orchard? How could she hope to grow apples when she couldn't manage more than the most basic life functions?

Suddenly she reached her limit of thinking and feeling for the day. As ever after she journaled, the energy drained out of her, leaving her depleted. She closed the book, shoved it back onto the shelf, stumbled up the stairs, and fell into a dead sleep.

⚷

The noise was slight but it was enough to wake Sam. He watched Celeste shove a notebook onto the shelf, turn off the light, and walk upstairs. Her gait looked odd, like someone who'd emerged from a coma and was having trouble using her legs again. He squinted, almost calling out in concern before thinking better of it. One thing he'd learned about Celeste, the only thing, was that she was private. His attempts to peer into her psyche and learn more about her—anything about her—had been a complete failure.

To say she was unexpected would be an understatement. When The Colonel told him he'd be going to Montana, he hadn't cared enough to pay attention. He was fleeing for his life, after all, with only the shirt on his back. If not for American Military Intelligence, he would be dead by now, probably several times over. They'd intervened on his behalf multiple times over the years, taking care of situations and arranging them so the outcome landed in his favor, albeit quietly. There had been a lot of coincidences in his world, thankfully not enough that anyone on the wrong side noticed. But if he had stayed, they probably would have. Sam had already survived too long in a world with a predictably short lifespan. Eventually someone would have started to talk and wonder why Din Chatti seemed to be made of Teflon, never in trouble, never in danger, always escaping harm at the last possible moment and in the most amazing way.

As ever, Sam felt a mixture of gratitude and resentment. Grateful that he'd been kept alive, resentful that he had to rely on the man who held his former love. The Colonel might be the main man in charge, but without a doubt it was Cameron Ridge who'd kept a particular eye on Sam the past few years, sending teams to pull him out of various scrapes. His only comfort was that Ridge likely resented it as much as Sam did. Not that Ridge wanted to see him dead. Or maybe he did, who knew? Sam didn't want Ridge dead. He just wanted him to never have existed to begin with, to magically erase him from the earth and Maggie's heart forever.

Unable to sleep now, his thoughts strayed toward Celeste. And such was his psychic misery over his own sad life that he was happier to think about hers. To say she was unexpected would be an understatement. After he safely arrived in Canada and made contact with the team, he found out he'd be staying with a woman, a former contractor for The Colonel. Sam had pictured someone old and stodgy, a weathered matron whose voice was as hardscrabble as her face. Instead he found Celeste. His first view of her hadn't left an impression, half delirious as he was with pain and blood loss. But then as he sat against the wall of the kitchen and tried to ignore the searing pain in his shoulder, he listened to her descend the stairs and braced himself, certain she would put him on blast for bumbling into her house in the middle of the night.

Instead she had eased into the room looking small and vulnerable, a skittish bunny with big eyes and small features. *There is no way this woman worked for The Colonel,* he thought. Perhaps she was some far-flung family member and he'd been mistaken. His interactions with her since had done nothing to clear up the confusion. He stared at her whenever she wasn't looking, trying to solve the mystery. The more he looked, the more he liked what he saw. There was something so… soft about her when she wasn't aware she was being watched. She examined each thing she found as if she'd never noticed it before, as with the pie. Certainly she'd had pie. He'd lived in Saudi Arabia for most of his adult life, and even he'd had pie.

He began to think maybe The Colonel had stashed her here to keep her safe for some reason. If the way she recoiled from any physical contact was any indication, perhaps she'd been hurt. If so, that person should be killed in some heinous fashion. How could anyone wound someone as small and helpless as Celeste? It was unfathomable.

I want her to trust me, he thought and then immediately banished it. There was no reason anyone should trust him ever again. In fact there was every reason in the world not to trust him after the things he'd done, the lies he told. He'd faked his own death to get out of his wedding, after all, eviscerating the person in the world he loved most, the person who thought he was trustworthy enough to pledge her life to. He only wanted to bestow friendship and kindness on Celeste, and yet even that was beyond his reach. He had nothing to give anyone, least of all someone as pure and deserving as Celeste, who seemed to be doing her best to care for him despite recovering from whatever she'd been sent here to recover from. He had no idea what it was, but he knew it was something. He of all people recognized the signs of trauma and Celeste had it in spades. It made him angry on her behalf, whatever it was.

His eyes strayed to the bookshelf and the notebook she'd put back. It was obviously her journal. His fingers itched to reach for it, but he couldn't, *wouldn't*. It would be a terrible invasion of privacy. He knew that, and yet he longed to solve the mystery that must lie within. Who was Celeste? Why was she here? How had someone so delicate, so vulnerable and innocent wound up alone in the wilderness of Montana?

Sleep stole over him again. He closed his eyes and vowed to solve the mystery another day. Soon, sometime soon he would figure her out.

CHAPTER 14

Once again something woke Celeste. She sat up from a dead sleep with a sharp intake of breath. As before, something was off. This time it wasn't a sound, it was something else. But what?

Her teeth chattered and she glanced at the now blank alarm clock. *Power's out.* Groggy and freezing, she stumbled out of bed and down the stairs, trailing her hand on the banister so she didn't topple. Strange how much ambient light things like appliances gave off. Now, with nothing on, it was all inky blackness. She couldn't see a thing, not the stairs, not even her feet.

She knew by counting how many stairs there were, and she knew when she reached the bottom. Even so she paused, taking stock of the stillness. It was disconcerting how quiet it was without the usual hum of the house.

"Celeste," Sam whispered, his slight accent making her name into a question.

"Yes."

"Are you all right?"

Her lashes fluttered. When was the last time anyone asked her that question? She couldn't remember. "I'm fine. The power's out." She started to take a step and paused, remembering she should also check on him. "Are you okay?"

"Yes," he said, sounding amused. Why, she had no idea.

"I'm going to light the heater." She tried to say it with confidence. Elliot had shown her how, it shouldn't be a problem. But so far everything in Paradise had been a problem. The house and barn were decrepit, the trees apparently sterile, the equipment unusable. Why should the heater be any different?

It was, though. As soon as she knelt beside it and clicked the button, the flame flicked to life and began to give out blessed heat. Enraptured, she plopped onto the floor in front of it and stared. A minute later, Sam meandered in and gingerly sat beside her, trailing one of the blankets from his makeshift bed on the couch.

"I have made fire," she announced.

He laughed and offered her half of his blanket. "You are very talented."

She stared at the blanket, pondering. Sharing his proximity, let alone his blanket, was an intimate thing. She must have hesitated too long because his hand tensed as he held it toward her.

"I won't hurt you," he promised, tone soft.

"No, I know. I'm not worried about that." Finally she took the blanket and eased a tiny bit closer, basking in the warmth from his body without letting on that she was enjoying it. A flame was nice; body heat was better.

"You should be. I'm much bigger than you," he said, then looked at her askance when she snorted a laugh.

"Sorry, I, uh, am pretty good at taking care of myself," she assured him.

"I suppose if you worked for The Colonel that is probably true, but it's hard to believe, given your high level of adorability."

She smiled a little, staring at the flame. It had been a long time since someone complimented her on her looks, if one considered being called adorable a compliment. Celeste did because she'd been called so many worse things. "That's part of what made me a danger. No one expects someone who looks like me to be able to..." she broke off, realizing how easily he'd gotten her to open up and talk about her job. *Danger, danger, danger.* Not only was her life classified, it was fully her own. Information was power. Giving it away put her at his mercy.

"I suppose," he said agreeably and she relaxed because he didn't probe further. "This is rather cozy, with the fire and the snow. How long do you suppose the power will be away?"

"I don't know. People in town made it seem like it could be a while. I have enough kerosene for a few days, and enough food as well. After that…" After that she had no idea. This was her first Montana winter. Learning by doing probably wasn't the best way with something that could kill you with frostbite or starvation, but she saw no other alternative.

"After that, we'll tunnel out, if we have to."

"You've clearly thought this through," she said.

"Life has prepared me for every contingency," he said.

"Same," she agreed.

"Sorry to have that in common," he said, and they sat a few moments in cozy silence. "Do you know what we need right now?"

"I'm going to guess pie," she said.

"You're a mind reader," he said. "Although I feel a little bad that by requesting pie I'm basically making you wait on me."

"You should," she said, tossing the blanket lightly at him as she sprang up. She found the flashlight she'd left on the table and propped it upright while she located the pie.

"I'm going to go out on a limb and say we can skip the plates. Just bring pie and forks."

"Now who's a mind reader," she said, clicking off the light as she tucked the pie under her arm and faced him. She sat down and he placed the blanket over her lap with his good arm. She opened the pie and set it evenly between them. "If you take more than your share, I'll know."

"How will you know? We can't see," he reasoned.

"I have special powers, very precise pie measuring abilities."

"That's terrifying," he said.

"You should definitely be afraid," she agreed. They tucked in and began to eat and that feeling crept over her again, the one from before. Something was oddly familiar about the moment, although she was certain she'd never experienced it before. It was as if she was finally getting a taste of the way things might have been, if her life had been different. As if something inside her recognized something that was happening and wanted to latch on to it. But that was insane. This man was a stranger, the new life strange and untenable.

"You're scowling. Did you get a bad bite?" Sam asked.

"How can you tell I'm scowling? You can't see me."

"I have special powers, very precise ability to read a woman's middle of the night mood."

She laughed and it might almost have been a giggle. "That actually is terrifying."

"I usually save it for the fourth date," he said.

"Did you leave a wife behind when you fled? A family?" she asked, her smile morphing to a stern frown. What if she was sharing pie and laughter with the sort of man who would leave his family behind to fend for himself?

"No." He took a couple of bites. She had the sense he wanted to say something and let him stew until he worked up to it. "The whole thing began with a wedding, actually. One I begged off attending."

"You weaseled out of a wedding and became a double agent arms dealer? That's some progression," she said.

"The wedding in question was mine. I faked my death and ran off. Are you okay?" he asked when she began to choke.

"That's a next level fear of commitment," she said when she finally worked the hunk of pie out of her throat.

"No, actually. I had no fear of commitment."

"I sense a story. Please continue, Brother Grimm."

"For the record, that is literally the nineteenth time in my life someone has called me Brother Grimm."

"Might be time to enter a new line of work, Death Dealer," she noted.

He coughed a laugh. "Touché. But enough about you, back to my sad tale. Given the suave way I bumbled into getting shot and passed out on your floor, it might surprise you to learn I was not always a ladies' man. In fact, brace yourself, I was rather gawky. It's almost like bringing a child from Jordan to middle school in America is a set up for being an awkward outcast."

"It worked for me," she said, and he laughed again, clashing his fork against hers to shush her.

"Do you want to hear my heartbreak or not?" he demanded.

"All of it, in its goriest detail, double bonus points if it still makes you cry."

"Only at night when I can press my face to my stuffed bear," he said. He took a breath and stared at the fire, like a Shaman about to deliver an allegory. Maybe he was: The Dangers of Being Born Into a Psychotic Family, Part One. "I met the girl my first day of freshman year of college, and she was adorable."

"I thought *I* was adorable," she muttered.

"There can be more than one adorable woman in the world. Don't be jealous. I certainly never got shot by her neighbor."

"We'll always have that," she agreed. "Proceed."

"Wonder of wonders, she seemed to believe I was adorable, too."

"Are we certain this isn't fiction?" she interrupted.

He held his fork aloft like a weapon. "One more insult and I will extend this monologue until the power comes back on."

She zipped her lips.

"Anyway, we were always together after that. Our relationship progressed naturally and easily until we became engaged."

"And then you realized you'd made a horrible mistake because why marry the love of your life when you could sell weapons to terrorists instead?" she said.

"It's the classic boy meets girl, boy fakes death, boy becomes a terrorist trope," he joked, eating another bite. "In reality, it was much more complicated."

"How so?"

"My father died in a car accident. Apparently he had been acting as the boy with the finger in the dam of family drama because afterward it all came flooding out."

"How so?" She tipped her head to study him. It wasn't possible that his family trauma was worse than hers, was it?

"My uncles threatened to murder my fiancée if I didn't break it off."

"That's pretty bad."

"They actually were terrorists, so I knew they meant what they said."

"So then you faked your death. I hope you were able to keep the deposit on your tuxedo."

"Has anyone ever told you compassion is your gift?" he asked.

"One guy. And then I killed him," she said, deadpan.

"Okay," he drawled. "Back to me."

"Pretty sure we never left there," she groused.

He sighed, annoyed, and she pressed a hand to her mouth, pushing back another giggle-snort. "Anyway, I promised to go away with them, but it wasn't enough." His tone turned somber and hers followed.

"They killed the girl?"

He shook his head. "My mother."

Her mouth made an "O" but no sound came out.

"Everything was rather a blur after that. My mother was gentle and kind, so much that she was able to draw my father away from the dangerous world in which he was raised. We had a normal, loving, carefree life before everything fell apart. The juxtaposition from before to after was too much for my mind to handle for a while. I was angry, to say the least, so angry that I lost my head a bit. In a matter of months I had gone from being in love, being the happiest man in the world to being a desolate, loveless orphan who, in the eyes of the law, didn't even exist anymore. Instead of rebelling against my uncles, I leaned into it. I became what they wanted me to be. I became what everyone in my life from before would have loathed."

Celeste understood that sort of anger. "Did it help?" In the beginning she had enjoyed her job a bit too much. The Colonel, prescient as always, took her aside and told her she shouldn't. *Hurting others won't fix what's gone wrong in your life. I didn't recruit you to be a vigilante. Find healing in some other way. This is the job and only ever the job.*

"For a time, perhaps. It was an outlet, at least. And the people I hurt were similarly bad people, or so I reasoned."

"Like Robin Hood," she said, another familiar path her mind had followed.

"I believe I substituted Batman, but the same basic premise."

"What changed?" she asked.

He gave another sigh, this one deep and sad. "The girl re-entered the picture."

"She tracked you down?" Celeste asked, incredulous. Was she impressed or horrified at that stalker level of devotion?

"With the help of the United States Government. She had not been lax in my absence, as it turned out. She became a spy and, as fate would have it, was assigned to my case."

"*Wow*," Celeste mouthed, though he couldn't see. "The chances of that must be astronomical."

"One would think. Someone up there either loves or hates me very much."

They stared at the fire a bit in silence, pondering, each wondering about the Someone up there and His role in their lives. And then they gave a collective shudder, remembering all the things they would rather leave unseen and unknown.

"And then what happened?" she prompted.

"Look who is suddenly interested in my story," he said.

"I'm a diehard romantic," she said.

"You only tuned in after the romance was over, everyone was dead, and I became a terrorist," he complained.

"I smell a new plot for Disney," she said.

He gave her shoulder a light shove. "What happened was this: My uncles were apprehended, and so was I. And then I was let go, with the caveat that I now work for the people who had saved me."

"And the girl?"

"Chose to remain with my replacement, the guy who has always definitively been on the side of good."

"Where's the romance or adventure in that?" she asked, affronted on his behalf. Clearly he still loved the woman and, from what she could tell, he had a lot going for him, terrorist past notwithstanding.

"Women these days. It's almost like they prefer men who aren't murderers and international criminals who ducked out on the wedding."

"You're probably better off without someone that shallow," she said, earning another laugh that abruptly faded.

"I'm not, though. She's married with a baby, and I'm theoretically happy for her. But for me there's no one else. Not in all these years have I strayed from my loyalty to her." He reached for the pie and paused when he realized there was only a bite left.

Celeste shoved it toward him. "You're pathetic enough to need this."

"Thank you for realizing," he said and downed the final bite.

CHAPTER 15

They woke in the morning in a huddled mass, curled together under the blanket like yin and yang. Celeste came to first, groggy and disoriented, unable to remember how she wound up in her current position. There was pie. Good pie, but was it enough to make her cast aside all her normal reserve and curl up on the couch with a stranger? Apparently.

After they finished the pie in the kitchen, the sun began to emit a hazy gray mist. They decided to watch it rise from the comfort of the couch. As the sun stole over the horizon, giving everything a rosy glow, they studied the landscape, pristine with fresh snow. Everything had felt so…cozy. The house was freezing, the warmth of the kitchen long forgotten and out of reach. But the body heat they generated under the shared blanket pulled them toward sleep, and that was how it happened. Without thought or purpose, they'd ended up…snuggling. *Only for warmth,* Celeste protested, but she wasn't certain she believed it. She was drawn to Sam for more than physical warmth, and that scared her. A lot.

"Well, this is awkward," Sam whispered, but he sounded more amused than sheepish.

"Yes," she agreed, tone stilted.

"For the record, I did not consciously spoon you," he said.

"I don't spoon," Celeste protested.

"Whatever you say, little spoon." His index finger rimmed her ear and it felt so good she immediately hopped off the couch, landing a few feet away in a jump worthy of the gymnast she had once secretly aspired to be.

"I'm going to shower."

Sam blinked up at her, brown eyes brimming with amusement. "The power's out."

"I'll improvise," she called, already heading toward the stairs. There was no need to improvise, however. Halfway up the power flicked on. The water would be freezing. She was tempted to jump in but knew she would immediately regret the rash action. While she waited for the water heater to do its magic, she performed a mini workout, jumping jacks, burpees, sit ups, push ups, squats and lunges. Her protesting muscles unkindly reminded her how infrequent her workouts had become since she retired. *I need to stay in shape. I need to keep myself in order. In every way.*

By the time she finished jumping around, she was warm and so was the water. She stepped beneath the spray, hoping it would wash away her confusing mix of thoughts and feelings. Celeste felt like she was standing on some sort of ledge. Across from her was the next part of her life, the person she wanted to be. Between that person and the ledge was a fathomless cavern she had no idea how to cross. Worse, she had no idea what the other side looked like, only that she needed to get there as soon as possible. But one thing she knew for certain, down to her marrow, was that the way did not lie with some man as her salvation, and especially not Sam who was temporary with a past as sketchy as hers. Since she was a child, she had only relied on herself because she was the only person she could trust to keep her safe. She hadn't changed that in fifteen years in the army and she certainly wouldn't change it now.

Resolved once more, she threw on warm, clean clothes and brushed her teeth, running a comb through her hair. She could dress up and look good when she wanted, could be stunning and possibly even mesmerizing. It was a skill that had served her well as an assassin, using her looks to distract targets. Everyone responded to beauty, especially egotistical men. But now, in this new life, she was content to remain as natural as possible. Though she couldn't articulate why, it felt good in that deep secret place she kept hidden to be as authentic as possible. *Simplicity,* she thought with a nod, vowing to write it down. Whenever she stumbled on a word she liked, one that pinged on her internal radar as important, she tried to write it down. She hoped journaling might heal all the things that had gone wrong with her before life. In the same way, she hoped capturing the new words and feelings might help her articulate the things she wanted for her future. So far the list consisted of *integrity, kindness, authenticity,* and now *simplicity.*

Maybe I'll become a shaker, she thought, inspecting her walls to see if she could affix pegs to them. Once on a school field trip she toured a Shaker Village. Their simple, homespun life made a deep impression on a little girl whose world was pure chaos. The shakers had died off because of their unbending embrace of celibacy. *Won't be a problem for me,* Celeste thought wryly, purposely ignoring the boyishly cute man now dominating her living room.

When she jogged down the steps, Sam sat on the couch, staring at her. The amusement on his face was the same as before she left. He might not have moved at all, except his hair was wet, as if he'd tried to clean himself up in the downstairs bathroom, which he probably had.

"I have towels and soap," she announced.

"I hope you used them," he returned.

She rolled her eyes. "I meant for you. I'm not the hostest with the mostest, so I sort of forget all the things I should probably be doing."

"You're doing fine," he said in that warm and reassuring way that made little prickles of what felt a lot like pain jab against her chest. Her heart was bundled, safe and protected in the solid cage she'd erected. Kindness, gentleness, all the good things she'd longed for as a child now butted against that cage, wounding her with their failed attempts to gain entry. She would not, could not open the cage and let anyone in. She'd learned that lesson on repeat in the hardest ways possible. Others could not be trusted, especially men.

"Just tell me if you need something, or feel free to get it yourself. I'm not territorial about things like about."

"About things like that," he repeated slowly, studying her as if compiling some sort of list about her.

Ignoring him, she went to the kitchen, turned off the kerosene heater, and poured two bowls of cereal, setting one in front of him on the table.

"Thank you," he murmured, staring at it.

"What's wrong?" she asked.

"Nothing," he said and picked up his spoon.

"I don't believe you," she said, pointing her spoon accusingly at him.

"That's your prerogative," he said, tossing her a smile before he took a bite.

"You're irksome," she said, and he covered his mouth to keep from spewing cereal while he chewed and laughed. "What?"

"Nothing. You're cute."

"Yesterday it was adorable."

"It downgraded when you left me freezing on the couch," he said.

"Then I guess you should prepare yourself. By the time you leave here, my inaccessibility will downgrade me to troll."

"Not possible. Also what's wrong with a little harmless flirting? I'm single. We both know this is a blip." He froze and stared at her. "Unless you're not single. You're not secretly married to someone who is going to now kill me are you?"

"No, I prefer to handle things like that myself," she said, draining her milk. "I'm single, by choice and for all eternity."

"Why?" he asked.

She glanced at her blank wrist. "Look at that. I have to be literally anywhere other than this conversation. Rain check. Also, I don't take rain checks."

"You're prickly. I like that."

She laughed. "You're odd."

His brows rose hopefully. "And do you like that?"

"No," she said, but she was lying. Despite his past, despite the fact that he'd confessed to being a one-and-done-with-love type person, despite everything, he had kind eyes and a sincere smile, two things she didn't realize were important until it was too late to look for them, until she'd given up.

"All I'm saying is you should think about it. How many times do you meet someone and share—hopefully mutual—attraction with the guarantee that nothing will come of it? We could fling and walk away, hearts intact."

"What a temptingly shallow offer. My heart is warm all over with the thought of being trampled and thrown away by you."

"So you're, like, a forever kind of girl," he mused.

"I'm a never kind of girl. You know those crows from that book they make kids read in high school English? Nevermore, that's me."

"Not to get too technically nerdy on you, but those were ravens. You can tell because the poem is literally called, 'The Raven.' And it's by Poe."

She pointed to her face. "This is me, not caring. Also, English is your second language. You should not know things about our literature. It's obnoxious."

Far from being offended, he grinned. "I know a lot about American history, too. It's a particular interest of mine. Quiz me, I'll impress you." He crossed his hands, awaiting her questions.

"That's becoming more doubtful by the moment," she muttered, tossing the dishes into the sink with a clatter.

"Fine, then tell me something about you," he commanded.

She remained mute, her back to him as she filled the sink with soapy water.

"What did you do for The Colonel?" he asked.

"Classified."

"Secretary? Attaché?" he guessed, hoping to provoke her.

"Both. I was secretary to the attaché," she returned, unperturbed. Better men than him had tried to poke at her, incorrectly guessing sexism would be her sore spot.

"Okay, you're once again upgraded to adorable for being an adorable liar," he said.

She was glad her back was to him so he couldn't see her smile.

"You're too short to be his personal pilot. Was it some kind of jester situation? Like you popped out whenever he needed a chuckle at your cuteness."

"Yes. I'm ever so glad not to live in that cake anymore. Quite the mouse and roach problem, not to mention the ongoing diabetes."

"You're not easily provoked. Wait, were you..." he pressed his palms on the table and leaned forward. "Or perhaps *are* you The Colonel's therapist? Does he pop in for a visit when he's about to go postal and you talk him down?"

She wanted to find a clever reply, but it was so funny she couldn't tamp down her giggles as she tried to picture The Colonel asking anyone for mental help or advice. And if he ever decided to "go postal," no one would ever find out because there would be no survivors.

"If you're going to add giggling into the mix, I'm going to have to come up with a new term to describe you. There must be a sweet spot somewhere between adorable and super fluffball kitten."

"How about 'tiny annoyed psychopath,'" she suggested.

"Ding! There we go, although it's kind of wordy. Let's shorten it to Tap, it's a timesaver."

She faced him, soapy hand on hip. "Are you actually trying to make me believe that other terrorists found you intimidating?"

"I'm a grown human male," he returned, causing her to sputter a laugh again as she faced forward.

"You're a weirdo," she said.

"I can be both things. Also, it feels good to let go of the bad persona, finally forever. I can get back to being the person I was before, if I can correctly remember who that was."

He sounded sad, and it echoed the sadness in her. "You'll figure it out," she assured him.

"How, though?" he asked, sounding genuinely curious.

That was the problem. She had no answers for him because she had no answers for herself. "Time or something, something."

"Ah, I finally figured out what you do. You're in charge of all those inspirational posters hanging in The Colonel's office."

She snickered again. "He doesn't have inspirational pictures in his office."

She didn't look, but she could tell he sat up. "Wait, have you for real been in The Colonel's office? No one goes in the inner sanctum."

She couldn't help but turn then, as she bestowed a smug raised eyebrow on him. "Some people do."

Far from being impressed, he shrank back. "You're not, like, you know, like, a secret mistress or something, are you?"

She gagged. "No! He's twelve million years old. And he's *The Colonel.* It would be weird and gross and, gah. Shut up." She pressed her soapy hands to her ears, but she wasn't trying to block him out; she was trying to block out all the memories she'd rather forget, especially the one where she hit on The Colonel during their first meeting. That sad girl existed a lifetime ago, but somehow she always lingered, ready to haunt Celeste at the merest suggestion of who she had been.

"Hey." She didn't realize Sam was standing beside her until he spoke softly, touching a finger gently to her forearm. What did her expression look like right now? Whatever it was, it must have been horrifying because he looked slightly terrified. "Hey," he repeated again. His tone was soothing and it worked to soothe her. "It's okay. I was joking. I know it's not like that. Five minutes of knowing the man and I know he would never...And you would never. I mean, I presume you would never, not only because it would be gross, but because..."

She dropped her hands from her ears. "Oh, sweet merciful cornflakes, stop talking."

His lashes fluttered and his lips twitched. "Sweet merciful cornflakes? Is that who you pray to?"

She took a breath and scrubbed her hand between her eyes a few times, clearing away the last vestiges of bad memories. "I made a bet with someone I used to work with, that I could stop swearing. I started using nonsense words instead and the habit sort of stuck. What?" He was full on beaming at her now.

"I think we've surpassed fluffy kitten and are well into the danger zone of cuteness. You could legitimately kill someone with lovability right now."

"If only that were true," she muttered, but halfheartedly. The conversation had left her drained, and they had only scratched the surface of the well of trauma inside her. Her eyes darted toward her journals, but it was too early to unburden herself. Once she opened that gate, she could only sleep afterword. She couldn't sleep all day with Sam in the house, even if they'd shared an abruptly shortened night.

"Hey," he said, bending his head to try and catch her eye. "I'm going to hug you now."

"Why?" she asked, immediately tense and suspicious.

"For one thing, I'm a hugger, but I've been surrounded by terrorists for most of the last decade. I could use a hug. But also, maybe so could you, it seems. It's a thing normal people do."

"Is it?" she said, having no idea if it was true. Did people hug? She knew families probably hugged, but did casual acquaintances do it, too?

"Yes, so don't read anything into it. I'm only hitting on you a little, like ten percent," he said. He put his good arm around her and drew her to him. She stood listless and uncomfortable in his embrace. "You're supposed to hug me back," he prompted.

She did so, but added, "I'm hitting on you zero percent."

"That's okay, I've upped mine to fifteen to make up for your deficit."

She snorted a laugh, accidentally inhaling his scent when she pressed her face to his chest to subdue it.

"Twenty percent and growing. You should know when we reach sixty, it's the critical phase and can't be undone."

"And what will happen then?" she asked, peeling back slightly to see his face.

He tucked a stray hair behind her ear. "Then we fall in love and live happily ever after."

"Now I'm terrified," she said.

"You should be. I snore."

"You're so weird," she murmured, but she returned to the hug because, as it turned out, hugging was nice. Even if it was a temporary stranger whose presence in her life made no rational sense. Maybe especially then because she didn't have to think about forever. She only had to think about each moment. Maybe, *maybe* she should take him up on his suggestion to throw caution to the wind and have a fling. What would be the harm if they both went into it fully prepared?

You know exactly the harm, she reminded herself.

Before she could allow herself to dwell, her phone rang, pulling her reluctantly out of Sam's embrace.

"No, don't, we were nearing fifty percent," Sam said, arms held beseechingly toward her. She waved a hand, warding him away, because there was only one person who called her, and he never did so unless it was important. And it turned out now was no different.

"We have a problem," The Colonel began.

CHAPTER 16

Celeste had lost track of the number of times the man had said that to her over the years. It was, in fact, the only reason he ever called her. Because the unique skill set she possessed, the one he trained her to have, was the one he called on for situations that needed to be dealt with. Briefly, her eyes flicked to Sam and away. Surely she wasn't about to be tasked with his demise, was she? Could she do that? She'd have to think about it, if that was the purpose for the call.

"How's the package?" The Colonel continued.

Her eyes flicked to Sam again. He was...aggravating and unexpected, but she was certain that wasn't what The Colonel meant. "Moderate."

He grunted, doubtless a commentary on her long pause. The man always seemed to have the preternatural ability to know what the people under his command were thinking. "I'm sending a team."

"Extraction?" she asked, half relieved and half disappointed. She would be glad when the arrangement was over, but she would also sort of miss him, at least for a while. For a short time it had been nice to know there were other people in the world stumbling through life, trying and failing to get it together and have everything go right.

"No. Recon. We haven't had a chance to debrief him yet."

"Pardon me, sir, but can't you do that after you extract him?"

"That's the thing, Sergeant Major. We can't, at least not yet. His departure set off a chain of events in an already overheated situation. We have to let things settle in that part of the world before we make any attempt to move him."

Her hand gripped the phone. Despite not being a great student of world events back in school, she'd learned an enormous amount by living and working all over the globe. Enough to say, "That could take years."

"Yes. I don't expect you to be tasked with him that long, obviously. We'll know better how to proceed after the team gets there. They'll be staying with you also. I've compensated accordingly. Buy yourself some new tires, Sergeant Major. They're not equipped for the weather you'll be dealing with."

And then he was gone. She didn't bother to try and ask how he knew the condition of her tires because of course he did. He probably knew what she was wearing right now and how she and Sam and slept curled together like homeless puppies last night. Fighting a blush —a *blush*—she turned away from Sam.

"Am I going to die?" Sam asked.

"Yes, but who can say when," Celeste replied, tossing her phone onto the counter as she continued to avoid his gaze. He was here *for the long haul.* Here in her house, in her space, in her healing place. How was she supposed to figure out her life with him standing in the way, being cute and charming and so weird that it somehow doubled the charm? *Assassin rule number one: don't fall for the terrorists, no matter how long their lashes.*

"Are you having some sort of mental break? Because you're staring really hard at that tacky wallpaper," Sam said. "Also, your fists are clenched like you're about to spin toward me and beat adorably on my chest in tiny frustration."

"There's no such thing as tiny frustration," she said, pressing her thumb to the middle of her forehead.

"Fair point," he agreed. "Are you allowed to tell me what that was about? Because I'm kind of getting the hint it had to do with me. And unless it was your bestie who is going to come give you a makeover that will kickstart our epic love story, it kind of feels like I should know about it."

"The Colonel is sending a team," she ground out.

He paused. "A murder team?"

"We don't call it murder if you're the bad guy," she informed him.

"Heh, heh. Sure, okay, but that's not exactly reassuring because, in the most technical sense and on a moral level, I'm not actually the good guy."

"They're not coming to kill you." She didn't add *yet* but it hung unspoken in the air between them. "They're coming to interview you."

Somehow that only made him tenser. "Did he say who?"

"No," she drawled.

He swallowed hard. "The girl, you know, the one I told you about."

"The jilted bride."

He winced. "Charming. Yes, that one. Did I mention she works for The Colonel? And so does her husband."

She laughed, which made him scowl, which made her laugh harder. "Quite a life you lead, Din Chatti."

He gave her a charmingly lopsided smile in return. "It's far less boring than I ever imagined it might be."

"He did not say who is coming because, you know, he's The Colonel," she replied.

"Can I ask you a question?"

She tensed. Dispensing information wasn't her strong suit and there was little she could safely tell him.

"Why does everyone call him The Colonel when he's a general now?"

She relaxed. "I can answer that one, or at least attempt to." She'd spent a lot of boredom-fueled down hours debating the same with special teams she sometimes worked with. "The working theory is that he was a colonel when he began assembling his teams, hand selecting people from obscurity into the realms. And it sort of solidified something, you know? A sort of unity and code. *You've been plucked by The Colonel.* Voila, the name stuck for all eternity."

"I see," he said, squinting at her in a way that made her wonder if he did see, if he could understand that she, too, had been selected by The Colonel, saved from obscurity. "Also I see what you did there. Plucked by The Colonel. Nice."

"The KFC jokes have been around for a while. They're not going anywhere, probably another reason no one wants to call him The General. Plus, I don't know. *General.* It's so...above. Calling him The Colonel makes him still seem like one of us, not one of them."

"Who is them?" he asked.

"Washington." She whispered it in the same way someone might speak of The Boogeyman. As if he might hear and punish you. Knowing what she knew about the government, it wasn't a far-fetched idea.

"So, not to belabor the point and make this all about me, but no one is coming here to kill me. Promise?"

She grasped his forearms in hers and looked earnestly into his eyes. "How about this. I promise you that if anyone is going to kill you, it will be me."

"You are the cutest little murder monkey ever," he said, giving her arms a squeeze.

"And you are..." her gaze slid to the side, distracted. "Bleeding."

"Ha, but I don't get it."

"No, you're seriously bleeding." She let go of his arm and pointed to his shoulder.

He glanced down. "I guess that explains why the room is swimming in and out of focus. I thought it was the height differential between us making me woozy." He sank heavily into a chair and rested his forehead on the table.

"Are you going to pass out again?"

"It's under consideration," he said. "Also, I should tell you I'm not great with the sight of blood."

"Seriously, you are the worst terrorist I have ever known," she said.

"Hey, do not disparage my terrorist skills. I have a lot of hidden assets," he said.

"Like what?" she demanded, crossing her arms.

"Maybe we could talk about this when I'm not bleeding out," he said.

"Typical man," she said, clucking her tongue.

"Celeste," he whined. *"Do something."*

She poked his good shoulder. "Stop bleeding."

"Do something better."

She uncrossed her arms so she could throw them in the air. "What do you want me to do? The town doesn't have a doctor, much less a hospital."

"Can't you sew it up?" he asked, twisting his head to make puppy eyes at her.

"I only know how to make holes, not repair them," she said. She bit her lip because he did look rather pathetic. "You're turning green."

"I'm too brown to turn green," he said weakly.

"Then you're turning olive. Maybe one of the team members will be a medic," she suggested.

"But when will they get here?"

"He didn't give a timeframe," Celeste said. She reached for her phone to double check, though she knew already, when there was a knock at the door. They froze and stared at each other.

"Could that be them?"

"I suppose it's possible, but knowing what I know of our lives, do you think fortune would be so kind?" She removed her gun from its holster and checked it.

"Were you wearing that while we hugged?" he exclaimed.

"Is there some rule against that?" she returned.

"Not a written one, but…rude."

"Next time I'll consult the 'So You're About to Hug A Terrorist' chapter in the 'Housing a Fugitive' handbook," she promised.

"Ex-terrorist," he said. *"EX.* I was a double agent. Why does no one add that part?"

"I'll be back. Sit tight," she said.

"I find your sense of humor lacking," he said, pressing a hand to his forehead.

Repressing a smile, she answered the door.

*E*lliot," she exclaimed, staring at him in wonder, almost seven feet of him as he towered over her in the doorway.

He held his hands up in supplication. "Not stalking you, I promise. I'm actually completely unfriendly and usually want nothing to do with newcomers."

"I believe you," she inserted and he snorted a laugh he immediately smoothed.

"I had a call up this way, and my wife has been worried about you."

She squinted, trying to remember if she'd met his wife. "Do I know her?"

"No, but what I lack in people skills, she makes up for. She's *friendly*." He grimaced and rolled his eyes. "Anyway, I promised her I would stop in and make certain you survived the night without power. It looks like you have, so I'll be on my way." He tugged his hat and turned to go.

"Wait," she called before realizing she was going to. Maybe this was a mistake, but what choice did she have? Sam might be injured more severely than either of them realized, and that could be terribly inconvenient. She licked her lips and darted a glance toward the kitchen, an action that did not go unnoticed by Elliot who narrowed his good eye and took a step toward her.

"Is something wrong?" he asked in a tight whisper, his gaze also moving behind her. "Is someone in your house? Are you being held hostage?"

"In a manner of speaking," she said, then realized he might not know she was joking. "No, not at all. I, um, I have a house guest and, um, he met with…an…unfortunate accident recently."

His gaze narrowed again. Anymore and she was going to appear like a wavy squint. "Let me guess: he was shot."

She nodded.

"Was he stealing Edward Jonas's cattle?"

"It's likely he doesn't know the difference between a cow and a buffalo," she said.

"I heard that," Sam called weakly from the kitchen. Elliot's ears pricked in that direction like an alert German Shepherd.

"He's harmless, I promise," Celeste said. "But he is wounded. Would you mind taking a look?"

With a nod, Elliot followed her inside.

CHAPTER 17

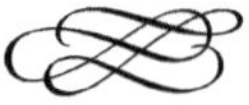

"I am not harmless," Sam said, eyes closed as he rested his head on the table and tried not to pass out. "I am dangerous and terrifying."

"Of course you are. Now open your eyes and say hello to the nice man," Celeste commanded.

He opened his eyes, which widened immediately. "Am I hallucinating or are you huge?"

"Maybe both," Elliot suggested. "What have we got here?" He took off his hat and began rolling up his sleeves.

"Are you a doctor?" Sam asked hopefully.

"No, I'm a *pizzaiolo*," Elliot replied.

Sam's panicked gaze darted to Celeste in question but she shrugged. "Maybe it's a Paradise thing."

"It's not a Paradise thing. It's an Italian thing. I make pizza."

"That cute little pizza place at the edge of town is yours?" Celeste said, face lighting.

Elliot winced. "Please don't call it cute. I was going for rustic, hoping for no ambiance entirely to keep it hidden."

"You thought opening a charming outdoor pizza oven in the idyllic setting of Paradise, Montana would lack ambiance?" Celeste said.

His good eye narrowed on her again. "Have you been talking to my wife? Because that's almost verbatim what she said."

"Excuse me, and not to interrupt this episode of *Diner's, Drive-in's, and Dives,* but is the man who is about to perform medicine on me not only a cook but also only in possession of one eye?" Sam asked.

"That about sums it up," Elliot said, using one of his massive paws to tug at Sam's shirt.

"It's either him or me, and if you've ever seen the pillow I tried to make in seventh grade, you'd want it to be him," Celeste said.

"This keeps getting better and better," Sam said, squeezing his eyes tightly closed as Elliot bent closer to take a look. He made his inspection in silence for a while before standing upright and rolling his sleeves back down.

"Well?" Sam asked when he couldn't take the silence any longer.

"I'm going to give it to you straight," Elliot began in a somber tone. "You've been shot."

Celeste laughed loudly and clapped a hand over her mouth.

"You two should take this routine on the road," Sam said, biting his lip against a groan of pain. Celeste, chastised, retrieved pain reliever and a glass of water for him, which he accepted and downed with a slight nod of thanks.

"I could stitch up the skin," Elliot continued. "I was a medic in the army and stitches aren't outside my realm. But I don't have my supplies, and I'm a bit worried about some of that tissue. The stitches might need to go a few layers deeper than I feel comfortable with."

"I think it goes without saying that I can't take him to a hospital because…reasons," Celeste said.

"Smooth," Sam inserted, wincing when she poked him in his good shoulder.

"It's amazing how many 'reasons' mysteriously arise in Paradise," Elliot said. "It so happens I know somebody who is good with sutures and trustworthy enough to take a look."

"The haberdasher?" Sam guessed. "A luthier?"

"You know a lot of words," Celeste accused before facing Elliot.

"Who do you recommend? We'll see whoever, and of course I'm willing to pay cash."

Elliot gave a nod. "I'll help you get him to your car, then you can follow me."

W̸hen he said he was taking me to a vet, crazy me, I thought he meant a veteran, like a retired army doctor or something," Sam said as they wound their way up a long ranch lane.

"Why would you think that?"

"I don't know, maybe because an animal doctor doesn't pop to mind as a first resource when one is about to expire from pain and bleeding. Also because it seems like a Montana thing, to leave the army and come here to try to find peace and resolution."

Celeste gripped the wheel, trying to ignore the fact that that was exactly what she had done.

"Maybe this is a bad idea. Maybe we should forget it. It seems wrong somehow to let someone who routinely looks at hooves and tails to get her hands on me," Sam said.

"You do what you have to," Celeste said, tone serene. If there was one thing she was well versed in, it was improvising life on the fly. In fact she was far more comfortable with that than the carefully contrived life she was currently trying to live.

"I'll say that the next time you have a hole that is about to be patched by someone who does routine sheep and cow castrations," he groused.

She laughed and turned it into a cough when he shot her a dark look. "I promise I won't let her castrate you," she soothed, reaching over the console to give his thigh a squeeze.

"That's what they all say," Sam replied, clasping her hand and giving it a squeeze when she tried to withdraw it.

They were still holding hands when they finally arrived at the house, a smallish farmhouse. Elliot stepped out of his tall truck and a man came onto the porch to greet them, tossing a wave as Celeste and Sam stepped from the car.

"See? He looks normal," Celeste said, sighing when Sam gave a stubbornly pouty look in reply.

"Mornin', Elliot," The man called. His voice had the booming quality of someone who spoke out loud a lot, like a teacher or drill instructor. He was used to making himself heard and understood, that much was certain.

"'Lo, Mitch. I brought your wife a customer," Elliot returned.

Mitch squinted, trying to see behind Sam and Celeste to whatever dog or cat or other animal they might be hiding.

"A two legger," Elliot added and Mitch nodded, gaze fastening on Sam's bloody shoulder with sudden understanding.

"Caldwell, you have a customer," Mitch said, turning his mouth to the side so it carried into the house. "She'll be out in a minute. She's feeding the baby."

"How is the baby?" Elliot asked.

"Good. I think he's going to make it," Mitch said.

Sam and Celeste had no time to absorb that before a woman who looked much too young to be a doctor, and much too young for her husband, appeared from the house, small bundle in her arms.

"Good morning," she said with a pleasantly cheerful smile.

"Hiya," Elliot greeted her, sounding suddenly so chipper and warm-hearted Celeste and Sam turned to study him instead of the woman. "We go back a ways. She's like my little sister," Elliot explained, scowling at their inspection.

"Can you finish up here?" Caldwell asked Mitch, handing him her bundle, which turned out to be a baby goat that bleated unhappily at the change off from wife to husband.

"Sure, but you know he's going to pout now," Mitch said.

"He'll recover," Caldwell said, giving the goat's head a little pat before regaining her beaming smile. "How can I help you?"

"Um," Celeste began, staring at the girl child/woman. How had she gotten so old that she was now doubting the veracity of the woman's degree?"See, Sam here…" She was usually adept at lying. She had to be. But this wasn't an insurgent and she wasn't on a job. This was her new place of residence, long into the foreseeable future. Why hadn't she thought up something to say about the situation? "You see…"

"Edward Jonas mistook him for a cattle rustler and shot him," Elliot said, nodding toward Sam.

Caldwell gasped. "In broad daylight?"

"No, it was the middle of the night," Elliot said. "He thought he was a rustler. In reality he was looking for his girlfriend."

Eyes turned speculatively toward Celeste. "You were at Edward Jonas's house in the middle of the night? Not to be mean, but he's kind of loony, even by Paradise standards," Caldwell said.

"Of course I was not at his house," Celeste protested. "I don't even know the man."

"Then why was he there?" Mitch asked, pointing to Sam.

"Because I didn't know where I was going. Nothing in this entire town is marked with an address," Sam said.

"That's because we don't have them," Mitch said.

"How does anyone get mail?" Sam asked.

"It's addressed to Paradise and then Jody at the post office sorts it," Caldwell explained.

"What if she doesn't know someone in the town?" Sam asked.

"Oh, she knows everyone," Mitch said, waving away his concern. "I'm still hung up on why you were stumbling around Edward Jonas's property in the middle of the night. Didn't you realize he would shoot first and ask questions later?"

"Yes, clearly I understood all the local customs and thought I'd roll the dice anyway," Sam groused. "I was lost. It had been a long journey."

"Why didn't you pick him up?" Caldwell asked Celeste.

"I didn't know he was coming," Celeste said.

"You surprised her? That's so romantic," Caldwell said, reaching over to console the baby goat who had started to bleat louder and struggle in Mitch's arms, trying to get back to her.

"And this is the thanks I get," Sam said, pointing to his shoulder. "This woman makes nothing easy on me."

"Sounds like she'll fit here just fine," Mitch said, giving Caldwell's shoulder a squeeze.

"Let's take a look," Caldwell said. "Also, if you could not mention this to anybody, I'd appreciate it. Obviously I'm not licensed to work on humans."

"Trust me when I tell you your secret is safe with us," Celeste assured her.

"I figured. Elliot only brings me people he trusts," Caldwell said. She led them to an office aside the barn. It looked new, with fresh white paint, a high stainless steel counter, and a couple of chairs. "Take off your shirt and have a seat, please." Meanwhile she washed her hands and put on a pair of gloves. She and Sam were ready at the same time. She inspected his wound a minute and stood back.

"Officially I believe you should see an actual doctor and have an x-ray to make certain there's no fragmentation or extensive damage."

"And unofficially?" Celeste asked.

"With some fancy stitch work, you'll be back in fighting shape."

"Okay," Sam said, sounding a little uncertain. "Are you allowed to give me something for the pain?"

"A topical rub," Caldwell said. "I don't feel comfortable pushing the boundaries enough to give you a shot of narcotics."

"I understand. A topical will be fine." He turned to Celeste and held out his hand.

"What?" she asked, staring at it.

"I need you to hold my hand," he informed her.

"Why? She's going to be stitching your shoulder."

He rolled his eyes. "For comfort, obviously. You are very bad at girlfriending. I'm writing a letter to the girlfriend board of commissioners. Expect comeuppance."

She scooted closer and gripped his hand while Caldwell began setting out equipment, smiling benignly. "What sort of comeuppance?"

"You'll be out of the running for girlfriend of the year, for certain."

"Good. I hate awards shows."

"Then double awards shows. And they'll make you share your feelings about me. In public."

"As time goes on, I find I'm more than ready to air my feelings about you in a public forum," Celeste said. Caldwell fought a snicker and bit her lip.

"You two are cute," she murmured when they darted her a questioning glance. "How long have you been together?"

"It's new," Celeste said. "We've run in the same circles for years, lots of mutual friends, but the timing was never right."

"That was why I surprised her. I wasn't certain of my welcome," Sam explained. "But of course she was thrilled to see me."

"More thrilled than Edward Jonas, at least," Caldwell interjected.

"*Barely*," Sam mouthed when Caldwell wasn't looking. He mimed pointing a finger gun at Celeste, reminding her of when she'd almost shot him.

"I'm going to apply the topical numbing cream now. It's cold."

"Yah," Sam said, squeezing Celeste's hand.

"*Such a baby*," she mouthed.

He nodded his agreement and tugged her closer, pressing his face into her as Caldwell opened the suture package. She started to sew and Sam swallowed hard, squeezing Celeste painfully tight. Unbidden her hand began smoothing over his head and he relaxed, taking deep breaths through his mouth.

"Almost over," Caldwell said after a few moments. And then it was done and she was cleaning up. "I would offer you a treat for being such a good patient, but I only have dog biscuits and alfalfa pellets."

"What do those taste like?" Sam asked, aiming for funny and coming off shaky instead.

"Oh, wait I have something," Celeste said. She let go of him, reached into her pocket, and took a mint she'd nabbed from the bank a few days ago.

"Thanks," he said, sounding unduly grateful for something that had been in her pocket a questionably long time.

"I hope this earns me a few points with the girlfriend board of commissioners," she said.

"You get all the points," he said, leaning forward to kiss her cheek. There was an unmistakable "zap!" when his lips touched her skin, at least on her part. And she thought maybe on his, too, because he sat back, blinking at her in a dazed sort of way.

"You're going to want to keep an eye on this," Caldwell said.

So mesmerized were they by staring at each other it took them a moment to realize she wasn't talking about the strange and budding attraction between them. "If it oozes, come see me. If it begins to smell bad, feel hot, get red streaks, I need to know. And, as I tell all my patients, make certain the nose is wet and the tail is dry."

"How does a girl such as you get to be a country vet in the middle of nowhere?" Celeste wondered aloud. It wasn't that she was skeptical that Caldwell was old enough to have an advanced degree. Rather that she was always searching for her own inspiration.

"Divine intervention," Caldwell said so sincerely they thought maybe she wasn't joking.

"I guess that leaves us out of it," Sam said, motioning between himself and Celeste.

"That's the beauty of it, it doesn't," Caldwell said.

They had no idea what she meant, and both were too wary of delving into a theological discussion with a stranger to ask. So they merely smiled politely and waited on her to dismiss them, which she did after tossing her gloves in the trash and reaching invitingly for the door.

CHAPTER 18

"That was odd," Sam said as they climbed back into Celeste's SUV.

"Which part?" Celeste asked. For her it had been those moments when she cradled him, giving comfort, and he responded by kissing her on the cheek. Easy affection was so far out of her comfort zone as to be declared odd, for certain.

"The part where a horse doctor sewed up my bullet hole and then talked casually about God like they're besties."

"I think her husband is a pastor," Celeste said. Now that she thought about it, she had seen him standing outside one of the two churches in town, changing the letters on the sign.

"Ah, well. There you go," Sam said, sounding relieved.

"Do you think she absorbed religion by osmosis?" Celeste asked.

"How else?" Sam replied. He was making pictures on the window with the fingers on his good side. For a second Celeste was tempted to snap at him to stop but in reality didn't care enough and let it go.

"It's sort of indicative of the whole town," she mused.

"The whole town is populated by veterinarians and pastors?" he guessed.

"No, the whole town is weird."

"How so?" He dropped his hand and faced her.

"It's hard to explain until you experience it for yourself. They're all very…individualized. Like a hundred years or so ago someone released the inhabitants of an insane asylum on a dare to see what would happen and what happened was that they settled down and reproduced, populating the town of Paradise."

"Let's go," Sam said, tapping the dash.

"What? No."

"Why not?"

"For the reason I said. They're weird. And nosy. You're supposed to be hiding."

"I can't hide forever. I could be here a while and we've already established me as your boyfriend. It would be weird to keep me hidden now," he said.

"Don't make good points when I'm trying to ignore the locals," she said.

"Please," he pleaded. "It's been so long since I interacted with everyday Americans. I've almost forgotten how."

"This is not the place to practice. Believe me. You're going to regret it."

"I regret nothing. Ever."

"Really?" She turned to survey him. She could do that here, where the only traffic consisted of an occasional cow that had escaped confinement from its ranch.

"No. I regret everything, always."

She faced forward. "What do you know? One more thing we have in common."

A while later she pulled into a spot on main street and turned off the SUV. "Are you certain about this? It's not too late to back out."

"Really? Because it sort of feels like everyone is already watching us. Kind of like a Hitchcock thriller where someone is always secretly staring."

"More like Hitchcock meets Doris Day," Celeste said as she caught sight of Maybe and ducked low in her seat.

"This is so exciting," Sam said.

Celeste gave him a look.

"Hey, if you spent three days stuffed in a box in the back of a truck trying to cross the border, you'd be excited, too," he said.

"All right, I'll give you that, but only because of the box," Celeste said.

"Yes. I knew I'd be able to use that someday to earn points," he said, pumping his fist in triumph. "Let's go exploring."

"There's not much to explore. Only this street. And it only has a couple of stores."

"But there are people," he said, beaming.

"You're really optimistically extroverted for a terrorist," she muttered.

He poked her.

"Fine, *reformed* terrorist," she amended.

"That's better. And I am definitely a people person. So let's go peopling." He rubbed his hands together in anticipation, causing Celeste to bite back further warnings. It was kind of cute to see how excited he was. It almost made her wish she shared his enthusiasm. Not that she was a misanthrope. People were all right, some better than others. But she had come here with the express purpose of trying to heal. She didn't see how that was possible surrounded by so many distractions. And people were always distracting, in one way or another. *Solitude.* When she got home, she would add it to her list of important things. Right now she yearned for solitude because solitude seemed necessary for healing.

Her glance fell on Sam, standing in the middle of the sidewalk and gaping around town with a fascinated smile, as if he'd landed on the Vegas strip at sunset. There hadn't been any solitude since he showed up. Strangely she didn't mind so much. It was kind of nice to have him there to fill the space. And despite everything, he was fun, upbeat, and cheery. Previous to his arrival she would have said someone like that would annoy her. Instead it lightened a little of the weight inside her. But since she couldn't put a name to it, she couldn't write it on her list. She needed more time to ponder, to figure out how to achieve the lightness Sam brought, but without Sam of course. Maybe she would try reading again. Maybe what she needed was to get out of her own thoughts. Sam definitely made her do that. Perhaps books would, too.

"It looks like books I used to read about the American West. In fact, I think I saw this place in a documentary," he said.

"You watch documentaries? I so would have beaten you up if we went to school together," she said.

"You would have had to get in a very long line," Sam said, unconcerned by her critique. He pointed across the street. "Is that a general store?"

"It's a hardware store. Hence the giant sign that proclaims 'Hardware Store.'"

"Can we instead pretend it's a general store? With checkers and a cracker barrel of dubious cleanliness?"

"Okay," she agreed, unable to deny him when he looked so excited.

"Do you think we'll meet the proprietor?" he asked.

"I guarantee it," she said, turning to cross the street. She felt a little bit proud that she actually knew Tony, the owner of the hardware store. *This must be what it's like to be a name dropper,* she thought as she heard herself add, "I'll introduce you. He's a personal acquaintance."

Sam whistled appreciatively. "Acquaintance. Wow. You must be a somebody."

She laughed, the giggle thing she hated and had spent years trying to suppress in order to be taken seriously. Sam seemed to like it, though. At the very least it made him smile down at her in a warm and cozy sort of way that made her smile harder in return. In fact they were so caught up smiling at each other they didn't realize someone was now standing in front of them until he spoke.

"New girl! You're becoming a regular. Who's your friend?" Tony said.

"You mean you don't know?" Celeste asked. She glanced at her watch. "The rumor mill is really slowing down."

"Elliot is strangely averse to telling me insider police information. But don't blame me for his morally upright code; he gets it from his mother," Tony said.

"This is Sam. He's staying with me a while," Celeste said.

"Hello, and welcome to Paradise," Tony said, putting out a hand. "Where do you hail from?"

"Canada, lately," Sam said, returning his shake.

"I've never heard a Canadian accent that sounded so Middle Eastern," Tony mused.

"I'm a melting pot," Sam said.

"I would say me too, but I basically arrived on a direct pipeline from Sweden," Tony said, motioning to his six foot, blond-haired, blue-eyed frame.

"This is some place you have here. I know I've only been here ten seconds, but if I could suggest changing the name to 'General Store,' it would be a real tourist draw," Sam said.

"Seeing as how I'm the only game in town, I could change the name to 'Opera House' and still attract the same number of people. It's really a nice racket. During tourist season I can sell anything if I affix a picture of a bear, moose, or huckleberry to it."

"Does Harvard know about you? You could teach a business ethics course," Celeste noted.

"Where do you think I learned it?" he returned. Someone from a back office called his name. "That's my cue, but let me know if you need anything. Might I recommend the huckleberry bear moose munch in aisle five? Makes good gifts to send back east, for those longing to get a taste of Montana." With a head tip toward aisle five, he was gone.

"I'm suddenly completely surprised there's no used car lot attached next door," Sam noted. "Let's get some of that moose munch."

"Why? It sounds disgusting," Celeste said.

"Yes, but it has huckleberries and bears and moose on it, so, you know." He shrugged and began heading in that direction.

"Who are you going to send it to?" Celeste asked.

That gave him pause. "No one. We'll save it for the next power outage."

She didn't reply because she rather liked the idea of having something to look forward to the next time the power went out which, if rumors were to be believed, could be any time it snowed or iced. They bought two bags of the stuff, which smelled so overpoweringly of huckleberry she knew she'd simultaneously hate it and eat most of it.

"Montana is going to make me fat," she groused. She had never been much of an eater, usually seeking food for necessity and not pleasure.

"I seriously doubt that," Sam said, his eyes scraping over her with approval.

"You're leering," she said, cheeks warming.

"A boyfriend's prerogative," he said, leaning closer to whisper.

"No more mileage from that," she warned.

"We'll see," he said, wagging his brows.

She turned away to hide her smile.

CHAPTER 19

They were about to leave the hardware store when they were waylaid by a stranger. Or at least Celeste thought she was a stranger, but she had her doubts when the woman greeted her by name with a cheerful smile, dimples pushing deep into soft, round cheeks.

"Oh, Celeste, hi. I'm so glad to see you."

She was that type of woman who made everything sound like it ended in exclamation points and Celeste was more certain they'd never met. That made it all the more confusing that the stranger was now speaking as if they were friends. "You are?"

"Yes, I was so worried. I plagued Elliot until he checked on you but the signal is spotty, per usual, and I haven't heard how you fared during the storm. But here you are."

"Ta-da," Celeste said, her bland tone a contrast to the woman's bright one. "You must be his wife, Missy."

"I am." She glanced at the bags of Montana Munch they were holding. "I see Tony convinced you to get the stuff. Careful, it's highly addictive. I can feel my pants getting tight from standing this close to it." Her voice dropped to a loud whisper as she confessed, "I have a bit of a weight problem."

"You look perfect to me," Celeste said sincerely. She was one of those people who tended toward being underweight. She'd always admired women who had curves. They looked so soft and feminine. Missy was one of those people, pleasantly rounded in all the right places.

She beamed at Celeste, making the dimples pop. "I knew I would love you, from all the descriptions, and I was right."

"All the descriptions?" Celeste asked, feeling a bit ill. What exactly were people saying about her?

"Oh, yeah," Missy said, nodding. "Fletcher's been raving. Apparently you're his white whale, and I quote, 'the one person in the world who has no idea who I am.'"

"That's…weird," Celeste said, recalling the odd conversation with Fletcher Reed.

"That's Fletcher. He's good people, though. The best, really, and I'm not just saying that because he's my boss and I'm trying to suck up. Who's the boy?" Her eyes flicked curiously to Sam who was quiet only because he was trying to sneak a bite of the munch in his grasp.

Celeste yanked it away. "That's for the power outage. We agreed."

"But I'm hungry. We can get more. Also pie."

"Oh, you got the pie," Missy said, face lighting again. Celeste wondered if she was ever sad and, if so, what her face was like. It probably crumpled pleasantly with tears that made her long lashes sparkle and stand out. Whereas Celeste looked like she was having a seizure if she ever gave in to tears, which she never did. Not anymore. "I'm so glad I put that on the list."

"Did you bake it?" Celeste asked. "It was amazing."

"It *is* amazing, and no, I did not bake it. I'm a connoisseur who has been trying to help Mrs. Hickman's home bakery take off. And, I don't know, it seems like a power outage deserves special food."

"It totally does," Sam said, trying to steal a bite of munch from the bag Celeste now held. She turned her back to him.

"Stop or I'll bite you," she threatened.

"Maybe I like that," he returned, causing her cheeks to heat and Missy to beam approvingly.

"Anyway," Celeste said, trying to regain some decorum, though she was certain her cheeks were staining red. *You were a soldier and trained assassin. You do not blush because a cute boy lobs innuendo at you, not anymore. Get it together.* "It was really nice to meet you. Thank you for sending Elliot to check on us."

"Sure, and if you need any more food recommendations, I'm your Huckleberry. Probably literally by now because I've eaten so many huckleberry-themed foods since arriving in paradise. Coincidentally I also haven't had a virus since then. Lots of vitamin C in huckleberries." She gave them a little wave and continued on her way while they stepped outside, blinking against the glare of sun on snow.

"Where to next, tour guide to the Paradise stars?" Sam asked, shading his eyes, which was rather a ridiculous thing to do when it was five degrees outside, but the snow/sun combo was that bright.

"The diner. But first I need to stop at the bank," Celeste said.

"Okay, but I'm already regretting not cleaning out the Moose Munch shelf. I'm going back for seconds and I'll meet you when I'm done."

"Don't let him talk you into buying anything else."

"I'll try, but if I come out with a boomerang that smells like huckleberry and has a picture of a grizzly on it, do not judge me. He's very persuasive," Sam said, spinning to go back inside the store.

Meanwhile Celeste crossed the street and yanked the bank door, stumbling when it didn't open.

"It's locked," a voice said. "They close for lunch on account of there's only one teller."

She turned to face the speaker, a cowboy who loomed large and unseen in the shadow. Celeste felt a prickle of apprehension that only increased when he stepped into view. Automatically her gaze fell to his teeth. She saw they were black and took a step back. He took a step forward.

"I've seen you around," the man said.

"Strange, I haven't noticed you at all," she said, which was true. He blended in with all the other cowboys she'd seen. They'd become

Paradise's background noise. With so many ranches nearby, they were a ubiquitous part of the landscape.

He chuckled, the sound harsh and foreboding like a rattler's rasp.

This is not going to go well for me, she thought. She'd met too many bad men not to immediately read the signs. Whoever this guy was, he was mean, nasty, possibly even dangerous.

"If you'll excuse me," she said, trying to step around him. Her attempt failed when he pivoted, putting himself in front of her, using his hulking size as an intimidating advantage. Celeste was nearly impossible to intimidate, however.

"You're a cute little thing," he tried.

She didn't reply. Once upon a time she would have, even if only to snark at him. But one lesson time and maturity taught her was that her words were hers to bestow. Other people didn't deserve them by virtue of being alive. They were hers alone to unleash, when she wanted to or not. The Colonel had taught her that, an actual lecture he delivered once when she was a newbie and eagerly trying to impress him with her nonstop flow of chatter. *Silence is almost always more powerful; use it wisely.*

"Why don't you let me buy you lunch," the man said, making it sound like a command more than a request.

"No, thanks," Celeste said. She attempted to take another step and he grabbed her arm in a painful grip that pinned her in place and would no doubt leave bruises. Celeste considered her options. She could break free, certainly. She could incapacitate him. For that matter, she could kill him. But it was the middle of the street and broad daylight and half the town was probably watching. If she put her skills on display in such a public manner, there would be talk about her, more than there already was. Anonymity was more important than saving face.

All the thoughts blazed through her mind with lightning speed, but before she could come to a resolution Sam was beside her.

"You're going to want to let her go, and don't ever touch her again," he said, but it didn't sound like him. Gone was the warm and friendly tone. Instead he sounded cold, imperious, and deadly. As Celeste studied him, he even loomed larger somehow, as if he were equal to the hulking cowboy. Only a moment ago she would have said he was smaller.

The cowboy dropped her arm and smiled at Sam. "Well, what do we have here? Welcome to Paradise, Osama."

"Your lack of originality speaks well of your intellect," Sam replied.

The man lost his smile. "Here's a friendly warning, fella. We don't like your type around here. Best not get too comfortable and be on your way, sooner rather than later."

"Actually, I plan to stay for the long haul. And I've found people to be quite friendly and helpful, people who matter, that is," Sam said.

The man took a small step closer. "I'm going to give you one warning: clear out and go away."

"I'm going to tell you what my cousin Osama used to say: Don't push me; I always push back."

It was that tense moment before someone took a swing and Celeste decided to intervene and break the tension. "All right, let's all take a breath here. Mister, I want nothing to do with you, and you know everyone in town is watching. Be on your way before this gets any uglier."

The man studied her for a moment, glanced at Sam, then pursed his lips and walked away with a swagger.

"Do you think he walks like that because something in his apparel is too tight?" Sam mused.

"I think he walks like that because something in his head is too small," Celeste returned.

He snorted. "Are you okay?"

"Yes. Was Osama bin Laden really your cousin?" she asked.

"No, I was quoting my cousin Osama Robinson. He has a job at a butcher, biting the heads off chickens. He gets an extra dime for every beak that remains intact."

She did the giggle-laugh thing that inexplicably made him smile.

"Do you think we have time to get lunch before the pinhead cowboy returns with reinforcements?" Sam asked hopefully.

"Maybe, but if we have to take down the reinforcements, we're definitely going to need extra calories," she said, leading the way to her SUV.

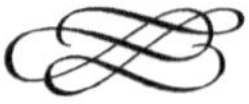

"Celeste, hi!" Avery called as soon as they stepped into the diner. Today she held a different baby on her hip. "Sit wherever, we're strangely un-busy at the moment."

Celeste and Sam chose a booth near the back. She situated herself so she could see the door, still edgy over the uncomfortable encounter.

"What's good here?" Sam asked, studying his menu.

"I'd go with the beef," Celeste suggested, not bothering to glance down.

"Which one? Most of the menu is beef," Sam said.

"I don't think it matters," Celeste returned.

Avery arrived with their waters, which she was somehow able to carry with one hand.

"Do you keep a supply of babies readily on hand?" Celeste asked.

"I wish, but no. This one's mine. The best perk of a family business is that I get to bring my family along," Avery said, kissing the top of the baby's head. "As we speak, my three year old is grilling burgers."

Celeste laughed. "Quite a talented lineup you have there."

Avery smiled and bestowed her attention on Sam. "You must be the boyfriend I've heard so much about."

Sam looked quizzically at Celeste.

"Not from her," Avery clarified. "No less than eight different customers in the last hour dropped by to give me the particulars. If the rumors are to be believed, you run a rug import business and have bought the ring but aren't certain you're ready to propose. This trip will be the bellwether."

"It depends on how many rugs she buys," Sam said.

Avery laughed and her baby waved its arms in delight, squealing as it reached for the string of her apron to chew. "Do you two know what you want or will you need more time?"

"We'll have the beef," Celeste said, gathering their menus.

"Which one?" Avery asked.

"Surprise us."

"Tongue and liver it is then," Avery said, tossing them a mischievous wink as she took the menus and turned away.

"It smells amazing in here," Sam said, inhaling deeply.

"It is amazing, or at least what I had the other night was." She stared toward the back, wondering how the magic happened. How were people able to cook things and have them taste delicious? Celeste hadn't had a lot of time to cook between world travels, but everything she'd ever attempted ended in flaming failure.

"Where'd you go?" Sam asked, stroking a gentle finger down the back of her hand.

"Hmm?" she said, shifting her focus to him.

"Just then, you looked so sad."

"I was thinking I'm not a good cook," she said.

"There's plenty of time to learn."

"I don't think it's my forte," she said. She'd bought cookbooks. It was like reading Greek, only worse because it seemed like something she should be able to understand. But all the books assumed one began with a base layer of knowledge. Celeste had nothing. Not one foster parent had ever taken her into the kitchen and showed her what a measuring cup was or how to chop something, likely because they didn't know. With few exceptions, she'd existed on a lifetime supply of convenience and takeout food.

"You seem like the kind of person who would be good at it," Sam said.

Her eyes flicked up, meeting his. "I do? Why?"

"You're thoughtful, purposeful, careful. *Soulful.*"

She felt herself blushing again and tried unsuccessfully to push it back. But no man had ever said those kinds of things to her before, had never made commentary on more than her looks. *You're hot,* only seemed like a compliment until around age fifteen. After that she'd longed for more and never received it. Until now.

"How does any of that translate to good cooking?"

"Good people make good food. Everyone knows that. It's science," Sam said, nodding at the profundity of his own statement.

She laughed, feeling light and buoyant. "Then why can't I cook?"

"I'm guessing because no one ever taught you how."

Her amusement slid to suspicion. "How did you know that?"

"Because you don't know how to cook?" he said, sounding confused. "I don't think cooking is an innate skill. No one arrives into the world with a chef's knife, thankfully for women everywhere. It's learned, passed down through generations."

"Yes," Celeste said slowly, sadly. Everything came back to that, her feral upbringing, the one that left her with nothing—untaught, untrained, alone.

"But it's not too late. Find someone to teach you. Avery, perhaps."

"She seems to have her hands full," Celeste said as they turned to watch Avery, bending at the waist to blow raspberries on her baby's neck. It was a poignant sight, the kind that should be captured in sculpture somewhere as the baby squealed and Avery beamed, happiness shooting out of her smile like lasers. Sam seemed equally somber and she wondered if the vision of Avery and her baby made him miss his own beloved mother. It was strange how they were both yearning for the same thing—a loving mother—though he'd had it and she never had. That was perhaps one of the most painful things Celeste was learning, that it was possible to grieve for things she'd never had. She began to fear the voids inside her might never be filled, that the aching chasm of longing for the life she might have had would go on forever.

"You should have a baby," Sam declared, startling her so badly she choked on air and had to take a few gulps of water before she could speak.

"What? Why would you say that?"

"Because you would be a good mother," Sam said.

Celeste shook her head at him. "I would be a terrible mother."

"Of course you wouldn't."

"Of course I would. I have no idea what to do with children, none whatsoever."

"So? You learn. Just because you don't know how doesn't mean you'll never learn. This defeatist attitude does not become you. You are Celeste fill in your last name. You worked for The Colonel doing fill in whatever you did. You can do fill in whatever it is you want to do."

"Wow, good pep talk. I feel very fill in unidentified emotion."

"Inspired. You feel *inspired*, Celeste," Sam said, touching his finger to her hand again.

"I might feel that way, if I had any idea what should fill in the blank at the end."

"Fill in the other blanks for me. I'll help you decide," Sam said.

She shook her head.

He slipped his hand in hers, giving it a squeeze. "Start small. What is your last name?"

"Smith."

He tossed her hand away. "You're lying."

"I am not. That's my actual last name."

"I'm not certain I believe you, but you have a nice hand, so I'm willing to keep holding it," he said, sneaking back to pick up her fingers and caress them.

"I'd like to see a Venn diagram of the things you say and the things serial killers say because I think there's probably a lot of overlap," Celeste said.

"Tell me what you did for The Colonel, and I'll help you make one," Sam offered.

She shook her head.

He stared at her in frowning frustration. "Your skin is perfect."

"That's going on the diagram," she told him and Avery arrived with their food.

As they left the diner, someone else called Celeste's name. She turned in time to see Maybe begin to dart across the road, right in front of a pickup truck. Before she could be flattened, a cowboy darted after her, picking her up around the waist and sweeping her out of harm's way.

"Maybe, there is *some* occasional traffic here. Woman, you have to look," the cowboy said, setting her down. "Dadgum, blasted…" he might have continued, but Maybe mashed her palm over his mouth, cutting off the flow of angry words.

"They should know to look out for me by now," Maybe replied, though she did check both ways before crossing this time, the cowboy in her wake with a grumpy expression. "Hi," she said again, waving frantically to Celeste as though they were at a great distance and not right next to each other.

"Hi," Celeste said, returning her wave with a weak flutter.

"I finished the list," Maybe said.

"The list?" Celeste asked, her eyes flicking automatically to the cowboy in question. He shrugged, so obviously he wasn't in on it.

"*The LIST.* Black teeth. Eligible cowboys. Although it looks like it might be a bit late for that." She smiled up at Sam and held out her hand. "Maybe Montgomery."

"Sam," he said, shaking her hand with a charming smile. He gave off such a little boy cuteness in that moment that it was nearly impossible to reconcile him with the man who'd coldly threatened a beefy cowboy only a short while ago. He took Celeste's hand and gave it a squeeze, making her realize she was wordlessly staring at him as she tried to puzzle the two sides of him.

"Sam and Celeste. That's adorable," Maybe declared. She rested her hand on the cowboy's bicep, bringing him into the conversation. "This is my husband, Baird. He provides the sanity, I have pizzazz."

"She has it in spades," Baird affirmed, shaking both their hands. "Welcome to Paradise. I've heard a lot about you both."

"Would you like to buy a rug?" Sam asked and Baird blinked at him, a deer in salesman headlights. "Joking," Sam said.

Baird gave a relieved chuckle. "I didn't think that particular rumor was true, but sometimes Paradise's rumor mill is eerily prescient."

"Did you come to help Celeste restart the orchard?" Maybe asked hopefully, clutching her hands together under her chin.

"Did I?" Sam asked, facing Celeste.

"That seems an insurmountable task at the moment," Celeste replied, fighting a climbing rise of panic. It felt as though the entire town of Paradise was counting on her to revive an orchard when she had never seen an apple not in sauce form until she was in basic.

"We'll think about it," Sam promised, smiling at her when Celeste tossed him a frantic look.

"My son, Jack, is coming home in a couple of days. Guess what he does," Maybe said.

"Poison snake milker," Sam said, causing Celeste to dart him a look again. "What? She said to guess."

"That would certainly make for more interesting party conversation, but no. He's a mechanic," Maybe said in a conspiratorial whisper.

"Congratulations?" Celeste tried, not certain what the announcement had to do with her.

"He can take a look at your machinery," Maybe said, clapping her hands together a few times in delight.

"Oh, I don't want to bother him," Celeste said.

"I think he would love it. He enjoys a challenge," Maybe said. "I'll send him out sometime, after he gets home. He'll be in town for a couple of months and is sure to be a bit bored, back with his parents after living the high life in LA."

"Awesome," Sam said, saving Celeste a reply, which was good because she had no idea what one should be. It felt like too much to have a strange boy promised to look at her decrepit machines and try to make them work again. If he could do so, it might change her entire world. Was she ready for that?

"It's settled then," Baird said. "In the meantime, you should come out for a meal sometime. Maybe's too modest to tell you she's the best cook around."

"I wouldn't say that because it's not true," Maybe said, but she flushed pleasantly at the compliment. Celeste was glad to see other women had the same embarrassing reaction to nice words sometimes.

"We would love that," Sam said and Celeste had to tamp down the urge to shoot him another exasperated glare. Why was he speaking for them as if they were actually a couple? Was he that good of an actor or was he that desperate for social interaction with the towns-folk? Maybe both things.

They said goodbye to Maybe and Baird, but before they could get in the car, someone else waylaid them.

"Celeste, wait."

"Not this guy again," Celeste muttered, bracing herself for another flow of crazy as she turned and forced a smile for Fletcher Reed, the town Boo Radley.

He was a bit breathless when he finally reached her. He bent over, pressing a hand to his side. "Oh, man. Going to fire my trainer. That fetal monkey growth hormone he injected into me was totally worth-less." He held up a finger. Celeste tossed Sam a pleading look, but he didn't catch it because he was smiling at Fletcher like he found his shtick adorable and not certifiable.

"Okay," Fletcher said at last, taking a deep breath as he finally stood upright. "So I was thinking about your orchard."

"Please don't," Celeste blurted. The last thing she needed in her life was another delusional man roaming her property. "That is, please don't concern yourself on my behalf."

"It's no trouble, especially because I think I found a solution."

"Which is…" she prompted when he remained staring at her with a

Cheshire grin, as if she should be able to plumb the depths of his unfathomable brain.

"Jack!" he waved both hands in the air, a jazz hands finale. Celeste couldn't stop herself from flinching away from him in terror, flattening her back against the SUV.

"Maybe's son?"

His happy smile dimmed. "Oh, did Maybe already talk to you? I was hoping to impress you with my mechanic connection."

"Well, I mean, he is her son," Celeste said.

"Yeah, but mine too. I mean, basically. Almost. Soon. Probably. We think," Fletcher said, nodding and tapping his temple.

Celeste's hand began creeping toward her door, trying in vain to open it so she could flee. "Yeah, okay. Well, you take care then."

"Wait, I wanted to ask you. Did you see Chloe the other night at the diner?"

"You mean the woman you kept frantically pointing to and mouthing, *This is Chloe,* that woman?"

He nodded, grinning again. "Well…"

"Uh…" Celeste darted a look at Sam who gave her a shrug. "She's very beautiful." She was beautiful, proving there was no accounting for taste sometimes. It was sad, really. Her life must be volatile in the extreme, married to someone as unstable as Fletcher apparently was. Not to mention the stigma over being married to the designated town crazy person.

"Yes," Fletcher said impatiently. "Obviously. She's gorgeous. But didn't you notice anything else about her? Didn't she look *familiar* somehow?"

"Uh…" Celeste glanced at Sam again, pleading for help. This time he mouthed, *no idea,* along with the shrug.

"I mean I guess maybe she looks a little like my former coworker's roommate's sister or something?" Celeste tried. Maybe he was one of those people who demanded an answer to every impossible question and would be happy, no matter how nonsensical it was. And when he threw back his head and laughed—hard—she thought that must be it.

"This is *fantastic*. Wait until I tell her. And Ira. He doesn't believe me. You'll have to tell him yourself."

"Okay, Ira, sure, okay, yes," Celeste said, nodding in agreement. Anything to keep him calm and happy. Her fingers finally found the door and she yanked it open. "Gotta go, bye." She opened Sam's door for him, tugging him hard when he was slow to sit down.

A few seconds later they were peeling away. Fletcher remained in their rearview mirror, smiling and waving cheerfully as they disappeared.

CHAPTER 21

"All right, let's hear it," Celeste demanded when they were a safe distance from Paradise. Sam had been unusually silent, so she knew he was thinking about it and trying to find the right words.

He took a deep breath. "First of all, you were right. Everyone in the entire town seems to have some sort of mental defect or quirk that makes them seem like an experiment gone wrong. It's a pharmaceutical goldmine, an entire untapped market for mass Quaaludes and Prozac." Before she could muster a smile of triumph, he continued. "And I love them. I mean, seriously and insanely love them. I want to alternately adopt, be adopted by, and/or marry all of them." He faced her, clutching his hands together. "I want to live here forever and always. Please may I?"

"What?" she said, half laughing, certain he must be joking.

"I'm serious. I *love* it. They're all so quirky and fun. You would never be bored here, ever. And I bet we've only scratched the surface of insanity. Think how much more is left undiscovered." He threw his hands wide, forcing her to duck out of the way or risk being clocked in the jaw.

"What would you do for a job? You know nothing about cattle ranching, and from what I can tell there isn't much else," she said.

"Spoiler alert: thanks to some fairly shady accounting on the part of my uncles, I don't ever have to do actual work again, if I don't want," he said.

"But don't you want? You're so young. You could do anything," Celeste said.

He shrugged. "Maybe. I'm sure I'll figure it out eventually."

She faced forward, staring hard at the horizon. "I definitely see how you fit here, but not me," she said.

"I'm going to choose to take that as a compliment. Also, you definitely fit. You just don't see it," he said.

"How do I fit? I am neither quirky nor fun."

He jutted an accusing finger at her. "You are quirky and fun and adorable. Paradise becomes you, admit it."

Instead she rubbed two fingers against her temple. "Great, it's catching. You seem to have caught whatever they have."

"A zest for life," he suggested.

"A delusional separation from normal society. Was there oxygen when you were trapped in that border-crossing box?"

"Based on the depth and soundness of my sleep, probably no. But I am telling you, this is a great town. The perfect place to have an orchard and start a family."

Celeste's heart began to beat hard because now they were moving from the theoretical to the possible and she didn't like it. "The orchard is dead and so is my desire to ever procreate."

"Were you quoting Elizabeth Barrett Browning, or did you make that up?" he rested his head on the seat behind him, studying her. They pulled up in front of her house and she shut off the car, leaving her hand on the ignition. "You planning to ditch me and take off again?"

"I'm thinking about it," she said.

"Hey." He reached over and touched her hand, pulling it off the ignition and holding it in his hand while he petted it gently like a gerbil. "Are you okay, for real? That guy grabbed you pretty hard."

She let out a breath, relieved to be talking about something she could actually wrap her mind around. "Believe it or not, that wasn't my first time being manhandled. And I'm fine, thank you for asking."

His free hand reached out and smoothed the hair at her temple, an oddly soothing and affectionate gesture. "It must be hard to be little and pretty and vulnerable when men like that exist in the world, ready to prey on you."

Her face had a mind of its own, leaning into his touch without her permission. "I've built up some pretty thick walls. I'm no one's idea of easy prey," she said.

"But you shouldn't have to have walls. You should get to be soft and vulnerable and protected."

His words smarted because she had never, ever been any of those things, not as far back as she could remember, not for a moment. She'd always had to be tough, to be hard, to take care of herself. Suddenly her eyes stung and she was mortified, afraid she might break down and cry in front of this man who had no idea the horrors of her past, nor would he ever, not if she had her way. He somehow saw her as better than she was, a first. No way would she disillusion him.

He leaned across the console and kissed the spot high on each cheek, directly under each eye. Celeste sucked a shaky breath and then, before she could open the eyes he'd kissed closed, he kissed her lips, a soft and gentle brush of affection.

"What was that?" she asked, backing away from him when the kiss was over.

"I just think we should," he whispered. If he had looked any less befuddled and shocked than she felt, she would have pushed him away. Instead she decided to give in and go with it.

"Okay," she whispered and, slipping her fingers into his thick, messy hair, pulled him close and kissed him with far more than tenderness or affection, though they were there too, mingled with fear and attraction and a touch of desperation. His free hand touched her waist and she felt a little electric thrill spiral through her. They were on the cusp of something neither of them condoned, with no idea how to stop, when the sound of crunching gravel finally broke through the haze.

Celeste lurched back, giving his chest a little shove as she struggled for oxygen. "Someone's here."

"What?" Sam murmured, smoothing his thumb over her bottom lip as he stared at it.

"People. People are here." She reached for her gun and checked it and he finally snapped to attention.

"Why are you always armed when I caress you?" he demanded. She laughed and he smiled, softening. "And why do these newcomers have the worst timing in the world?"

Celeste wasn't certain if it was the worst timing or the best. She and Sam had definitely been on a runaway train to nowhere good, and she was both glad and sad for the reprieve. Did she want to have a fling with Sam? She had never decided, but she knew it was something she needed to think about before anything else happened between them. There should be logic and discussion and no soft lips involved whatsoever.

"Oh, no," Sam said, staring at the mirror in his visor. "It's them."

"Who?" Celeste asked. Had the cowboy from before followed them home and brought backup? And why was she absurdly hopeful that was the case? *Better to deal with it now than let it linger.*

"Them. The team. It might be her." He squeezed his eyes closed.

"Her who?" she asked, still a bit dazed from the kiss.

"*Her* who. My ex. It could be her and her husband. Would The Colonel be that cruel?"

"To you, maybe. Probably not to her."

He relaxed, nodding. "Right, yes. No one can be cruel to her. It's impossible." He took a breath.

Celeste tossed him a scowl he missed. She wasn't jealous. She *wasn't.* But no one could be as angelic as he made his ex out to be. It was, to borrow his word, impossible.

She holstered her gun and stepped from the car, squinting again in the bright sun/snow mix. At first she didn't recognize the man who stepped from the other car, caught in the glare as he was, but as he came closer her smile grew until it beamed.

"Leo," she called, waving like Maybe had earlier. She had always liked Leo and she hadn't seen him in years, way too long.

"Celeste," he returned, sounding equally as happy to see her. They didn't hug, of course, former marine and soldier they were, but they did clasp hands mid-air, sort of an affectionate high five.

"So you know him," Sam said, and was it Celeste's imagination or did he sound a bit testy?

"We go back a ways," Celeste said. "Wow, how long now?"

"Marrakesh, October 24th, fourteen years ago," a woman said, and now everyone turned to face her. She had been so still and silent no one noticed her at first. Now she stood beside Leo, tempering his wild energy with her steady presence. They were like panther and keeper, Celeste thought, smiling wryly to herself.

Leo put his arm around the woman's shoulders and gave them a squeeze. "This is Esther. Esther, this is Celeste and, I presume, Sam."

"No," Sam said testily. "I'm the other terrorist she keeps on standby for occasions such as these."

"Reformed terrorist," Esther amended and Sam beamed.

"I like her very much," he said.

"Me, too," Leo said, giving her another squeeze. His glance slid to the house. "Is it okay if we go inside?"

"Sure," Celeste said, jumping to attention with a flutter. These were the first guests she'd had—Sam didn't count, foisted on her without notice as he'd been. What if they thought the house was terrible? "I don't have any food. I didn't know when you were coming, and…" why hadn't she thought to buy extra while they were in town? At the very least she could have gotten another pie. The house might not be impressive, but the pie definitely was.

"I brought food," Esther volunteered, holding a plastic box aloft.

Celeste paused and faced her in amazement. "You did?"

Esther froze, now looking uncertain. "Was that okay? Leo gets hungry, so I brought some bread and a coffee cake. Also cookies."

"Did you stop at a bakery?" Celeste asked, amazed they'd been able to find one on their snowy journey.

"She made it," Leo said and there was no mistaking the beaming pride in his tone, or in his expression as he smiled down at Esther.

"If it's too weird, we don't have to eat it," Esther said. Celeste realized she was still staring at her in openmouthed astonishment.

"It's fantastic," she said at last. She had never personally known anyone who could make things. To her baking was like something from Harry Potter, pure fantasy.

"It's science," Esther said, placidly unaware of Celeste's awe. "I can show you how, if you want."

Sam poked her, nodding. Celeste smiled up at him. "I like her very much," she declared.

"I know, right?" he agreed and the four of them went inside.

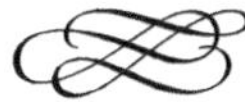

CHAPTER 22

Leo stood in the center of the room, swiveling his head in a slow inspection. "Wow, Celeste. This is so nice."

"Thank you," Celeste said, trying to relax. Leo was a friend. There was no reason to believe he was judging her. And she thought Esther's deadpan expression had more to do with Esther than distaste over Celeste's lack of decorating finesse. Sam sat on the couch, arms crossed. Esther and Leo remained standing, as if they were waiting for something. At last Celeste realized it was her. "Sit?" She waited until they chose their chairs and sat beside Sam who scooted closer. He seemed antsy, more so than he had been, and she thought maybe he was still uncertain if they viewed him as the enemy, even after Esther's affirming statement.

"Could we maybe get this over with?" he asked.

"Is that okay with you, Leo?" Celeste added. She didn't want him to think she was a challenge to his authority or his case. That might make him defensive, which could make things worse for Sam.

"You think I'm the one in charge?" Leo said with a chuckle. "Nah. Esther's the lead investigator on this case."

Esther gave a tentative half smile when everyone turned to survey her. Celeste wondered what her background was. It must have been impressive if she usurped Leo, who had been a lieutenant in the marines and sidecar to military intelligence for as long as she could remember. It surprised her further that an alpha male like Leo not only willingly handed the reins to Esther but had also clearly fallen for her. *Wonders never cease,* she thought with a little bit of hope. If an old timer like Leo could change, there might be hope for her, too.

"That's a little better," Sam said, softening as he gave Esther a smile. There was something wholesome and gentle about her that made everyone in her radius want to be kinder by proxy. Leo had always been a restless ball of energy, especially at work. The fact that he now sat placidly to the side with his arms loosely crossed could only be an effect of the soothing woman who sat beside him, head tipped to the side like a curious bird as she studied Celeste and Sam.

"I'm ready to begin," Esther affirmed. She turned to Leo who pulled out a recording device and switched it on. She gave a little nod and then she was off, throwing out a blitz of questions and names attached to precise dates impossible for anyone to memorize. But somehow she had. She used no laptop, no notebook, not even a pen. Her hands were empty and crossed in her lap as her unending flow of words went on and on, peppering Sam with questions about what seemed to be every arms dealer in the Middle East and Northern Africa.

Celeste's mesmerized gaze left her a moment to turn to Leo who gave her a little head nod, as if to say, *I know, right? Can you believe it?* No, she could not. She had never seen anything like Esther, not during her fifteen years as a soldier. She was like a walking, talking computer. And yet she remained kind, keeping Sam at ease so the endless barrage of questions didn't feel like an interrogation at all.

"That brings us to two weeks ago and the event that led to your defection," Esther said. "Are you okay to continue?"

"Let's finish it," Sam said, swiping his hand wearily over his eyes. He looked so…depleted. It echoed in a part of Celeste she thought was long gone, the selfless part of her that wasn't solely focused on her own survival. Her hand slid unbidden toward his leg, bestowing a little pat. It wasn't much, but for her it was monumental. She had comforted someone, a man, a *handsome* man, and absolutely nothing was in it for her. He gave her a tired smile and clasped her hand, giving it a squeeze. She felt Leo's eyes on her and avoided his gaze.

Esther began again, rehashing the events of the two weeks and the crisis that had led to Sam's arrival back in the states, basically an extended version of what he'd already told her. A sale of a self-guided missile went wrong when a man named Alfred Komeni tried to use a child from a local village as a test of Sam's loyalty. He blew his cover, saved the kid, and fled for his life.

Sam reached the end of his story. Esther remained staring at him, expression blank. He squirmed.

"Was there something else?" he prodded.

Leo held up a hand, halting him. "She's thinking, hold on. She has to replay the script in her head to make certain she didn't miss anything."

Everyone was silent a few minutes until Esther relaxed her posture and sat back. "No, that's everything. Thank you. If you don't mind, I'd like to find a quiet place to type and file my report."

"Sure," Celeste said. "I assume you're staying here."

"We can get a hotel. We have a stipend," Leo said, sounding exhausted. It must have been a long day with the flight and time change. Celeste remembered those days well and gave him a sympathetic smile.

"That's a nice thought, I'm sure, but you'd be hard pressed to find a hotel within a hundred miles. It's okay, this house has four bedrooms and three bathrooms."

Leo whistled, impressed. "So fancy, Celeste. You're in the bigtime now."

"If by 'bigtime' you mean barely habitable and completely sterile, then yes. But I do have clean sheets and towels, and Esther brought food. Beats that grotto in Cairo."

"Any day and twice on Sunday," Leo agreed, holding his hand up for a high five. "I think that was the last time I saw you. How long ago was that?" He addressed the question to Esther who provided an immediate answer.

"Three years, four months, and seven days."

"Wow," Celeste whispered, impressed. "That's amazing, Esther. That you know Leo's schedule that well."

"Actually, I read your files as well. I like to be prepared, and I took note of all the times you crossed paths with Leo," Esther said.

Sam, who looked half out of it after his long interview, suddenly perked up. "You read Celeste's file?"

"I read everything," Esther clarified.

"What did she do for The Colonel?"

Three mouths pressed together in sealed lines.

"Oh, come on. Please? Not even a hint?" Sam pled.

"Sorry, but you don't have the classification to know," Esther explained, which was kind of her because Leo and Celeste were happy to leave him twisting in the wind, uninformed.

"But I'm one of you guys. Sort of, in a reformed terrorist kind of way," Sam said.

"And yet in another way we can be hauled before a tribunal and sentenced to death for breaking the law," Leo said, pretending to ponder. "It's a tough decision, for sure."

"That's a bit extreme," Sam pouted.

"Come on, I'll show you upstairs," Celeste said, herding them out of the room.

"I'll remain here, alone and ostracized as usual," Sam called, but everyone ignored him.

Meanwhile Celeste gave Esther and Leo a tour of the house, ending upstairs where she deposited them to freshen up. Sam was still on the couch, staring dazedly into space when she returned.

"How are you holding up?" she asked, sitting down beside him.

"I think my life just flashed before my eyes, in a visceral sort of way," he said, sounding dazed.

"Any regrets?"

"All of them, and yet I'm kind of sad it's over, and how crazy is that? I'm back in the US, out of the double agent racket, and now what?" He looked at her as if she could provide an answer.

"I'm working on my own stuff over here," she informed him. "You're on your own."

"Maybe that's why we're, you know…" he trailed off leadingly.

"What?" she said.

He huffed an annoyed sigh. "Attracted to each other, dummy."

"I know, but I wanted to make you say it."

"You take more than you give." He said it in a flippant tone as he made a cage of his arms and put them around her, but for Celeste the words hurt because they were true. She had no idea how to open up and let anyone in, least of all men.

Sam pulled her close, nuzzling his nose against her neck. "You smell good."

"How? I use cheap soap and no perfume," she said.

"Maybe it's your natural scent. Au de Celeste. Speaking of which, how long did you and Leo go out?"

"How does that relate to soap?" Celeste said.

"It doesn't. I was trying to trick you into revealing secret information," he said. "I'm a master interviewer."

"You're no Esther," she said.

"Yes, but who is? I feel like if she'd been alive during the forties, we would have won the war in the thirties."

"That makes no sense," Celeste said, drawing in a sharp breath when he pressed his lips to her neck.

"I'm tired and you're befuddling me with your good smells and such," he said. "What are the chances we could compel Esther to cook supper for us?"

"Better than the chances of compelling me," Celeste said. Her idea of cooking from scratch was using a manual can opener.

"You could learn," Sam said, pulling back to give her a sincere look. Or maybe it wasn't sincere. Maybe chocolate brown eyes gave the illusion of making everything seem sincere. But the softness in his expression wasn't her imagination. And when he gave her a little squeeze and kissed the tip of her nose, she melted a little. "Why are you looking at me like that?"

"I'm trying to decide if I should wait to kiss you until I hear Esther's verdict about whether or not I have to kill you," she said.

"Always kiss first, kill later," he said.

"That's coincidentally the same thing my drill instructor said," she whispered, brushing her lips against his.

Leo's step in the next room alerted them to his imminent return. By the time he entered, they were a respectable distance apart.

"Celeste and I were just talking about when you guys used to date," Sam said.

Leo laughed. "Trying the sneak attack, huh? Can't say that I blame you, but Celeste and I never dated. Not for lack of trying on my part. I asked you out three, maybe four times?"

"Something like that," Celeste said, unconcerned.

"You really never went out?" Sam said.

"She always said no," Leo said.

"In your defense, Leo, I said no to everyone."

"I know. That's why you were the white whale, the golden goose. The unobtainable and pristine Celeste." He pressed his hands prayerfully together and gave her a little bow.

"I'm glad to see I created mystique and not resentment," Celeste said. "I never wanted to earn the reputation of being cold or aloof. I just wanted to do my job."

"What job was that again?" Sam asked.

"No one who knew you ever thought you were cold," Leo assured her, ignoring Sam. "Just too good for us losers, in all the ways."

"You're nice," Celeste declared. She'd always liked Leo. He never took her refusals personally, never turned on her and badmouthed her when she turned him down. He'd remained a pal. Truthfully, she had been a bit tempted by him for that very reason, because he'd been kind and good. But she'd held off, partially because of the rangy, unsettled feeling he always gave off. It was gone now, in the wake of Esther.

"You seem so happy, Leo," she added.

"I am happy, Celeste. So happy." Unbidden, his eyes flitted toward the stairs and Esther. "But it's more than happiness, you know? It's like all those broken little pieces are knitting themselves back together." He wove his hands into a knot and held them aloft.

"I'm glad. Congratulations. Are you going to make it official? Put a ring on it?" Celeste asked.

"I'm going to make it official, but there will be no ring. Esther's religion forbids it. We're engaged though, it's happening."

"Not to backpedal on the happiness, but you sound a tad defensive," Sam noted.

"Sorry," Leo said, relaxing his tense posture. "Esther's from a big, connected, protective family. I love them, I *do*. But it's hard, you know? To go from being completely alone to that. They have ideas about things, about everything—when we should marry, where we should live. Esther's ready to run away and change our identities, but I'm trying to stall her, to see if we can come to some sort of workable solution."

"You don't want to start life with a new family as the bad guy," Celeste guessed.

"Exactly," Leo said, nodding in relief that she understood.

"Plus take it from me: running away and changing your identity isn't all it's cracked up to be," Sam added.

"To staying put," Leo said, holding his glass of water aloft.

"To healing all the broken pieces," Celeste agreed, adding her glass.

"To falling in love," Sam said. He had no water, so he merely held his hand up.

"You look like someone who has a question," Celeste said, sipping her water before setting it down.

"I do," he agreed, taking her water and drinking a hearty amount. "What was your job for The Colonel?"

"Trust me when I tell you that you don't want to know," Leo interjected. "Cause if she tells you, then she has to kill you."

"Might be worth it," Sam mused, eyeing Celeste.

"I've seen the tapes, friend. Believe me, it's not," Leo said, downing the rest of his water.

CHAPTER 23

It was almost dusk by the time Esther finished her report. She arrived blinking into the living room like someone who woke on planet earth without a clue about how they arrived there.

"Celeste, I feel the need for a little fresh air. Is it okay if I explore your orchard?" she asked.

"Yes," Celeste said. "Would you like some company?"

"Yes," Esther said, reaching for her jacket.

They walked a few moments in silence, Esther breathing deeply to restore the oxygen she'd likely depleted while typing in a darkened room.

"I'm so delighted for Leo, Esther. He seems so happy with you," Celeste said.

Esther murmured something, a word Celeste couldn't discern. She leaned in to hear better. "Pardon me?"

"*Mudita,*" Esther said louder. "It means taking delight in the happiness of others, and it's a rare gift. Thank you, Celeste."

It was one of the nicest things anyone had ever said to Celeste, and especially a woman. She felt a warm little glow that someone of Esther's caliber had found something good to say about her, the same sort of feeling she got whenever The Colonel approved of her. As if she wanted to keep growing and doing better to earn more praise. But neither did she want to appear as pathetically over-eager for acceptance and approval as she felt, so they meandered in silence a few moments until Esther spoke again.

"It's so beautiful here, and you have so many lovely trees."

Celeste stopped short. "Thank you, but aren't they all dead?"

In answer, Esther reached around her and scratched at a piece of bark, pointing. "The bark is still green, they're alive. They've been neglected, for certain, but nothing a little trim and feeding won't fix."

"They're…they're alive?" Celeste said, not sure how to feel. She had written the trees off as a loss, their revitalization impossible. But now that they weren't, what should she do next? "I have no idea what to do with them. I've never even kept a cactus alive."

"It's not so hard, once you learn the basics. My family has an orchard."

She said it so offhand, as if everyone's family owned land and trees that made sustainable fruit. "They do?"

"Yes, they're quite into cider and jam," Esther said, her hand still lovingly caressing the tree.

"How did they learn how to tend the orchard?" Celeste asked.

"My grandfather taught my father, before that his father taught him."

Celeste's heart sank. *It always comes back to that.* "That definitely won't be my case."

"Just because your father died doesn't mean you can't find someone to teach you," Esther said.

Celeste froze again. "My father's dead?"

Esther's head whipped around, eyes widening with horror. "You didn't know?"

Celeste shook her head.

Esther began wringing her hands together. "Celeste, I'm so, so sorry. I'm not good at reading visual cues or picking up signals. I read your bio, and I assumed… I'm so sorry."

"Esther, it's really all right. I assumed he was, but I wasn't certain. Clearly we weren't a tender, loving family. Is…is my mother…?"

"Also gone," Esther said softly.

Celeste sank to the ground, landing in a hard cold heap. Her parents were truly dead. She'd thought of them that way for a long time, but to hear it made official left her feeling off-kilter somehow. Now she was an orphan, not in the technical sense, but an actual orphan. "How did they die?"

Esther sat softly and gracefully beside her, tucking her dress around her legs. "Your father got hit in the head during a bar fight between prison stints six years ago. He never regained consciousness. Your mother had a stroke in her halfway house four years ago. I'm so sorry."

"It's okay," Celeste said. "I mean, it's not. It never has been, but it is what it is. They were never my parents, not really. Only in the biological sense. I'm not certain I ever lived with them for more than a few weeks."

"You lived with your mother for eight months when you were two. It didn't end well," Esther supplied.

"How did you possibly find that?" Celeste asked. She was certain the state's records were not part of her bio.

"Our hacker is really good at finding hidden things. And at the time you were an anonymous person, part of my investigation. I like to dig deep. Sorry."

"You really don't have to apologize, Esther. You were doing your job, I get it. It's kind of funny, though, that you know more about me than I do. I'm amused, not offended."

"That makes you rare," Esther said. "You're incorrect, though. I only know the facts of your life, not any of the feelings. Those are what matter."

Celeste thought it was the best summation of her life she'd ever heard. "Esther, can I keep you?"

Esther gave a little smile in reply. "I don't think Leo would like that arrangement. He doesn't care for long distance relationships, and we seem unable to function without the other anymore."

"Does your family like Leo?" She drew her knees up to her chest and wrapped her arms around them. The cold was seeping into her bones, but she was having such a good time talking to Esther she didn't care.

"They love him," Esther said, nodding. "My mom loves to say, 'Oh, that Leo,' with a little shake of her head because he's charmed her so well. And my father has been teaching him about woodworking." Her happy expression slipped a tiny amount.

"Is there a but in that sentence?" Celeste asked. In Leo, she recognized a kindred spirit. They hadn't been close enough to spill their secrets to each other, but there was a sameness there, a hard outer shell that kept the world at bay. If he could find happiness, did that mean there was hope for her?

"I love my family very much. I know how blessed I am and I appreciate all they do for me," Esther said.

"But…" Celeste prompted.

"But they are driving me cuckoo," Esther exclaimed, pressing her fingers to her temples.

Celeste laughed. "Even the best families get on each other's nerves sometimes, I imagine." She had to imagine because she had no idea. But if someone hovered over her shoulder, always interfering, it would drive her crazy, too.

"I'm from an extremely conservative upbringing. Leo and I don't live together. We won't until after we're married, and that's fine. But my parents have ideas on when the wedding should be. It's as if they have a list of hoops Leo has to jump through to prove himself. But he's already proved himself to me, and we're adults, Leo especially. He's been so patient, but I think that's because it's all new. And, well, the truth is that Leo and I are together most hours of the day and evening at work. Our lives are extremely intertwined and have been for a long time. It's tiresome to have to separate for a few hours to go to different apartments, not to mention the waste."

She frowned a little, and Celeste thought it was probably as close as she came to being petulant. At first she didn't say anything. Over the years, learning to use words as an economy had taught her how much other people needed to be heard. Sometimes people simply needed to vent, and that was okay. Not every problem had a ready solution. But as she sat there, wishing she could do something to help Esther, who was so lovely and kind and gentle, she got an idea. In the words of The Grinch, a "wonderful awful" idea.

"Esther, I know something about Montana you might not realize," Celeste said, leaning forward to grip her arm.

"It's the 41st state? Nicknamed 'The Treasure State,' attained statehood in 1889, the state animal is the grizzly bear…"

Celeste interrupted her with a laugh. "Okay, scratch that. You know a million times more about Montana than I probably ever will. But the thing I know, it's about you: Montana has no waiting period for marriage. You can get a license and get married that minute."

Esther blinked at her, lashes fluttering. "I'm not really good with subtext and reading between the lines. Could you maybe spell out for me whatever you're saying?"

"What if you got married while you're here, a ceremony for you and Leo to make it official, then you could have another ceremony for your parents later."

"Oh." Esther sat up. "Could I do that?" She curled her fists and pressed them to her mouth. She seemed to be seeking Celeste's permission, so she gave it.

"Well, you are an adult," Celeste said, poking her. "And you said your parents approve of Leo. There's some disagreement on the timeframe, that's all. This is a compromise, a way for you to both have your way."

"I'm not certain they'll see it that way, when the truth is revealed, but I'm also not certain I care," Esther said. She hopped to her feet, started for the house, and stopped short. "But it's almost night time, Celeste. Surely no minister will marry us on such short notice."

"Leave it to me," Celeste said, reaching for her phone. "I know a guy."

"You're not going to have to do a job in return for this favor are you? Because we can only cover up so many dead bodies in this part of Montana," Esther said.

"Esther, please. I'm a professional. No one would ever find the body. Now go get your man. It's time to get you married." She made a little shooing motion toward the house and started to dial.

CHAPTER 24

In the end, Caldwell's husband, Mitch, agreed to meet them at the church. And as long as he was satisfied that Leo and Esther were a proper couple, with a proper commitment to the vow they were about to undertake, he agreed to perform the ceremony. After a five-minute conversation, in which they distilled their lengthy and complex history, he happily agreed to marry them. Celeste stood as witness for Esther, and Sam stood as witness for Leo, a fact which amused them all, given how much of Leo's life had been spent tracking terrorists, many of whom had worked directly with Sam.

It was so late by the time the ceremony was over that the diner was closed. Esther insisted on stopping by the market to pick up ingredients so she could make supper, despite Celeste's attempts to deter her.

"Let her do it, she likes it," Leo said, and that was how Celeste ended up sitting ringside while a bride prepared her own wedding feast of the best chicken salad Celeste had ever eaten.

"So you really just cook the chicken, cut it up, and add a few other ingredients," Celeste said, awed. Esther didn't use a recipe, of course, so Celeste was writing down everything she said, a mishmash of shorthand with things like "probably a teaspoon of salt. Pepper if you want it, Leo doesn't like it."

"What did you think went into it?" Esther asked.

"Magic beans," Celeste said. "I've honestly never seen a real person cook anything before. I've watched shows on TV, but the food is already prepped and then after they come back from commercial, it's all ready, thereby furthering the illusion that it's been done by secretive gnomes when no one was looking."

"It's very simple," Esther assured her. "And usually the simplest food is best. A pot roast is literally a piece of meat in a pot with some salt on it, cooked until it's tender. Mashed potatoes are boiled potatoes with salt, milk, and butter mixed in."

"But how many potatoes? How much milk and butter? How do you know when they're tender?"

"You're overthinking it. Relax, trust your instincts."

"I have no instincts."

"You do because you know what tastes good, right?"

Celeste nodded.

"Then start there. Make a list of foods you like and practice making them until they taste right."

"What if they're garbage?" Celeste asked.

"Then get new ingredients and start again, taking care not to duplicate whatever you did wrong. Look at this chicken." She stepped aside so Celeste could see the breasts she'd taken out of the oven. "This is what it looks like when it's no longer raw. You have to check it near the end because overcooked chicken is awful. But so is raw chicken. It should look like this, with some juices still flowing. That's how you know it's going to be good."

Celeste nodded, jotting notes like she was about to be graded. That was how she always felt, she realized, as if she was about to take a test for which she was wholly unprepared.

Leo was taking a shower and Sam sat at the table, head resting on his arm as he watched Celeste and Esther. During a lull while Esther shredded chicken, he caught Celeste's eye and crooked his finger, drawing her over. When she was close enough, he pulled her into his lap and gave her a squeeze.

"I think you're pretty cute," he whispered.

"Have I been downgraded again?" she asked, resting her head on his chest. She tried to ignore how good it felt, this unexpected sense of belonging she felt with him.

"No, it's an additional layer, cute on top of adorable. If you add one more, you'll go atomic and be able to make people explode with the power of exponential cuteness."

"Wow, you're like a nuclear physicist or something."

"Nah, I'm just an everyday guy who loves bombs enough to sell them to men trying to take over the world," he said.

"Sort of an unsung hero," she said.

"They'll probably make a Marvel movie about me," he agreed. "What with my tragic backstory."

"But what is your super power?" she tilted her head to stare up at him.

"The ability to keep starting over. When we moved from Jordan to the US when I was ten, I thought that would be the only time. And then my parents died and I moved to Saudi Arabia to join my uncles, I thought that was it. Then my uncles were arrested and I became a spy, that really seemed like the end because I thought I would be killed. But everything changed again, and here I am in Montana. And I don't know, Celeste, this time is turning out to be pretty good. Maybe the best. Might be a keeper. What do you think?"

He looked handsome and earnest as he stared down at her, but Celeste had no reply. How could she? Less than two hours ago she learned both her parents were dead and her reaction had been to plan an impromptu wedding. She was badly broken, completely in tatters, didn't even know how chicken got to the table. What could she possibly offer this man whose own life was so painful she somehow looked like a solution?

"It smells so good in here. I'm starving," Leo announced cheerfully from the doorway.

"You're always starving," Esther said, but affectionately.

"And you always feed me," Leo said, easing close to hug her from behind. The sweet action reminded Celeste it was their wedding night and they were about to eat supper with strangers. She jumped up and began pulling out dishes while Esther arranged their food and Leo poured everyone's drink.

The meal was cozy and warm and affectionate. It made the house feel the way Celeste had always wanted things to feel—alive, peaceful, loving, and fun. She avoided Sam's eye the remainder of the evening, but she felt him watching her. And his words kept a continuous echo through her brain. *This time is turning out to be pretty good.* No matter how many times she kept shoving them away, they circled back around. She wanted nothing more than to escape to her room, this time with her journal, but she couldn't allow Esther to clean the kitchen on top of everything else. She volunteered, and this time Esther and Leo were happy to make their escape together, holding hands and trying not to sprint in order to cocoon themselves in the privacy of their room.

Celeste watched them go with a fond smile.

"You look happy," Sam noted, reminding her he'd stayed behind and still needed to be dealt with.

"They're sweet," she said.

"Why are you so afraid of me?"

She tensed, almost dropping a slippery glass. "I'm not."

"You're a bad liar."

"I'm an excellent liar."

"You can tell me why you're so bunched up inside. Was it the job? Did something happen? Is that why you retired so early?"

"I can't talk about my job," she said.

"Can't or won't?"

"Both."

He came to stand beside her and picked up a dishtowel.

"You can't dry dishes with one good arm," she said.

"I know, but I hate feeling useless." He tossed the towel onto the counter with a frustrated sigh. "Celeste, I'm thirty two years old, and I've only ever had one girlfriend. There have been other offers, other opportunities, but I haven't wanted any of them because the possibility was never there, the indefinable connection. I feel it with you, that potential for something more. But I need something from you, anything. Some assurance that I'm not hanging on this thread alone."

She pulled her hands out of the water and faced him. "I honestly don't know what to say."

"You could start by telling me that maybe you feel it too, this pull between us. That it's not all in my head."

She gripped his shirt in both her hands, feeling relieved. The now was easy to handle. It was everything before and after that terrified her. "Of course I feel it. I felt it that first moment I walked into the kitchen. Bad guys aren't supposed to be boyishly cute. It's very confusing."

"I'm a reformed bad boy," he reminded her, kissing the tip of her nose.

She closed her eyes and inhaled deeply. "As for the other stuff, I don't have a lot to offer."

"That's not true. You have everything to offer," he said.

That's because you can't see inside me. You don't know about my past. Instead of saying any of that, she hugged him. Her ear pressed over his heart, comforted by its steady thump. He hugged her in return, as best he could with his injured shoulder. His head nestled against hers and it was so perfect, so right. If only they could freeze time and not have to worry about the future or the past.

"My trees are alive," she murmured.

"My heart's like a turnip," he returned.

She snorted a laugh. "What?"

"I don't know, I thought we were using garden euphemisms. What are you talking about?"

She eased back so she could see his face. "Esther said the fruit trees are alive. If I can figure out how to take care of them, I think I could grow apples again. This could be an actual working orchard."

His jaw dropped. "That's spectacular. Isn't it? You don't look happy. I thought you'd be happy."

"I'm too overwhelmed and terrified to be happy," she explained.

"It's going to be okay," he declared.

"How do you know?" she asked.

"Because it's my super power, starting over. Starting over doesn't get much bigger than spring renewal and growing new fruit from once dead trees. Also it turns out I'm deep now, since arriving in Montana. Got to start writing this stuff down for my memoirs. How do you spell unfathomable greatness?"

"E-g-o," she said.

"You can't trick me. That's eggo," he said and Celeste collapsed against his chest in a fit of giggles. On the day she found out both her parents were dead, it wasn't how she expected to end the evening. But as Sam waited for her to turn out the lights, walked her to her door, and kissed her goodnight, she didn't think about her parents or her journal or anything but the warm feeling of contentment spreading through her chest.

And for the first time in forever she fell asleep without journaling, snuggling beneath the covers warm and happy, a slight smile on her face.

CHAPTER 25

In the morning Esther taught Celeste to make bread while the men went to the barn to "fix the machines and do man things."

"This seems like a terrible way to spend the first morning of your honeymoon," Celeste noted as Esther bustled around the kitchen, setting out bowls and ingredients. It didn't escape her notice that she'd been there less than twenty-four hours and it already felt more hers than Celeste's.

"Of course it's not. Leo and I spend all our time together. It would feel silly to designate a day where we can't be with other people, just because we're married now." She stopped short and blinked a few times, a bread pan Celeste didn't know she possessed held aloft. "Oh, my goodness, we're married now."

Celeste laughed and Esther snapped to attention, shaking herself out of her trance. "That might take a while to get used to. Anyway, the most important part of bread, and really the only thing you can mess up, is the yeast. It needs to be fresh and still alive in order for the bread to rise. And you don't want to kill it with water that's too hot." She spoke while running the tap with her finger under it until she was satisfied it was the correct temperature. She filled a measuring cup and held it out to Celeste. "Stick your finger in."

Celeste dutifully complied.

"Notice that it's warm, but not too warm. If you can't hold your finger in it for a count of three, it's too hot."

"What if it's too cold?" Celeste asked.

"Better too cold than too hot. From here on out, I'm going to tell you what to do and you'll do it."

"Okay," Celeste said, tone uncertain. She needn't have worried, though. Esther was a patient teacher who broke everything into simple steps and explained them along the way. In no time she was kneading her newly formed lump of bread dough, her first ever, and it was with a little bit of sadness that she tucked it into a bowl and put a cover on. "I'm going to miss it," she admitted.

"You'll see it again soon," Esther assured her.

They sat at the kitchen table with mugs of coffee and some of the bread Esther had brought between them.

"You're my first female friend," Celeste admitted.

"I don't have many, either," Esther said.

"Why? You're perfect."

"I'm autistic." She waved a hand in front of her face. "I lack a filter, am unable to read social cues or understand sarcasm. Complex social hierarchies are beyond me. I never fit when they're established, and they're always established. People find my plain spoken nature off putting and odd."

"I don't. I love it," Celeste blurted.

"You sound like Leo," Esther said. She took a sip of coffee and set her mug down. "He told me about you, before we arrived. He said he asked you out a bunch of times."

"That doesn't bother you?"

"Leo had a past before we met. It doesn't affect the now or our future," Esther said.

Celeste let out a little breath, staring at the dark abyss of her coffee. "I wish everyone felt that way. Other women don't like me."

"Because you're pretty?" Esther guessed.

"No. I guess they probably had good reason. Back in the day I had a well-earned reputation as a man-eater. Men who were taken were sort of my preferred delicacy."

"Don't you find it a bid odd when women blame the other woman in that scenario instead of their significant other? If a man is truly committed, he can't be taken. Personally I'd be more worried about any man who'd let himself be distracted to that degree. *Acrasia,* a lack of self-control."

"That's a good point, and a testament to your maturity as a woman. But also, I was predatory."

"I can't help but notice your repeated use of the past tense," Esther said.

"It's been a long time. When The Colonel recruited me, I decided to turn over a new leaf."

"It would seem you have. Look at you, a homeowner and bread maker with money in the bank and a man who, even to someone who is bad at reading context clues, obviously adores you."

"He doesn't know me. Not really," Celeste said.

"Let him."

Celeste shook her head. "I can't. You know what's in my file, and that's bad enough. If you knew all that's unwritten…"

"What? Do you think I wouldn't like you anymore? That I might run away because you're so unclean I can't stand to be in the same room with you?"

Celeste didn't reply, but she swallowed hard.

"Celeste, when I look at you I see *probity*, integrity and uprightness. Honesty. A woman who spent fifteen years doing an impossible job few people in the world could even contemplate."

"I appreciate that, so much. And I'm trying hard to believe it. But when you spend the first eighteen years of your life being told the opposite, the competing voices get a little confusing. I haven't yet figured out a way to drown out the first one. But I'm trying."

"That's all any of us can do," Esther assured her. "Sometimes people are blessed with an amazing family and system of support and sometimes you have to seek it yourself, to make your own community. I fell in the first category. I was sheltered, so Leo was my first exposure to people who were alone in the world. Since then I've met a lot more people like you and him, enough to make me realize the people in the second category far outnumber the people in the first. And do you know what's amazing to me?"

She paused. Celeste shook her head, unable to fathom.

"People who are broken and hurting so often go into the kind of work you and Leo did. They become the helpers—soldiers, policemen, nurses, firefighters, and EMTs. Because they want to help other people like them. Despite everything, despite all the pain, you have these great big hearts, filled with care and compassion, hoping to make the world a better place than the one you sprang from. That's a miracle. And you *do* make the world a better place, Celeste. Don't let yourself believe otherwise. And maybe now that you've retired you'll have time to make the community you never had and always wanted."

Celeste didn't know what to say. It was like Esther opened a bottle of healing salve and dumped it all over her wounded pieces. No one had ever said anything so kind and gentle and encouraging to her before. At last she took a shuddering breath and spoke. "If Leo ever becomes stupid enough to let you go, I will literally kill him."

"Get in line behind this pacifist," Esther said, tipping her mug to Celeste in a little toast.

Together, they finished their coffee in companionable silence.

By the time the men returned from the barn, the bread was in the oven and it was time for Esther and Leo to fly home.

"Did you get everything fixed?" Celeste asked.

"Yes, if by 'fixed' you mean we gave up immediately and threw rocks at old tin cans instead," Sam said. "It smells edible in here. What sorcery is this?"

"I have made bread," Celeste announced.

"You are very talented," Sam replied, tugging the hem of her shirt.

"She is," Esther agreed. "My star pupil, for certain."

"Also your first and only?" Celeste guessed.

"Don't get caught up in the details," Esther replied, snaking her arm through Leo's. He gave her a squeeze and kissed the top of her head.

"Is it weird how much I'm going to miss you guys? Can't you come live here? Communes are coming back in style, I think," Celeste said.

"Our boss is weirdly picky about us actually showing up to work. But Montana is freaking fantastic. How about if we come back sometime?" Leo suggested.

"Anytime. My door is always open. Literally, apparently, because Sam stumbled through it in the middle of the night," Celeste said, snaking her arm through Sam's, unconsciously mimicking Esther's pose.

"In my defense, I'm really good at breaking into places. Criminally so," Sam said.

"La, la, la," Leo said, mashing his palms over his ears.

"You should come to DC to visit us," Esther said. "Especially because we're going to be living in the same house now."

"At long last," Leo said, giving her another squeeze. "Also, I second the invitation."

"We'll keep it in mind," Sam answered for them, as if they really were a couple. He held out his hand for Leo to shake and then Celeste hugged both of them goodbye. They followed them to their car, remaining on the porch as they loaded up.

Esther paused with her hand on the door and faced Celeste. "Next time I see you, you're going to be *effulgent*."

"What's that one?" Celeste asked.

"Look it up," Esther replied.

"That's how you know you've breached the inner sanctum, when she starts making you do the work yourself," Leo said. With a final wave, they got in the car and drove away.

Celeste pulled out her phone and looked up the word. Effulgent: shining forth brilliantly, radiant. "Why can't Esther be my mom?" she said, tucking her phone away.

"Because she's many years younger than you?" Sam guessed.

"The use of the word 'many' in this case is extraneous and hurtful," Celeste replied.

He picked her up and gave her a squeeze. "Sorry. Also, I missed you."

"We've only been apart a couple of hours," she said.

"But it hasn't been the same. Don't get me wrong, I liked having Esther and Leo here, post-interrogation, but I also liked it when it was Sam and Celeste time."

"Sam and Celeste time makes it sound like we're a seventies jazz lounge duo," she said.

"Not to brag, but I can actually play the triangle and the recorder, in case you'd like to learn to back me up on 'Hot Cross Buns' and take the show on the road."

"We should probably wait until you're no longer being hunted by all the people who want to kill you," she said.

"That's a good point. We'll have plenty of time to practice."

"Maybe years and years," she said.

He sucked a sharp breath. "I kind of like the sound of that, more and more. Also, I want to kiss you very much. I'm having lip withdrawal. It might deadly."

"Probably best not to take chances," Celeste agreed. She angled her face upward, startling when the oven timer beeped loudly.

"Is that the kissing alarm?" Sam asked, taking a step back as he set her down.

"It's my bread."

"Your bread," Sam said, following close on her heels as they hurried to the kitchen. He hovered nearby, making appropriate noises of awe when she pulled a perfect loaf from the oven.

"It's so pretty," Celeste whispered. She couldn't believe she had actually made bread. Esther pretty much instructed her on a molecular level, but still. She made food, completely from scratch like a real person.

"Are...are we allowed to eat it?" Sam asked as they continued to stand still and stare at it for several long moments. "You're not going to scream and snatch it out of my hands and tell me I'm eating your baby or anything, are you?"

"Yes, but I do that with all bread, not just the ones I've made," she clarified.

"Oh, that makes it normal then," he said.

"We can eat it, but it's hot. We should probably let it cool."

"If only we could think of some way to pass the time. Think, man, think," he said as he removed the oven mitts she was still inadvertently wearing.

"A walk? Like the three bears."

"I'm more interested in what Mama Bear and Papa Bear might have gotten up to on their own without the baby," he said, putting his hand on her belt loop and using it to tug her close.

"I didn't think it was possible to make a children's story inappropriate, but congratulations on your accomplishment," she said.

"It's all in the tone," he said. "Tell me something."

"What?"

"Anything. Tell me anything and also everything about Celeste."

"Oh," she said, spirits dimming. The morning had been so good. The last thing she wanted to do now was talk about herself.

"Start with something small and easy."

"Nothing is easy," she said.

"What's your favorite food?" he prompted.

"This bread I just made," she said.

A smile tugged at his lips. "Don't try to use your adorability to distract me. What's your favorite color?"

"Gunmetal gray," she said.

He snorted. "Your favorite color is coincidentally the color of your gun?"

"It goes with everything," she said.

"You're hopeless," he said, but he was smiling.

"That's what I've been trying to tell you," she said, standing on her toes so her lips brushed his. He gave up talking and gave in to the kiss, tugging her impossibly closer, one hand pressed against the small of her back, flattening her against him. The sound of tires on gravel once again registered, breaking them apart.

"Someone's here," she said.

"You know, for an orchard in the middle of nowhere, you get a lot of intruders," Sam said.

"Tell me about it," she replied, tapping his chest.

"Hey, I was here first. I have break-in dibs on the proprietor."

"If only I had a nickel for every time someone claimed break-in dibs on me," she said, shaking her head.

"How many nickels would you have?" he asked curiously. "You've never actually told me your dating history. Or anything else. Hint, hint."

She ignored him and withdrew her gun. "You can't take out your gun every time someone asks you a personal question," he said.

"Watch me," she said and opened the front door.

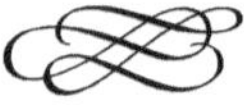

CHAPTER 26

As soon as she glimpsed the new arrival, she tucked her gun away. They parked and a man, or maybe boy, stepped from the driver's side. Ever since she reached thirty, Celeste had a harder time transcribing the age of anyone younger. The girl who stepped from the passenger side was definitively a girl, short and petite with a heart-shaped face and distinctively auburn hair.

"I recognize you," Celeste called.

The boy and girl froze and glanced at each other.

"You're Maybe's son," Celeste continued.

The boy, Jack, pointed to his chest. "Me? I'm the one you recognize?"

"Yes. You look exactly like your mother, except taller. It's uncanny."

"Do you recognize her?" he asked, pointing to the girl. Celeste gave her a once over. She was pretty in that unique way that made everyone do a second look, but her face didn't look familiar.

"Sorry, no. I don't think we've met. I'm Celeste."

"I'm Jack," he said. He slid an arm around the girl and cinched her against him. "This is Mare, my neighbor, best friend, lamp post, and all around light of my life."

"I see what you did there," Mare said, giving his chest an affectionate pat. To Celeste she called, "It's so nice to meet you. My dad has told me a lot about you."

Maybe that was why they expected Celeste to recognize her; she had apparently met the girl's father. "Oh, who is your dad?"

"Fletcher Reed," Mare said, tensing as if for some sort of reaction. Poor girl. It couldn't be easy to be the daughter of the town eccentric. Celeste tried not to let the pity come through in her tone when she replied.

"Right, yes. We've met a couple of times."

"Yes, he told me. He told everyone," Mare said, now sounding amused.

"Okay," Celeste drawled and Jack choked back a laugh before composing his features.

"My mom said you have some equipment that's giving you a bit of trouble," he said.

"Yes, but only if it's no trouble for you to look at it," she said, still feeling uncertain over the imposition.

"I'd love to take a look. I have a bit of downtime while Mare is…" he paused and glanced down at Mare who shook her head imperceptibly, warning him away from whatever he was about to say. "…doing what Mare does. I've always admired this place. Anything I can do to get it up and running would be a bonus."

"Great," Celeste said. She motioned to Sam. "This is Sam."

"I'm not sure there's a lot left to do," Sam said. "I took a look at all the machinery this morning and tightened a bolt. That probably fixed it. I mean, it didn't when I tried it, but there's probably some sort of delayed effect that will only take place after you try your hand at it a few hours."

"I'll make sure and give you the credit," Jack said and Celeste knew right then she liked him. He was a decidedly gorgeous boy, tall and sandy blond with piercing blue eyes, a good counterpart to Mare's exotic beauty. But there was no conceit in him. He appeared as humble and hardworking as Celeste guessed he might be, after meeting Maybe and Baird.

They walked together to the barn, Sam and Celeste in the lead, Mare and Jack bringing up the rear.

"This place is so great," Mare exclaimed. "I can't believe I lived here my whole life and never knew it existed."

"My mom brought us here once," Jack said, looking around the interior of the barn with a fond smile. "Actually she got lost here once and my sisters and I spent a few hours pretending we ran the place."

"Was Tansy the one in charge?" Mare guessed.

"No, actually that time it was Caldwell. It was her birthday so Tansy threw her a bone."

"Caldwell is your sister?" Celeste exclaimed.

"One of them," Jack returned. "I take it you've met her. Do you have a pet?" He looked around a if a horse or llama might suddenly appear.

"No, but, um…" Celeste glanced at Sam for a rescue.

"Her husband married our friends yesterday, sort of an impromptu wedding. They're nice people, Caldwell and Mitch," Sam said.

"Yes, they are," Jack agreed, but the words trailed away as he caught sight of the machinery he'd been dispatched to inspect. He began to roll his sleeves up, already calculating where to begin.

"I just took some bread from the oven," Celeste announced unable to snuff the note of proud disbelief from her tone. *Bread. I made bread. With my hands. Unbelievable.* "I'll check back later, please let me know if you need anything."

"We'll be fine," Jack assured her, tossing her an absent smile as his attention returned to the equipment.

"I'm going to stay and watch for a while," Sam said. "Bestow my wisdom and such." He stared at the machinery, too. Maybe it was a guy thing. Celeste didn't see the draw and Mare was already withdrawing a book and what might have been a manuscript from the bag she'd brought. Celeste eased away and headed toward the house, feeling restless. She checked her bread, assured herself it was still real, and headed for the living room.

The bookshelf caught her eye, along with her journal. She headed there now, withdrew it, and sat down, pulling one of Sam's blankets over her lap. Her pen hovered over the paper. Where had she left off? Fourth grade. That was a bad year, and one that needed to be addressed, but suddenly she didn't want to. All of a sudden she wanted to write something good and happy, so instead of dredging up past trauma she wrote about everything that happened after Leo and Esther arrived, spending a long time talking about the bread, the burst of stress relief she'd felt as she kneaded and shaped the dough.

When she was finished, she felt as drained as ever, too much to re-shelve her notebook. *I'll close my eyes for a minute,* she thought, curling up on the couch like a squirrel settling in for winter.

Seemingly only a moment later, Sam sat beside her on the couch, smoothing a hand gently over her hair. "Hey. You had a big weekend. No wonder you're sleepy."

She didn't tell him that while on a job it was routine for her to go days without slumber, mostly because she enjoyed the tender minis-trations a little too much. So she nodded instead. "How's it going in the barn?"

"Good. Jack made a list of all the parts he's going to need."

"Does he think he's actually going to be able to fix it?"

"Looks like. Apparently he's some sort of boy genius with a wrench. Although he did say my bolt definitely needed tightened, so I think I have some latent instincts as a natural mechanic."

"You're very talented," she said. His hand was still smoothing the hair off her face. The gesture was so soothing her eyes slid closed again.

"Hey," he nudged her. "Is your bread for eating or only for looking? Because it looks and smells as good as its maker."

"I don't know if I should be flattered or creeped out," she said.

"Probably both. But I'm suddenly starving." He took her hand and began insistently tugging. Her journal slid off her chest and landed on the floor with a hard smack.

"Oops, sorry." He bent to pick it up as she lunged and they barely avoided knocking heads. "I can put it away for you. I know where it goes," he offered.

Celeste sat up, eyes narrowed in suspicion. Her heart was beating hard at seeing all her most personal history in his hands. "How do you know where it goes?"

"Because there's a gaping hole on the shelf and I saw it there before," he said. In contrast to hers, his tone was calm and smooth, likely because he didn't understand the dire importance to her. The pages within contained her worst memories, all the bad things that had ever happened to her, along with the most shameful things she'd done. Her cheeks burned with the thought of all the things she'd so carelessly written. She should probably burn it before anyone read it, but she couldn't. Bad as it was, it was as if she needed some written record of her life, if only to bear witness to the atrocities.

Sam shelved the book and spun to face her, head tipping as he studied her tense features. "How do you wake up so pretty? It's uncanny."

"I do?" she said, pressing her hands to her overheated cheeks.

"All flushed and girly."

"I don't think of myself that way," she said. She thought of herself as tough, capable, and independent. But seeing the warm approval in Sam's eyes made her understand the value in the girly flush, and now she wasn't certain which she preferred.

"Celeste," he whispered.

"What?" she asked, staring at him with big eyes, heart thumping. She had no idea what he was going to say next and she was both terrified and excited to find out.

"Let's eat bread."

She blinked a few times, clearing her sleep-induced fog, then, laughing, led the way into the kitchen.

Sam sat at the kitchen table and watched Celeste bustle back and forth, trying so hard it made everything inside him turn to a full, rolling boil. She was so *earnest* in her attempt to be domestic. He had no idea why the bread was important to her, but it was. He could see it in her expression as she unmolded the bread, gazing at it in rapt fascination when it turned out perfectly.

After staring at it a while, she searched the drawers until she located a knife, attempted to make a slice, realized it was the wrong sort of knife, and returned to the drawer again. After finally making a slice, she placed it lovingly in her hand, turned toward him, stopped short, and pivoted back to the cupboard for a plate. She put the bread on the plate, started toward him again, stopped short once more, pivoted away, and spread the bread with butter. When she finally came toward him, plate of bread in two hands like a beloved pet, he thought his heart might burst.

He took the time to properly appreciate it when she set it gently before him, picking it up to sniff and inspect like a fine glass of wine. "This looks incredible."

She clasped her hands behind her back, flushing again, and now he was caught up staring at her.

He had only loved one woman in his life, the woman he thought he would love forever. Maggie had burst onto the scene like a sunbeam, filling his life with her warm energy. She was bright, confident, witty, and fun. He had loved those things about her, but she came to him whole and unbroken. Though they'd had a good relationship, she hadn't needed him, not really. That was how he was able to walk away, because he knew she was resilient enough to eventually recover.

Celeste was something altogether different. There was something so incredibly vulnerable about her, something that made him want to wrap his arms around her and protect her from life's blows. And though she wouldn't tell him what they'd been, he knew she'd received more than her share of them. Too many, perhaps. She was trying so hard to get wherever she was going, and he wanted to help in any way possible. Maybe forever.

He'd been a good kid. He respected his parents, got good grades, had a pleasant, happy-go-lucky attitude. And then life pigeonholed him into being the bad guy, or maybe he pigeonholed himself. For a while he'd tried to find redemption working for the government, and he thought he had, as much as such a thing was possible. And now with Celeste he felt he once again had the chance to be the good guy, to stand in the gap and protect her. More than that, he *wanted* to. Plus he hadn't been joking. She was certifiably adorable, but with a hint of toughness that made her over-the-top hot. Like a woodland creature wearing a leather jacket and riding a tiny Harley.

"Is it not okay?" she asked, making him realize he'd been staring at her too long.

"Let's see." He picked it up and bit into it while she tried to pretend she wasn't waiting anxiously on his judgment. "It's perfect," he said, mouth still full. "Why don't you have some and sit with me?"

She jumped to attention and cut herself a slice, sans plate this time, and sat beside him. They ate in companionable silence until their bread was finished. Celeste stood to clean up, but Sam pulled her into his lap.

"Thank you for the bread." He nuzzled her neck, inhaling deeply. The scent of her went straight to the heart of him, and when she nestled closer and relaxed into his embrace, he thought his heart might actually explode. He wanted more. In fact, he wanted everything. The care she bestowed on him was nice, but earning her trust seemed like a bigger coup, a clear indicator that he wasn't in this alone. "Why does the bread matter so much?"

She tensed, as she always did when he asked her a question. When she relaxed and let out a breath, he thought perhaps this was it: she was finally going to let him in and give him a real answer.

"Everyone loves bread," she said.

He tried and failed not to be disappointed by the flippancy. On the other hand, she was letting him hold her and he also understood that wasn't something normal for her, not if the way she'd held herself carefully away from him in the beginning was any indication. Maybe he needed to back off, be patient, and allow things to take place in incremental stages.

"What are you going to work on next?" he asked.

"I don't know. Maybe I'll make a list. What about you? What are you going to work on?" she asked, tipping her head back to inspect him.

You, he thought. If he wanted a project that would make his life better and bring happiness, it would be seeing Celeste open up and succeed. Out loud he said, "I'm sure I'll think of something."

"Confidence is key, at least according to that Fletcher guy," she said, resting her head on his good shoulder again. "You know he thinks he's famous. He can't believe I don't recognize him."

"Let him have his delusions. Maybe he's been through a lot."

"I suppose, but famous in Paradise? Come on. What would he be famous for?"

"Cow herding?" Sam suggested. Celeste did that giggling thing he was beginning to adore, as if she couldn't stop the laughter from escaping and immediately wanted to recall it, but it was too late. Someday maybe she would laugh freely and without hesitation. "Butter carving," he added, biting her neck when she tried to stop her laughter again. This time she was unable to. Her whole body shook with it, spreading an answering warmth through him. *This,* he thought, giving her a squeeze. *I want more of this; I want all of this.*

CHAPTER 27

Celeste couldn't believe she'd willingly gone to town again. Was she a glutton for punishment? Possibly. But Sam's words kept ringing in her ears. *What are you going to tackle next?* She had made bread and watched Esther make chicken salad, so attentively she thought she'd be able to repeat it. It was time to master something else, something completely unnecessary but wholly appealing for reasons she'd rather not contemplate.

"Oh, hello, Celeste." When Sheila Hickman, a woman she'd never met, opened her door and greeted her by name, she didn't even bat an eye.

"Hello, Mrs. Hickman."

"If you've come for a pie, I'm sorry to tell you I'm fresh out," Mrs. Hickman said. Celeste hadn't bought the pie from the woman herself. She bought it from the market. But she was already becoming used to the speed of light relay system in Paradise. Of course Sheila would know that Celeste had bought one of her pies. And of course she would call her by name as if they were old friends when in fact they'd never been introduced.

"Actually, I was wondering if maybe you could show me how to make your pies instead," Celeste said, biting her lip as she waited for the woman's reply. She never asked people for things, hated to depend on anyone or owe someone something. The longer she remained in Paradise, the harder it was becoming to remain aloof. She was over her head here. First Minnie had helped prepare her for the storm, then Tony had arranged all the things she needed to buy, and then Elliot carried her heater upstairs and showed her how to light it. And now this.

"Well," Mrs. Hickman drawled, and it was clear to Celeste she was going to say no.

"I'll pay you," Celeste blurted. "For your time and ingredients."

"It's not the money, my dear. It's, well," she paused and glanced furtively around, as if they might be overheard though there were no houses nearby. But given Paradise's apparent ability to read minds and hear even the smallest whisper, it wasn't a far-fetched fear. "There's a bit of jealousy over my pies. They're kind of a closely guarded secret."

"Oh," Celeste said. There was no way to make someone give up her secrets. Unless… "It's just that I have no idea how to bake. And my friend…"

"Sam," Mrs. Hickman interrupted with a nod.

"Sam," Celeste agreed, glossing over the fact that her cheeks flamed, "He loved that pie I brought him, I mean *really* loved it. And it's not only that I don't know how to make that pie specifically, it's that I don't know how to make any pie. I don't know how to do anything. I don't know how to cook. I never had a mother." She had intended to sound plaintive and ended up sounding pathetic, but since that was an authentic representation of her actual feelings, she let it linger, leaning in to the fact that her eyes tended to go wide and her lips jut unhappily when she was sad.

"Oh," Mrs. Hickman wailed, pressing her index fingers beneath each of her eyes to try and stop *her* sympathetic flow of tears. "All right, but please don't tell anyone. And please don't enter a pie in the fair, okay?"

"I promise," Celeste said, holding up a hand like an oath taker.

Mrs. Hickman stuck her head out the door, looked both ways, then held the door open and ushered Celeste stealthily inside.

She was slightly nervous, as she followed Mrs. Hickman through her cozy house to her kitchen in the back. What if it was like the cookbooks and the woman began at a level that was over Celeste's head, causing her not to be able to understand anything?

"This is a kitchen, and this is an oven," Sheila said slowly, gesturing to the white behemoth in the corner.

Celeste smiled and nodded, took out her notebook, and wrote it down. And then she took a breath. Everything was going to be okay.

Three hours later Celeste left Mrs. Hickman's house with a perfectly imperfect strawberry-rhubarb pie. Celeste chose the filling, reasoning that no one could object to the lesson as long as Mrs. Hickman wasn't giving away her huckleberry secrets. The pie wasn't as beautiful as the ones Mrs. Hickman made to sell. In fact it looked like it had been made by an overzealous ten year old, (a fact which set Mrs. Hickman's mind at ease because she was not training her replacement in the competitive Paradise tourist pie market.) But Celeste couldn't have been happier or prouder with her first effort. It was so much simpler than she'd thought it would be, and every bit as rewarding. As with the bread, it soothed her to put her hands in the dough and create.

People are meant to make things with their hands, she thought, making a mental note to add *creativity* to her list of important words.

She wanted to go straight home and show Sam the pie, knowing he would be as excited as she felt. But there was the practical matter of supper. Last night they finished off the last of the chicken salad Esther made. Celeste had plenty of canned and frozen food on hand, but she couldn't bring herself to eat it, not after realizing what she was missing out on—real food made by a real person and not in a factory somewhere far away.

Instead of heading away from town and toward home, she turned instead toward the market. Again. *I must be setting some kind of Paradise record for consecutive grocery visits.* At the moment she didn't care. All she could think about was creating something in the kitchen.

But as soon as she parked and wandered into the store, she was immediately overwhelmed. There were so many options and she had no idea what to do with any of them. All she knew was chicken salad, which was good. But they had eaten it two days in a row already. How long would it take to become malnourished by eating only chicken salad? Probably not as long as it would take to become sick of chicken salad.

"Celeste, hi."

Maybe spoke from very nearby, making her wonder how long she had been standing there while Celeste stared at the meat display, wondering what the difference was between London broil and rump roast and why it mattered.

"Hi," Celeste said, smiling. She didn't have to fake it today. Maybe was a little scattered and eccentric, but she was sweet and sincere. "Thanks so much for sending Jack. I think he's going to be life changing."

"Well, he was for me," Maybe said. She motioned to the beef display. "Are you trying to figure out what to make for dinner?"

"Yes," Celeste said, but it came out sounding like a question.

"It's the worst. I have to menu plan for the entire week, otherwise I lose my train of thought and will to cook. And sometimes we go to the diner anyway. Other times we eat leftovers because I've never acclimated to cooking for just me and Baird and cooking for three teenagers is a vastly different experience, so we always wind up with hordes of extra food. What's that, Maybe? Stop weirdly monopolizing the conversation and shut up? Okay. Sorry." She gave Celeste an apologetic smile and pointed to her mouth. "Once I get going, it's hard to stop."

"It's fine," Celeste said, realizing with some surprise she meant it. She had enjoyed the little glimpse into Maybe's life. It was surprising to her that she cooked every day with no children at home. And sometimes they ate leftovers? Somehow she'd pictured regular people eating something new and delicious each day, not rewarming food they'd already eaten. That was something Celeste did—bought takeout and made it last three days.

"What are you considering? Perhaps I can help," Maybe said.

"I don't know," Celeste drawled, making an inspection of the beef again. "I don't know how to make anything and I don't know what these things are." It was getting easier to admit her incompetent helplessness. "I want to learn to cook, but I haven't found anything that's basic enough for beginners. And I mean *basic*." Sheila Hickman levels of basic. Celeste supposed she should have been insulted when Sheila held up a box marked BUTTER and said, "This is butter," slowly and carefully, but she hadn't been. Because that was how little confidence she had in her ability to learn or understand this new thing.

Maybe glanced at her watch. "What are you doing right now?"

"Talking to you?" Celeste said, confused.

Maybe sputtered a laugh. "Good one. Are you free the next few hours? Is Sam expecting you?"

"I didn't really give him a time for my return. I'm free."

"How do you feel about chili?" Maybe continued.

"Good, but I'm losing the thread of the conversation," Celeste said.

"I have that effect," Maybe said, shaking her head sadly. "What I'm trying to say is that you should come home with me and I'll teach you how to make chili. Then you can take it home with you and that can be your supper."

"Oh," Celeste drawled. "Would that really be okay?"

"I'd love it," Maybe said with so much sincere enthusiasm Celeste believed her. "Why don't you ride with me? I'm terrible at having people follow me. I tend to space out and forget and then it's three weeks from now and I suddenly remember and wonder where you are."

"Sure. What ingredients do I need to buy for chili?" Celeste asked, turning helplessly toward the meat again.

"None," Maybe said.

"None?" Celeste swiveled to inspect her, confused. She wondered if everyone was equal parts confused and charmed when dealing with Maybe, or if it was only her.

"My husband is a cattle rancher. If we don't have at least a ton of beef in the freezer at all times, along with the complete ingredients for impromptu chili, the Montana Cattlemen's Association will show up and drag him away in the night." She turned and walked away before Celeste could protest or even respond. All she could do was trail helplessly in her wake. They piled in her truck. She remained silent until they were out of Paradise because it seemed like Maybe was the type of person who was easily distracted and shouldn't talk while trying to navigate parking lots and pedestrians.

"If you already have all the ingredients for chili, why were you at the market?" Celeste asked.

"I went to see if they had any fresh fish," Maybe said.

"I didn't think the market here carried fish," Celeste said.

"They don't, but I'm optimistic. One of these days when I decide I'd like to have something other than beef, some fresh cod or mahi-mahi will magically dangle from the grocery's ceiling like a thought bubble," Maybe said.

"Are there any vegetarians here?" Celeste asked.

"Sure. Except here we call them cows," Maybe said, smiling at Celeste when she laughed. "So how's the orchard going? Jack said he put some parts on order for you."

"A lot of parts, I think. He's a sweet kid."

"He is that," Maybe said nodding her agreement. "It's kind of a crapshoot when they're little, you know? You do the best you can and hope they turn out okay, and then when they do it's like winning the best lottery in the world. Moving to Montana was the best decision I ever made. No, one of the best decisions. Having them to begin with was pretty great, and marrying Baird, of course."

"Baird isn't their father?" Celeste guessed.

"Not biologically, but they're all pretty close. And they call him Dad, even Jack now sometimes. He was the lone holdout, not wanting to trample his dad's memory. My first husband was killed in an embassy attack."

"Dar es Salaam?" Celeste said.

Maybe turned to her in shocked surprise. "How do you know that? Nobody ever knows that. It was like it never happened here."

"I was there. I saw the plaque with the names of the soldiers who died."

Maybe blinked at her, speechless.

"I was in the army. I went a lot of places," Celeste explained.

"But you're so adorable, like a little sugar glider or something," Maybe said.

"The cuter you are, the more places they let you go," Celeste said, smiling when Maybe snorted a laugh.

"Wow, I can't believe you saw the plaque. I've only ever seen a picture of it, and of course I have the flag. Rather, Jack has the flag. Would you mind telling Jack sometime that you've seen it? It's always been a big deal to him, the fact that his father died a hero."

"I can only imagine," Celeste said. "And I'd be happy to talk to him about it."

They'd been driving a while, in the opposite direction Celeste usually went. "Is your house far?"

"It's about another forty minutes. This is our land, though."

Now it was Celeste's turn to be speechless. She looked out the window at acre after acre of fencing, dotted by the occasional cow. "All of this land belongs to you?"

"Technically Baird, but I guess legally it's half mine. Still feels weird to think that. And someday it will belong to my kids, Baird's already drawn up his will to sort out the legalities. If you knew where I came from." Maybe paused and stared thoughtfully through the front windshield.

"Somewhere bad?" Celeste asked, somewhat hopefully. She was always looking for a fellow trauma survivor. If someone like Maybe could overcome a bad childhood, there was definitely hope for her.

"No, nothing like that. I had a good life with good parents and a good, if somewhat boring, older brother. But I got married two weeks after I graduated high school and had my first baby nine months later, followed by two more in two years. My husband was gone because of the army, of course. And then he was really gone, killed when the kids were three, two, and almost one. And then my mom died that same year. My dad got remarried immediately and moved to Florida, along with my brother. I thought I understood what it was like to be a single mother while my husband was deployed, but then I had a new understanding of the word *alone*. I coped by doing what needed to be done, every day, day after day after day. I got up, went to work, did all the heavy lifting and hard work of parenting, made the Halloween costumes and birthday cupcakes, drove the kids to various lessons and events."

"How did you end up here?" Celeste asked when Maybe paused and became thoughtfully silent with remembrance.

"My great uncle died and left me his house, a should-have-been-condemned heap of junk. To this day I have no idea what shook me out of my stupor and made me think I should come here and start over. A miracle, probably, because I had gotten so used to being numb I could barely feel the strain and stress and pain of life anymore. And then I came here and it was terrible, at least at first. The kids were miserable and I was gobsmacked with confusion, completely overwhelmed by culture shock. And then Baird stepped in like some kind of avenging angel, rescuing us all in different ways, in the ways we needed to be rescued. And I, able to breathe and relax and not have to be 'on' for the first time in eighteen years, had a complete and total breakdown. Really freaky stuff, like my brain and body broke. Completely bonkers." She tapped her head and faced forward, shaking her head.

Celeste stared at her, unable to believe someone as sweet and vibrant as Maybe not only had a breakdown but felt free enough to share it with a stranger.

"What happened to make you better?" Celeste asked, wondering if she should take out a paper and pen and take notes so she could apply it to her own life.

"I needed to finally deal with the trauma I'd been avoiding. It was exhausting to always be on the move and doing what needed to be done, but it was also an excellent distraction, a handy way of never dealing with all the pain I'd been dealt. When I finally held still long enough to let it catch up with me, it did so with a vengeance, like a shovel to the face. And, being the mature grownup I am, I tried to run away again. But this time Baird came after me and just…let me feel. He held me and sat with me in the pain, didn't try to fix me or tell me it was going to be okay. He made it okay for me to be sad. I lingered in the sadness a while, marinated in it. Those were some dark days. Not a lot got done. The house was messy, the beds unmade, the meals uncooked, the laundry unwashed. Sometimes he would come home from a long day on the ranch and find me lying on the floor, staring at nothing, doing nothing. And I would see him and realize how much time had passed and I would cry and apologize for all the things I hadn't done. And do you know what he did?"

Celeste shook her head.

"He lay down on the floor beside me, gathered me close, kissed my cheeks, and said, 'So what? So what, Maybe, it's only laundry. It's only a little dust. We have plenty of food in the freezer. So what?' I had spent so much of my life in crisis mode, stressing over every moment, over every possible outcome of every day. You have no idea how powerful it was to hear someone say, 'So what?' Because then I started to ask myself, 'So what? So what if I'm almost forty and still have no idea what I want to be when I'm a grownup? So what if I'm not going to win housewife, cook, or mother of the year? I'm doing my best, and right now my best is going to have to be good enough.' After that I stopped trying so hard to be perfect, to do all the things and be all the things. I started trying to be okay with average, with ordinary. Some days I get everything done, I rock being a wife, mother, and grandma. Some days I wear two different shoes and forget to open the glass door before walking onto the patio. So what?" She shrugged. "So much of life is letting go of the vision in your head, of the person you think you should be, of the way you think your life should look. I'm not perfect. I never will be, ever. I'll always be that person with my head in the clouds who talks too much and often says the wrong thing. But I'm trying my best. I'm taking it moment by moment. And I'm happy; I'm fulfilled; I'm *content*."

Celeste would kill for "content." She didn't say so because, unlike Maybe, she wasn't comfortable baring her soul to a stranger. Or anyone, really. But she had a lot to think about. "I have to admit I'm a little envious. Baird sounds like a wonderful guy."

"He's the best," Maybe agreed. She darted Celeste a covert glance. "Sam seems like a good guy."

"He does," Celeste agreed. "We don't know each other that well."

"Ah, early days," Maybe said with a knowing nod. "Those are fun times. Also terrible. But mostly fun."

"Why terrible?" Celeste asked.

"Because you don't know what he's thinking. You don't know if he likes you as much as you like him, if it's going to work out, if he's *the one.*" She took her hands off the wheel to make air quotes. Celeste gripped her seat when the truck yanked sharply to the right. "That doesn't seem normal. Maybe there's something wrong with the tires. I'll have Jack take a look."

Celeste bit back her reply. She thought it was more likely something wrong with the driver who probably shouldn't use her hands to talk, at least not while driving. She'd bet Jack had to take a lot of "looks" at vehicles after his mother used them. And even after one interaction with the kid, who seemed almost angelically good, he probably did so with a smile and no longsuffering sigh whatsoever.

"I just don't have good luck with cars," Maybe muttered to herself.

Celeste turned to the window to hide her smile.

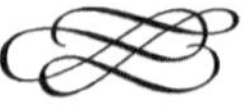

CHAPTER 28

A few hours later, Sam was awed and impressed when Celeste arrived home with chili and pie, both of which she'd made herself.

"Did you know that chili is such a contentious topic it's inspired wars?" Celeste asked as they sat down to eat their bounty.

"Really?" Sam asked.

"Yes, at least in the Montgomery household. Apparently when Maybe and Baird first got married, she made chili the way she'd always made it and he asked her why she put ground beef in her tomato soup. She thought he was joking, but he wasn't. He told her chili wasn't chili unless it was made with chuck roast."

"This has both things in it," Sam noted, staring at his bowl.

"Yes, apparently the way to compromise in Montana is to double the beef. But then the beans were an argument."

"There are beans in here," Sam said.

"Maybe won that one. Because fiber."

"Ah, she played the constipation card," Sam said, nodding. "My mother used to do that."

"But then there were the spice wars."

"India?"

"Chili powder versus actual chili peppers. And Maybe put sugar in her chili and she said that was the only time Baird has ever tried to sleep on the couch," Celeste said.

"I guess when Shakespeare said 'the course of true love never did run smooth,' he must have been referring to chili," Sam noted.

"You're pretty hot for a nerd," Celeste said, reaching for her glass of water.

"Maybe I'm just a nerd and everything is hot," Sam said, also reaching for his water.

"They compromised on the chili by doubling that, too," Celeste said, adding another dollop of sour cream to her chili to try and cut the heat.

"It's good, though. So good," Sam said, pausing to shovel a few bites. "Did you have fun?"

"Yes."

"You sound surprised."

"I guess I am. I thought I would come here and be a recluse and look at me, peopling. Plus I learned to add something to my growing list of edible things. And, I don't know, it was informative."

"How so?" Sam asked.

He was one of those people who actually listened when he asked a question, as if he cared and had a vested interest in the answer. He set aside his spoon, focusing solely on her.

"I guess I had this vision of being a grownup as having everything together, no more problems. But Maybe's had a lot of problems. And she and Baird don't always get along. They hash things out and power through. It was like stepping inside a TV show, but better because it's real."

"You never watch TV," he said.

"I've always been too busy. I'm pretty out of it, as far as pop culture goes," she said.

"Me, too. I kind of have a thing for Bollywood, though."

"Really? That's what you're into? Elaborate costumes and belly dance routines?" she said.

"I'm shocked I haven't performed one for you," he said, pushing her water closer when she choked. "Do you know what I overheard at the hardware store the other day?"

She shook her head, still too busy gulping water to answer. "Someone said Fletcher was on some kind of show."

"Oh, is that why he believes he's famous?" Celeste said.

Sam nodded. "How much do you want to bet he was an extra on some police drama ten years ago and still brings it up at parties?"

"I wouldn't take that bet. The man has crazy eyes." She wound her finger around her ear.

"He's no Ranbir Kapoor," Sam agreed.

She gave him a blank look.

"Famous Bollywood actor," Sam explained.

"Ah. What did you do all day? You never said."

"I read some of the books from your shelf, I hope that was okay."

"Sure. I bought a bunch of stuff and never read it. I've never been a reader, can't get into it," she said.

"You should try reading picture books," he suggested.

She froze, spoon held aloft. "Are you making fun of me? Because I *can* read. It's not a learning disability, just a low boredom threshold."

"Of course I'm not making fun of you. And picture books aren't only for children."

"They're literally in the kid section of the library," Celeste said.

"No, no, no. That's all wrong. My mother was a professor of children's literature. She loved picture books, thought they were the highest form of art and self-expression. They have stories *and* pictures. She believed if someone didn't think they liked reading, they should start with picture books to spark their interest. Because you become captivated by the story, and then you want more stories. Like starting with milk before solid food."

"That's kind of brilliant."

"So was my mother," he said, shrugging.

They ate a few moments in contemplative silence until he spoke again. "Why do you believe there must be so much distinction in what is for children and what is for adults?"

"I don't know." She did know, though. In her world growing up, adults had all the power. She couldn't wait to be an adult, when she was a child. And now that she was an adult, she associated childhood with her former misery. For her, there was a clear distinction.

"It makes me a little sad to think of you unable to do fun things because you regard them as childish."

"Like what?"

"Playing in the snow."

"That's one example. Also, it was cold and wet. I'm fun."

"What do you do that's fun?"

"I…" Suddenly she couldn't think of one thing she had ever done, merely because it was fun. "Sometimes I run."

"Sometimes I do, too, if I'm being chased. Give me something else, an actual fun activity."

"It's classified," she said, scraping up the last of her chili.

"Lies. You won't tell me because you can't, because you don't believe in doing fun things," he said.

"I'm fun," she said, banging her spoon on the table.

"Prove it," he said, one eyebrow quirking.

"How, exactly?" She said it slowly, suddenly wary. What if their ideas of fun were vastly different?

"Play with me."

"Play what?"

"Hide and go seek."

"Why? To prove I'm not stuffy?" she said.

"I never said you were stuffy. And the answer to why is why not? We have time, we have energy, I think it will be fun."

"I don't know if you're normal," she said sincerely, studying him. Celeste felt like she had spent most of her life looking for a yardstick, trying to find a baseline of normality. Sam seemed well adjusted and happy, shockingly so for someone who was essentially running for his life. But was he what she should aspire to be? And was the key to his happiness his willingness to embrace carefree fun?

"Let me assure you I'm not, but then who is?" He dabbed his lips with his napkin and carefully set it aside, waiting for her answer.

"All right. Let me clean up, and then we can go…play."

"No. Play first, clean later."

"That doesn't feel right," she said.

"You're trying something new. Trust me." He stood and reached for her hand, pulling her up beside him. "The dishes will be here when we get back. In fact dishes will always be here. Chores can wait, fun cannot."

"Now who sounds like a motivational poster," she groused, but she allowed him to lead her outside. He led her to the space beside the barn and put his hands over his eyes.

"I'm going to count to a hundred. You hide."

"Hide and seek? That's your brilliant..."

"One, two, three..."

"I can't play hide and seek. I'm thirty thr..."

"Four, five, six..."

When it became clear he wasn't going to stop until he reached a hundred, she squeaked and leapt to attention, scurrying for a good hiding place. And because she was small and had long ago learned to be good at hiding, he couldn't find her. Not after he counted to a hundred, not after ten minutes of searching. She watched him from her space in the barn rafters, wandering in and out of the barn, checking behind equipment and in each stall.

"All right, I give up," he announced at last. He stood in the middle of the barn, his back to her. Celeste pondered what to do. Should she keep hiding and make him work harder to find her? *I miss him too much,* she thought, rolling her eyes at her pathetic internal dialogue. She was not a teenager anymore, unable to function without her boyfriend, fake or otherwise. But they had been together all day every day for days. Being apart today took a toll, more than she would have expected.

She decided to give in, but she wanted the element of surprise. Spying a rope tied a few rafters away, she silently picked her way to it and grabbed on, planning to climb down. What she hadn't counted on was the age of the rope and mildew. Only a few feet down, the rope snapped, sending her plummeting about ten feet. She landed on her back and all the air rushed out of her lungs so quickly it felt like they collapsed.

Sam spun in time to see her fall, a horrified expression on his face. He darted forward, but not in time to catch her. He knelt beside her and clasped her hand.

"*Ya eazizaa*, are you all right?" His hand pressed to her forehead and he stared in her eyes, likely checking for signs of life.

For a second she felt panicked; there was no air in her body and she couldn't seem to draw a breath. And then slowly, painfully, her lungs reopened. She gasped hard, taking in the max amount of air. It came out in a slow whoosh, and then she spoke. "I'm your darling?"

His lashes fluttered. "You know Arabic?"

"A few phrases."

"I'm going to skip over the how and answer the question, but only because you're injured. Yes, you're my darling." He lay down beside her, his hand making gentle passes over her hair. "Are you all right?"

"Yes." She flexed her fingers and wiggled her toes to make certain.

He smiled at her.

She smiled in return.

His smile slowly slipped and he bit his lip, his eyes focusing on her cheek instead of her eyes. "Celeste."

"Yes?"

"I think maybe I'm falling in love with you."

"Oh," Celeste said. The air left her in a whoosh again, like she'd taken another tumble off the rope. "I…"

He touched his finger to her lips, shushing her. "I didn't say it to receive a reply, especially one you're probably not ready to make. I just…felt it and needed you to hear it. You can think about it. Get back to me." He shifted closer and kissed her cheek.

"All right," she said. She felt muddled but also soft and fizzy all over. She hoped it was a response to his statement and not some latent nerve damage from the fall.

Instead of urging her to get up, Sam eased closer and slipped his arm over her, surrounding her with his steady warmth. She rested her head on his shoulder, nestling. "Even though I fell off a rafter, it's been a good day," she noted.

"Even though I don't have a home and am being hunted by an international terrorist, it's been a good day," Sam agreed.

Celeste swiveled her head to face him. "Of course you have a home. This is your home. You *are* home."

"I feel like maybe I am, which is rather extraordinary," he said. His thumb traced a gentle path around her ear.

Playing hide and seek had been fun, but she liked this far better. "I might never get the hang of being normal," she informed him.

"So what," he whispered, giving her waist a squeeze.

"So what," she repeated to herself, then she took his face in her hands and kissed him.

CHAPTER 29

The following few weeks were peaceful, gentle, *healing*, and not merely for Celeste. Sam was changing, too. For a few days after Esther and Leo left, he had slept. And slept. And slept. It was as if now that he'd finally found a place to rest, all the years of running finally caught up. No more subterfuge, no more pretending to be the bad guy when what he secretly wanted was to be good.

Celeste had already passed through the sleeping phase. While Sam napped, she organized the kitchen, arranging things where she could find them and writing them down when she had no idea what they were. Those items she began stacking in a corner of the kitchen. By the time she was finished arranging, the stack was massive. She brought her laptop to the kitchen and looked up each item, labeling it with its proper name and what it was used for as she went along— sifter, egg beater, egg separator, strawberry huller. The items had clearly been purchased before modern technology, but Celeste kept them regardless. She liked that they were old fashioned.

On one of her organizing forays, she found a stack of yellowed cookbooks, decades old. Some of them were too outdated to be of use —what was aspic, and why had people ever thought it was a good idea to eat it? Three of the cookbooks proved both promising and timeless.

She spent the next few days poring over *Betty Crocker, Fanny Farmer,* and *The Joy of Cooking,* once again pausing to write down and lookup terms she didn't know. It was laborious and she was putting in more effort than she'd ever given schoolwork. But in the end she had earmarked a stack of basic recipes to try.

This time she approached the process differently, or at least with a different attitude. It didn't have to be perfect and probably wouldn't be, given her lack of experience. She only had to try, and if she failed she would try again. Somehow giving herself permission to fail made her succeed, or perhaps it was because she changed her definition of success. Maybe having the courage to try counted as success.

In any case, she and Sam dined on beef stew, chicken kiev, and salmon chowder that were at the very least edible and, some lesser critics might say, almost good.

The parts for Celeste's equipment came in and Jack spent a few days working in the barn, getting everything in working order. Celeste paced outside the barn on those days, feeling like a 1950's father-to-be in a hospital waiting room. What if he couldn't get them working? Worse, what if he *could*? Then what? What about the trees?

That answer began to sort itself, too, when Esther forwarded her father's contact information, along with the number for the local state extension agent. With shaking hands, Celeste emailed Esther's father and called the extension agent. He contacted an arborist and they set up an appointment to inspect her trees.

I might actually be doing this, Celeste thought, staring dazedly into space.

Sam walked by the room, caught sight of her zombielike visage, picked her up, and sat down with her in his lap. "Why are you in a panic spiral?"

"I'm just sitting here. How can you tell I'm in a panic spiral?" she asked.

"Because you're just sitting here. You're almost never not doing something. You only freeze when you're too stressed to function."

"Huh," she said, regarding him. She hadn't realized that about herself until he said so, but now she saw it. She functioned well under physical pressure, but too much emotional stress and she shut down. "I guess I'm feeling a little overwhelmed by the orchard."

"Why? It seems like things are going well. Jack has almost all the equipment up, the tree guys are coming, and Esther's dad sent you that list of recommended reading," he said.

"It's a lot of things," she said.

"But you're Celeste. You can do anything," he said with so much confidence she might have believed him, minus all the hidden things she knew that he wasn't privy to.

"I can't, though," she said. She could feel herself curling inward, gripping his shirt in both hands like a lifeline as she shrank.

"Why not?" he asked.

"Things don't work out. A lot. Most of the time, actually."

"How so?" he asked with forced casualness. He had been trying not to pressure her to tell him things, personal things about her life. But it was always there between them, a gnawing tension and awareness that she only allowed him to know the most surface information. Adding to Celeste's growing guilt and discomfort was the fact that some of the things he thought he knew weren't even true.

"Nothing. I'm rambling."

"Celeste," he said, making her name a tired sigh.

She froze. She knew that tone, understood the exasperation and pending end of his patience. *Here it comes.* "What?"

He didn't respond for several agonizing beats. "Nothing. Is it all right if I take the car to town? I'm expecting a few things."

"Yes, of course," Celeste said. She started to ease away, but he held her firm, giving her a squeeze.

"I want to love you. I wish you would let me." He kissed her forehead, grabbed the keys by the door, and then he was gone.

Celeste meandered to the bookshelf, pulled out her journal, and flipped through it. She felt a sense of urgency, mingled with a large dash of helplessness. She so badly wanted to unburden herself, to write down everything that had gone wrong in her life and find a way to fix it. She felt desperate for a rescue from the quagmire she'd created, the secretive cage of self-protection. The only way that made sense was to write it all down, fix it, and then emerge into the world healed and whole. But what if that was wrong? Or, worse, what if it was right and it didn't work? What if she wrote her entire life story and she was still as broken as before she started?

She sank to the floor, book in hand, and began reading, page by page, line by line.

S am drove to town distracted and miserable. There was a not so small part of him that was annoyed with himself more than with Celeste. Why couldn't he be happy with things the way they were? Why couldn't he settle for the status quo? He and Celeste had fallen into a happy routine. He was certain he loved her, and he thought maybe she loved him, too. Why couldn't what they already had be enough?

Because it isn't, that annoyingly insistent little voice reminded him. He didn't want part of Celeste; he wanted all of her, even the ugly inaccessible parts she tried to keep hidden. It was growing harder not to be hurt by her refusal to tell him, especially when he saw her writing in her journal night after night. He had started to become jealous of a notebook, but how could he help it? The book got all her secrets while Sam sat by and tried to pretend the continued rejection didn't sting.

He pushed aside his sadness in favor of being social. Paradise had come to mean a great deal to him, along with its inhabitants. He felt well on the way to being friends with several of them, felt an unexpected sense of belonging in the last place he would have imagined. He was half Jordanian, half Saudi, an American citizen turned double agent, former arms dealer, reformed terrorist, and yet he felt like a local. People were excited to see him whenever he arrived in town. They treated him like a celebrity, more so because he was part of Celeste's orchard. It became clear to him very quickly that the town wanted her to succeed in remaking it.

He paused to have four conversations before he could reach the door of the post office. Once inside, he paused and sniffed. *Smells like maple,* he thought. Jody, the postmaster, hastily shoved something back inside a box and closed it before brushing her hands together and smiling at Sam.

"You got some boxes."

"Excellent," he replied.

"From big cities. New York, Washington, Boston," she continued, probing in her not-so-subtle way.

"Yes, I needed some things. Clothes and such." He'd been slowly restocking his life, first with toiletries, underwear and socks, then with actual clothing, a laptop, and phone. He was beginning to feel not only normal, but *settled*, another unexpected development. As a double agent, he imagined a time when he would have to flee for his life. He pictured himself wandering for years, possibly for the rest of his life, never feeling at peace, never feeling at home. But Celeste was right, this was his home. More than that, he was beginning to realize she was his home. If he had to leave Paradise and start over somewhere else, he would be okay, as long as she went with him. She had a way of curling into him, balancing his weaknesses, easing into his soft spots with tender comfort. He was finding healing through her gentle attention and affection. She gave him space, let him be, offered silent support, didn't judge his past, in short acted like a true friend. His only regret was that she wouldn't open up and let him do the same for her.

Jody nodded. "Right. I keep searching for a little box. Ring size, you know? We're all hoping." She held both hands up to show him both sets of crossed fingers.

Sam laughed. This was his first full conversation with the woman, and yet she felt comfortable probing into his marriage plans with Celeste. But that was the way in Paradise, he was learning. Each person's life wasn't solely his own. The town viewed itself as a collective, but not in a communist way. More like a family. It was mind boggling, but also sort of wonderful, especially for someone like him who had been so long without family.

"You'll be the first to know." He said it in a joking way, but she responded with a sincere nod.

"You bet I will," she said, tapping the mail slot behind her.

Mental note, never order jewelry through the mail here.

He thanked Jody, headed back to his truck, and was waylaid by Fletcher Reed. Unlike Celeste, who thought the man was always two seconds away from donning feathers and declaring himself a chicken or something similarly insane, Sam found him amusing. So he fancied himself famous. What was the harm? He seemed nice enough.

"How's it going?" Fletcher asked.

"It's…" Sam began and then somehow ran out of steam before he could finish the lie. "Okay," he said at last.

Fletcher glanced at his watch. "Wanna grab a coffee?"

"Yes," Sam said because the alternative was going back home and he hadn't worked through enough of his feelings to face Celeste yet.

"So what's up?" Fletcher asked as soon as they were seated in the diner. Avery brought coffee, followed by pie delivered with a breathless smile by her three year old son.

Sam appreciated that they were cutting to the chase, but he wasn't sure where to begin. Without a doubt he knew Celeste wouldn't want him to spill any of her information or their private issues. On the other hand, how was he ever supposed to fix what he couldn't figure out?

"How did you and Chloe meet?" Chloe was quiet, a bit shy, sharp contrast to her gregarious and outgoing husband.

Fletcher gave him a wry smile and shook his head. "You really don't know. Amazing. You and Celeste are meant to be. To answer your question, we met as kids and grew up together. It was *not* love at first sight. We're opposites in almost every way. It took a while for that to actually attract. We reconnected after she came to Paradise. I fell in love, both with her and the town."

Sam remained quietly thoughtful, breaking off little pieces of his pie without actually eating them.

"Was there a reason you asked? Is everything okay with you and Celeste?"

"I wish I knew," Sam said, tossing aside his fork. "Celeste is the most incredible person I have ever met. She works harder than anyone I've ever known. The woman never stops. It's as if retirement gave her a blank slate she feels she has to fill with a list of accomplishments." He thought of yesterday, when Celeste went to her first story time at the library, nervous and excited and trying not to be. When she saw Celeste checking out so many picture books, the librarian suggested she join the weekly kids' circle. Celeste had been willing to undergo the humiliation of being the only non-parent there, merely because she wanted to begin again, to learn to appreciate books from the ground up, starting with children's stories. Some days Sam loved her so much he felt like his heart couldn't take any more.

"Does that bother you?" Fletcher asked. "Her attempts to accomplish things?"

"No. Yes. I don't know." He rubbed his hands over his eyes. They felt gritty, despite the fact that he finally felt caught up on sleep for the first time in a decade. That was another great thing about Celeste: she had let him sleep, hadn't bugged him or badgered him or guilted him for being so unproductive. She was so caring, so kind, and she didn't even realize. "I guess I want to know why she's a blank slate. I want to know everything, and she won't let me in. I don't know how to show her that she can trust me, that all I want is to love her."

Now it was Fletcher's turn to be thoughtfully silent as he stared at his pie. "Maybe you can't."

Sam blinked at him. "You mean give up?"

"In a manner of speaking. Give up trying to fix her. Give her space and time to come to her own realizations. If you manhandle her into opening up before she's ready, it will make things worse. You might damage her further; she might not forgive you."

Sam felt the bottom drop out of his stomach and suddenly regretted the pie. "I don't want to hurt her, to damage her," he exclaimed, then lowered his voice when a few people darted him looks.

"Do you want to fix her?" Fletcher asked.

"Of course I do," Sam said, tossing his arms wide in frustration.

Fletcher shook his head. "You can't."

They stared at each other. Sam's frustration was palpable. Fletcher seemed to be letting the words sit for a while so Sam could soak them in before he continued. "You can't fix another human being. You can only love them. The question you have to ask yourself is whether you're willing to love her as she is, secretive and closed off, or if you can't. If you need her to open up and let you in or it's a deal breaker, so be it. There's no shame in having boundaries and declaring them, as long as you do it with integrity. If you're willing to take her as is, then you work on yourself, on your own longsuffering patience."

"Are you some kind of counselor or psychiatrist?" Sam asked.

"Nope. I'm a messed up guy who's trying to do better for his family. And I learned a lot of things the hard way, this lesson specifically. Chloe had some issues, stemming from our childhood. I had to give her time and space, had to let her come to me in her own way."

"It sounds easy in theory, but we live in the same house, see each other all day every day. I tell myself I'm going to let it go, and then I'm confronted with the reality of how little she lets me in, and I get frustrated."

"Maybe you need some actual physical space," Fletcher suggested.

Sam sighed and rested his fist in his hand. He didn't want to leave Celeste, not even for a moment. The thought of being apart hurt so deeply it erased all doubt about his feelings for her. Also, "I have nowhere else to go."

Fletcher leaned forward with a calculating smile. "I can fix that."

⚷

*C*eleste felt like she hadn't made any headway whatsoever. By the time Sam returned several hours later, she still sat on the floor clutching her journal. And she still didn't know how to be what he wanted her to be, to do what he wanted her to do.

He entered quietly and sat silently beside her, reaching out a hand to touch her temple. "Hi."

"Hello," she said.

"I was thinking maybe I would go away for a while," he said.

"Oh. Where?"

"Fletcher invited me to stay at his guest house for a while."

"Fletcher has a guest house?" she asked.

"Apparently."

"You're not afraid it might be a secret lair or dungeon where he's going to make crazy person paraphernalia from your hair and teeth?" she said.

He laughed and shook his head. "No. Whatever he is, I think he's harmless."

"Oh."

They sat in heavy silence a while. Celeste's nose felt hot. At first she thought maybe she was getting sick, and then she realized the truth was worse: she was about to cry. She hadn't cried since…she couldn't remember the last time she cried. She sucked a shaky breath, trying to press back the pain, press back everything.

"Celeste," Sam said, making her name a question.

She squeezed her eyes closed, trying to block him out, trying to block out everything.

"Your phone is ringing," Sam said gently, breaching her apparent breakdown.

Her eyes flapped open. She reached for her phone and held it to her ear. "We have a problem," The Colonel said, and then a gunshot rang out

Celeste dove for Sam at the same time he scrambled to cover her. They ended up rolling a couple of times, landing flat on their backs, side by side. Miraculously Celeste maintained her hold on the phone, probably because it was The Colonel and she was certain he'd have answers.

"You were saying there's a problem," she said and tossed Sam a smile when he snickered.

"Komeni is on the move. We think he might have caught wind of Sam's location and could be planning to take him out in person."

"I think he's already here," Celeste said.

There was a pause, then, "That's not possible."

"Begging your pardon, sir, but we're under fire from someone."

"I can have a team there in less than five hours. You'll have to hold them until then."

"Yes, sir," she said.

They disconnected and Celeste tossed her phone aside.

"Was that The Colonel?" Sam asked.

Celeste nodded.

"What did he say?" he asked.

"He had some intel that we might soon be in trouble," she said, tossing him a wry smile as another shot rang out.

"How good is his intel?" Sam asked, smiling when she laughed out loud. He reached over and took her hand. "Do you have an extra gun? I'm a pretty good shot but my gun's upstairs."

"I think I could rustle one up for you," Celeste said. She closed the gap between them and kissed him. "I don't want you to go."

"Are you only saying that because you think we're going to die?" he asked, stroking his finger on her cheek.

"No."

"I don't think my presence here is helping you. I don't want to pressure you or push you into something you're not ready for," he said.

She took a breath and rested her head on his chest. As she lay down, she caught sight of her journal, lying sad and discarded on the floor. She closed her eyes and forced herself to begin.

"My name isn't Celeste."

Sam's hand froze on her head. "It's…not?"

She shook her head. "I mean, it kind of is, but it wasn't originally. It wasn't my birth name."

"Are you allowed to tell me what that was?"

She took another breath and made herself look at him. "Nevaeh."

"Heaven spelled backwards," he noted.

She nodded, smiling sadly. "It was an ironic name choice for parents who never wanted me." A shot pinged off the siding and she sat up with a huff of frustration. "Hold on a minute."

He watched as she walked to the entry closet and pressed her hand to a spot beside it. A panel sprang open. She typed a code and another door opened, another closet. Perhaps closet was the wrong word; an arsenal sprang open. Forgetting that people were actively trying to kill them, Sam popped up and came to a halt beside her, openmouthed.

"Wha…" he began, but that was as far as he got.

"You're not the only one with enemies, not the only one being hunted. I wanted to be prepared." She selected a couple of guns and some ammo, turning to him in invitation. "See anything that looks good?"

"Wha…" he stammered again.

"This one is good," she supplied, handing him a gun and an extra clip of ammo before closing the armory.

Sam sat hard on the floor, staring at the gun in his grasp, only half cognizant of how it got there. Meanwhile Celeste moved to a window and stared outside. That got his attention.

"What are you doing? Get away from the window," he exclaimed. He tensed, ready to spring and tackle her to safety, but she turned to him with a smile.

"They're bullet proof. I had them put in before I moved in," she said. As if to prove her words, someone outside shot at the window. The bullet repelled and bounced away as if it were rubber.

"Still, I'd feel more comfortable if you weren't making yourself a target," Sam said. He patted the space beside him.

She sat and pulled her knees up to her chest. "There's only one truck. I can't see inside it. Maybe they're waiting for reinforcements. I can't imagine they would come unarmed, knowing what they know about you. And what they don't know about me. It seems like a good idea to wait a bit and let them tire themselves out."

"Okay. Why did you change your name from Nevaeh?" Sam said. He didn't care about the men outside. He'd spent too much of his life running and hiding, pretending to be someone he wasn't. He had no plans to leave Paradise, now or ever again. If Komeni wanted him, he'd have to come and take him. Until then, he wanted to know about Celeste.

"I only have vague memories of my parents. It's like I can sort of see them, but it's as if I'm only seeing their reflections by staring in a pond and there are all these ripples, distorting everything. I know for certain they were wholly unprepared for a child. They were never even together, not really. A fling that turned into a baby that was easily flung away. My mom abandoned me three times. The state kept giving me back. It wasn't until the fourth time that a police officer intervened. Apparently the state wanted to give me back again and he put his foot down, made them come get me, and take me somewhere else."

"Where did you go?" Sam asked softly. He didn't want to interrupt the flow of her memories, but she stopped talking and he both wanted and needed her to keep going.

"Foster care. It's true that people only want to adopt babies. By the time I was processed and my parents' rights were terminated, I was far past being a baby. No one wanted me at that point. I bounced from home to home, never connecting. I can't say any of my foster parents were neglectful or abusive. They provided my basic needs: some food, some clothes, a place to sleep. But none of them went over and above, none of them loved me or trained me or invested in me in any way. I got a basic education from school, I learned to read and write and do basic math. But no one ever taught me how to function outside of that."

Another shot pinged off the siding.

"That is getting really annoying," Celeste groused.

"How did you wind up working for The Colonel?"

She shook her head. "I'm not there yet, not even close. The Colonel is the best part of the story, the part where things start to turn around. Everything that came before is why I am the way I am."

"The way you are, you say that as if it is a bad thing. I love the way you are, the person you are."

She didn't reply and she wouldn't look at him. Instead she drew her knees impossibly closer, curling into herself the way she did whenever she didn't want to face something. He was afraid she was done talking, but she started again.

"When I was in fourth grade, my foster family had an older biological son. He took a shine to me, paid me special attention. I loved it. It was like having a real brother. Except then he began sneaking into my room at night. The worst part is that I liked that, too. Because no one had ever told me that wasn't something that should happen. I had no idea what was going on, only that someone seemed to love me. Someone finally noticed me.

"I was moved from that home soon after. I never knew why. If they found out what he was doing, they didn't hear it from me. I became, not surprisingly, extremely promiscuous. Now that my eyes had been opened to a new way to get attention, I began to seek it from other boys. The day after my tenth birthday, I lost my virginity. And I kept going, blazing through an endless string of boys, trying to pretend those few minutes they spent with me meant they saw me, they loved me."

She paused, opened her mouth, closed it again, took a breath, and continued. "By the time I reached high school, I had earned a nickname: The Original Mattress Factory. Because that's what I was, a mattress. But I didn't get that yet. I chalked the nickname, the stares, the whispers, the rumors, all of it up to jealousy. Guys liked me; girls wanted to be me.

"I joined the army and thought I should probably start fresh, turn over a new leaf. But that's not so easy. Everything felt like high school all over again. The only way I knew how to fit, to stand out and be special, was to be that girl again, to be The Mattress. And then The Colonel came along. He recruited me, with the caveat that I stop doing what I was doing. And I did."

"Just like that?" Sam asked.

"Would you believe me if I told you no one had ever told me to stop before? No one cared enough to even notice what was going on, what I was doing to myself. He was the first and only person in my life to actually look at me, to acknowledge my pain, and offer me a way out. Of course I took it, but..."

"But..." he prompted when she once again paused.

"But I didn't know how to function in the new reality I tried to create. The Colonel let me pick a handle, I chose Celeste, an homage to my heavenly birth name. When I started plotting who I wanted Celeste to be, I knew I didn't want men to be part of the equation, so I cut them out completely. Since I started working for The Colonel, I haven't had a date. I haven't had a relationship. I said no to every man who asked me out. Eventually they stopped asking. I've been celibate and completely alone. My world was my job. And then I retired, moved to Montana, and this terrorist stumbled into my orchard." She rested her chin on her knees, staring straight ahead, afraid to try and make eye contact. There was a particular sort of terror, now that she'd unburdened herself and let go of everything she'd been hiding. He was the first and only person she'd ever told. But there was also relief, a certain freedom that came from dragging all one's demons into the light of the day. *No more hiding,* she thought, letting out a complete breath for the first time in a long time.

Sam was quiet, staring thoughtfully at her while she continued to avoid his gaze. "Celeste," he began at last, and then paused. "Do you prefer Celeste?"

She nodded. Nevaeh was someone else, someone who lived in shame and fear and sadness. Someone who no longer existed. Maybe someday she would learn how to reconcile the two, but for now she preferred to keep them separate.

"Celeste," he tried again, but she sat up, sniffing.

"Do you smell that?"

Surreptitiously, he put his nose to his armpit and inhaled. "No."

"Smoke." She stood and walked to the window, gasping when she looked out. "No."

"What?" Sam asked, hopping up to stand beside her. What he saw made him almost physically sick. They had a propane torch and were using it to light the orchard on fire, tree by tree.

Celeste squinted, pressing her face farther against the glass. "Sam, that's not Komeni."

"How can you tell?" Sam asked. He had to speak past a lump. Her trees, her precious trees, filled with so much promise and potential.

"Because he's wearing a cowboy hat. That's the idiot from outside the bank." She checked her gun again and tucked it away. "This ends now."

"What? You can't go out there," he said, overcome by immediate panic. There were two of them and they were armed. They were huge, she was little. "I'll go with you," he said, checking his own gun.

"No, you stay here and cover me if I need it." She paused and gave him a cocky smile, the first one he'd ever seen from her. "Spoiler alert: I won't need it."

And then she was gone. She opened the front door and marched out, stalking toward the two men like a woman on a mission. Sam watched, gun at his side. *Should I shoot them?* He was an okay shot, but not perfect. The chance of hitting Celeste was too great. Besides, the men weren't doing anything yet, hadn't even noticed her advance until she stepped behind the big one, the leader, and tapped him on the shoulder.

He set aside his propane torch and faced her, a look of cold amusement on his stupid face.

"Well, well, well, you're not the one we want, darlin'. Send out your boyfriend. We'd like to have a word."

Celeste was angry and that was no good. Anger clouded her rational mind, causing her to be unable to make the sort of snap decisions she needed to make. She took a breath, pushing it away, reminding herself she was a soldier, not a woman in love, not the owner of an orchard that was now on fire.

"Get off my property. I'll send you a bill for the damage you've caused," Celeste said.

He smiled. "I don't think you understand, sugar. We're not leaving until we get what we came for. Your boyfriend needs to know he's not welcome here. We don't like that type."

"You're the one who is not welcome. This is your last chance to leave." She glanced at the smaller man behind him, obviously his toady. He grinned back with the spacy dimness of one not used to thinking for himself. "And take your trash with you."

"That's hardly friendly," the oaf said. "Me and Jed, we want to have some fun. We'll get to him, but now that I think about it maybe we should start with you. After all, you're the one who brought him here. Maybe you need to be taught a lesson about staying away from the wrong kind."

"If you like. I haven't had fun in too long myself. Of course, I think our definitions are different," she said. She withdrew her gun. Jed, the idiot on standby, shifted nervously. The oaf simply smiled.

"Aw, you're not going to need that. You best put it away before someone gets hurt."

"I didn't expect to agree with you on anything, but here we are. I'm going to slip it back in my ankle holster."

The oaf turned to Jed. "She got an ankle holster. Ain't that cute? Girls these days think they're so tough. They ought to teach them better, though. Strength always wins." Celeste bent over to refasten her gun. As she stood up, the oaf's hand shot out and gripped her bicep like a vise. She looked at his fingers.

"You should let me go," she warned.

"I don't think so," he said, smiling. "Let's go back behind the barn and have some fun." He began tugging her, back stepping toward the barn.

"I prefer to have fun right here," Celeste said. She was still half bent over with the knife she'd retrieved from her ankle. She used it to slice the tendon at the back of the man's knee. With a scream he went down, landing hard on his useless knee. Celeste grabbed him by the hair at the top of the head and peeled his head back, pressing the tip of her knife to his windpipe until it drew blood. "I'm going to give you one more chance to get off my property."

He flailed, trying and failing to grab her and fling her away. Being small and fast always worked to her advantage. She knew how to stand, how to hold herself just so, always darting and flitting out of range. By now the pain in his knee had to have fully registered, the realization that he could no longer stand, that he might never stand again.

"Shoot her," he called to Jed. "Shoot her and get her off me."

Jed shifted uncertainly, vacant cow eyes flicking from Celeste to the oaf and back again.

"You heard what he said. Shoot me," Celeste commanded.

Shaking now, Jed raised his gun and fired, as slowly and clumsily as everything else about him suggested, so slow it almost felt like slow motion to Celeste as she moved out of the way, putting the oaf in the bullet's path instead. By the time his body hit the dirt, she had her gun back out and trained on Jed.

"Drop it," she said, and he did. His gun clattered uselessly to the ground as he stared at the oaf.

"Is he dead?" tears and snot leaked out of every hole on his face.

Celeste didn't answer because she didn't know. At the moment her priority was securing the man who was still standing. "On your knees."

"Don't kill me," he pled, fully blubbering now. He dropped to his knees and put his hands on his head. Behind him she rolled her eyes. Clearly he had seen one too many mafia movies. Still, it was a handy reach for her to secure his hands with a zip tie and she did so, securing his feet and trussing them together like a calf. And then she stood over him, finger jutting in his face like a warning.

"When the authorities get here, you let me do the talking, do you understand? They're going to take you to jail, but if you think I can't get to you there, you're wrong. You'll let me handle this, or I'll track you down and finish the job. Are we clear?"

He nodded and turned his face to the grass, using it to wipe away the messy goo that covered him. Celeste checked the oaf. He had a pulse, but it was weak. She debated the merits of finishing him and found none. He was in God's hands now. If he made it, he made it. If not, so be it. Anything beyond this point would be a step beyond justice and into vengeance, something she swore an oath against years ago.

A truck barreled down her long driveway. Celeste shaded her eyes as recognition hit: Sam must have called Elliot. Overhead she heard the distinctive hum of an airplane. It swooped low and dropped something, either water or chemical foam that subdued the raging fire in her orchard. Too late, though. Half of her dry and decrepit trees had already succumbed. She turned her back, not wanting to see the destruction.

Elliot screeched to a halt and hopped down. "Celeste, are you okay?"

"I'm fine," she said. Belatedly she realized he might find her placid tone odd or off-putting. After all, her orchard was in shambles, she'd spent the last hour or so under siege being shot at, a half dead man lay at her feet, another tied up like the world's worst Thanksgiving turkey.

Elliot regarded her in silence, one eye blinking slowly as he took in the scene. "I see," he said at last, and she wondered if he did. He had been in the army. He had to have garnered at least a passing acquaintance with the sort of training she'd had. "What do we have here?" He toed the oaf with his heavy boot before squatting next to him, checking for a pulse.

"They wanted Sam," Celeste explained.

"And they got you instead," Elliot said, darting her a wry smile.

She shrugged, aiming for innocence. "My land, my rules."

"Now you sound like a true Montanan," he said. "So what happened?"

"This one," she pointed to the oaf, "grabbed me and made threats. This one," she thumbed toward Jed, "stepped up and tried to offer protection. I don't know if he meant to shoot him or it was an accident. Either way I'm safe." She glanced down at Jed who stared up at her in wonder. "Thanks. They'll probably take it easier on you, knowing that you tried to defend me like that." He blinked a vacant calf blink and licked his lips.

Elliot studied him. "Anything to add?"

"It's like she said," Jed agreed.

"Huh, I see," Elliot drawled again. "This is all very conveniently packaged and wrapped up for me."

"Merry Christmas," Celeste returned, and he laughed.

"I need to call the state for a transport, in case anyone needed to practice their assigned script some more before they get here," Elliot said. Jed nodded obligingly while Celeste remained stoic and silent. "Is Sam okay?"

Her glance slid toward the house. "It's been a big morning, lots of information. I take it he called you."

"Yes. He sounded fairly frantic on the phone, mostly about the fire." Elliot scowled at the ruined orchard. "I'm sorry, Celeste."

"It's all right," she said, but she didn't believe it. She was only starting to get to know the trees, had recently taken steps to fertilize them. Only three days ago she pruned her first four, tentatively and with lots of back and forth communication with Esther's father. And now half of them were gone, wiped away in an instant by the irrational hatred of the man at her feet.

"I don't know why people are so ugly sometimes," Elliot mused. "But there's good, too." By the smile on his face, Celeste knew he was thinking of his wife, Missy, whose kindness and good cheer must go a long way to counteract the things Elliot had to deal with.

Celeste turned away from that, too. She was happy for Elliot, glad he'd found some goodness in the world. She thought maybe she had, too, but what if she hadn't?

When she realized she was now staring at the house—the silent, empty house where Sam made no appearance, she turned away from that, making a circle of all the places she didn't want to look. In the end she turned her eyes skyward and reached for her phone. "Excuse me, I have to make a call."

Elliot chuckled softly. "I bet you do."

She wandered a few steps away as The Colonel picked up before the first ring.

"Situation contained," Celeste said, in lieu of hello.

"What exactly was the situation, Sergeant Major? Because it's not one of ours," The Colonel said.

"A local, unhappy with the shade of Sam's skin."

The Colonel grunted. "All the idiocy in the world we have to deal with, and that's the frosting on the cake."

It was all hate, something Celeste had realized long ago. Whether the tribalism took place in Afghanistan or Palestine or the United States, it always boiled down to hate, at its core.

"How many pieces do I need to pick up?" The Colonel asked.

"He's still intact for now. Not sure he's going to make it," Celeste said.

"And the package?" The Colonel asked.

"Still safe," Celeste said. Sam was safe, but then what? There was no time to think about that now.

"It's too late to scramble the team. They're already wheels up and will be there within the hour."

"I apologize, sir," she said.

"Don't, Sergeant Major. When we got your call, we took a peek at Komeni and it worked to flush him out. We managed the extraction and he's in custody. The team that's coming to you will do the wrap up. After that, your package is a free agent."

She swallowed hard. What would Sam do with that freedom? "Yes, sir. Thank you."

"And what about you, Sergeant Major? Is retirement everything you thought it would be?"

Celeste read the coded message. *Do you want to come back?* "It's... different than I expected, but..." She didn't know how to tell The Colonel she was still trying to heal. They didn't have the sort of gooey heart to heart conversations that took place on television.

"But necessary," The Colonel finished the thought for her.

"Yes, sir."

"We'll touch base when this is over. I'm going to want eyes and ears on the package for a while."

"He's solid, sir," Celeste assured him. Whatever Sam had done before, he wanted nothing to do with it now. Of that much Celeste was certain.

"I don't disagree, Sergeant Major. But Komeni's not the only one who wants him gone. It would benefit us all to babysit him for a while, to keep him safe. If only I knew such a person and such a place capable of such an undertaking." He cleared his throat.

At any other time Celeste would have smiled. By now she knew the man well enough to understand when he was making a pointed joke. But it had been a morning and a half and she was fresh out of humor. "Yes, sir," she muttered instead.

The Colonel hesitated, a signal that he'd caught her tone and read all that she left unsaid. "I've been around a long time, Sergeant Major. Trust me when I tell you things have a way of working themselves out in the most surprising manner sometimes."

He was gone before Celeste could fathom a reply, not that she knew what it might be. Was The Colonel secretly a romantic? Add that to the mystery that surrounded him, one that would likely never be solved.

By the time she finished her phone call, the state chopper arrived, followed by the medic. Two helicopters that landed on the far side of her property. Two troopers got out, followed by two medics. Celeste reached to the ground for some dirt, smearing it on her face. She put her hands in her hair, tousling it, and then widened her eyes a few times, mustering some tears. Her eyes felt gritty, the tears a little too ready. She walked to Elliot, who was now talking to the troopers as the medics bent over the oaf, checking his pulse.

Elliot glanced at her and did a double take, noting the fresh tears and dirt. "Sorry," she apologized, using the back of her hand to wipe her eyes. "it's been a rough day."

The troopers nodded at her in sympathetic understanding, towering over her much smaller size. One reached out to give her shoulder a reassuring pat and Elliot turned away, choking on a laugh he tried to turn into a cough.

The door to the house opened and closed and Sam eased out, coming to rest beside Celeste. She darted him a glance and found him studying her, eyes big and brown and brimming with concern.

Her eyes darted away, filled with real tears this time. She couldn't take his warmth and care, not right now, not with all she had told him still hovering uncertainly between them, a rejection waiting to happen. He reached for her hand. She crossed her arms, pretending not to notice.

The troopers weren't interested in talking to her, probably not wanting to traumatize her further after her "difficult ordeal," as the one who'd patted her shoulder said at least three times. She nodded along, biting her lip as she stared sadly at the ground. At one point she felt Jed's eyes on her. When no one was looking she shot him a glare, sliding her finger over her throat in an unmistakable gesture of warning. He nodded furiously, wiping his face in the grass again.

"It's like she said," he yelled, even though no one had asked him a question.

"You already told us," the trooper said impatiently.

"Yeah, but I really mean it. It happened just like she said. *Exactly*."

"Okay, now shut up," the trooper said, turning to his colleague with a shake of annoyance.

Jed turned imploring eyes to Celeste. She gave him an approving nod and he relaxed a little, apparently falling asleep.

"That one wouldn't know a bull from a potato," one of the troopers muttered.

Celeste was inclined to agree. She was glad she hadn't had to take him out. It was no fair to exterminate someone too stupid to understand the rules of the game.

Almost as soon as the troopers and medic and Elliot finally cleared the scene, a new chopper landed. The timing was so precise, it was almost as if it were planned, as if they'd been circling, which they undoubtedly had.

They tumbled out in tactical gear, Leo and a man Celeste didn't recognize, followed by Esther, a sharp contrast to the men with her long dress and big, windblown hair.

"Celeste, are you okay?" Esther asked, bestowing a tight hug.

"I'm fine," Celeste said, hugging her in return. At the moment she was more worried for Sam, who had turned tense and stoic as soon as the men stepped from the helicopter.

"Celeste," Leo's cheerful voice boomed. "You're not supposed to have this much fun when you're retired."

"It's a laugh a minute," Celeste agreed.

"Let's keep it to a dull roar from now on. This is my boss, Cameron Ridge." Leo gestured to the man beside him. If possible, Sam grew even tenser.

Celeste had a feeling he was the same lieutenant she met long ago, the night she helped the SEALs during their raid. But since the memory of that night was especially unpleasant, she didn't bring it up. "Sir," she said, extending her hand for a shake.

"Sergeant Major," Ridge said, returning her shake.

Sam quirked an eyebrow in her direction, giving her the side eye. "Sergeant Major," he muttered. But then he also extended his hand for a shake. "Cameron."

"Sam," Ridge returned. If possible, he sounded as tense as Sam. Clearly there was some history here Celeste wasn't privy to.

"I haven't had a chance to congratulate you yet. On the baby. Congratulations."

"Thank you. I think you'll understand that Maggie wanted to name him Cliff and I had to veto," Ridge said, lips twitching.

"Cliff Ridge," Sam said, shaking his head slowly. "That sounds about right for Maggie. Good call on the veto." They chuckled and a little of the tension eased. Ridge glanced at the house.

"Is there a good place to talk privately? There are some debrief items we need to go over."

"Of course. If that's okay with Celeste?" Sam turned toward her, seeking permission, and she didn't like it. She had told him it was his home. Did he not want it to be anymore? She gestured toward the house, trying not to stare as he and Ridge walked away.

"I'm going to take some pictures of the scene for our files," Leo said. He squeezed Celeste's bicep and turned away, withdrawing his camera.

"Let's check out the orchard," Esther suggested.

"What's left of it," Celeste murmured, trying not to sound as forlorn as she felt.

CHAPTER 32

They couldn't get too close to the orchard. The trees still sizzled with live coals and ash, the acrid smell of smoke hung heavy in the air.

"All your beautiful trees," Esther said.

They hadn't been beautiful to most people, but Celeste thought Esther understood. They had been beautiful to her because they represented a fresh start. Now, as with everything else in her life, they'd been destroyed. She folded herself carefully to the cool earth and surveyed the damage, telling herself her eyes watered because of the smoke. Certainly not because she was grieving for fruit trees.

"It's so sad," Esther said, sitting gently beside her.

They were silent a few moments, and it was nice, almost like an homage to the nature that had been lost. In any case, it eased some of the ache in Celeste's chest to have someone share and understand her misery. She took a breath and let it out slowly.

Esther turned to face her, tipping her head as she made a study of Celeste's features. "I'm not great at intuiting people's emotions, so tell me if I'm wrong, but you seem sad about something more than the trees. And I don't think it's the guy you've shot, given your job history."

"I told Sam about my past. My real name. Basically everything that's not classified." She rested her chin on her knees.

Esther paused thoughtfully again, digesting. She seemed to be trying hard to think before she spoke, to not blurt the first thing that came to mind. Celeste wondered if that was Leo's influence. He'd always been diplomatic that way. "How did he take it?"

"I don't know. We were interrupted by..." she gestured to the sad remains of her orchard.

"Oh," Esther said, facing forward. Now she rested her chin on her knees.

"How's married life?" Celeste asked.

"I spent a long time searching for the right word, only to discover it didn't exist in English. So I found it in Balinese: *Ramé*. It means both chaotic and joyful."

"And how did your parents take it?"

"Shockingly well," Esther said. "It turns out they weren't as into all the rules for our marriage as I thought they were. In fact when I told them we were already married, they were relieved. The stress of wedding planning was getting to them. They told all my hundreds of kinfolk we eloped, and that was that." She dusted her hands together to demonstrate and then faced Celeste. "Which brings me back to you. Sometimes people surprise us. They don't fit in the boxes we've created for them; they don't react the way we think they're going to. I'm not an expert, but I really think Sam cares about you. Give him a little time and space to adjust to the surplus of new information, and I bet he'll come around, too."

"I hope so," Celeste said.

"But also, either way you'll be okay. Platitudes and feel good sayings aren't my comfort zone; raw truth is. And that's the raw truth, Celeste. No matter what happens, you're going to be all right. You're healing and growing. I can see the changes in the short time I've known you. This life you're creating, it's going to be amazing, with or without the cute boy with the big brown eyes." She reached over and squeezed Celeste's shoulders and, despite everything, Celeste believed her. She even managed to laugh.

"You still notice cuteness, even after you're happily married?"

"It took twenty four years for me to notice men. I don't think that switch can ever be flipped back off again," Esther mused.

"Believe me, it can," Celeste replied. She hadn't allowed herself to get close to a man or be interested in one the last fifteen years. But Esther was right, with or without Sam she would continue to heal. Just because she wanted it to be *with* didn't mean she wouldn't eventually move on.

Esther moved closer and slipped her arm around Celeste's shoulders. "I brought you some cookies."

Celeste laughed. "How did you have time to make cookies before a mission?"

"I already had them at work," Esther replied. "When I heard we were coming here, I scooped them out of the break room and back into their container. Maggie was not thrilled. She gave me a five minute lecture on the effects of oatmeal on lactation, until I opened up the container and gave her two."

"Maggie is Ridge's wife?" Celeste asked.

"Sam didn't tell you?" Esther said.

"Why would Sam tell…oh. Maggie's the girl from his life before."

Esther pressed her lips together, looking miserable. "I have got to stop telling you things."

"No, you don't," Celeste said, resting her head on Esther's shoulder. "I like you exactly as you are, Esther. Please don't ever change or think you need to."

"You sound like Leo," Esther said fondly. "You two might be the only ones who don't get offended by my incessant blurting."

"That's what makes us the best," Celeste said.

"Absolutely," Esther agreed, giving her shoulders another squeeze.

They chatted about nothing at all until Leo came for them. "I think we're finished. How are you two holding up?"

"Better, if I could keep her," Celeste said.

"Sorry, she's too vital, both to the country and to me personally," Leo said, sitting on Esther's other side. "It's nice here, Celeste. Peaceful."

"Charred," Celeste noted, staring at the ruined remains of her twisted trees.

"Sometimes the best things come after a fire," Leo said

"That's pretty deep talk for a guy I once saw race a fifteen year old across the Nile," Celeste said.

"Oh, man, don't remind me. I got a parasite from that. But I had a pretty massive soul-scorching fire of my own. And look at me now." He bumped Esther's shoulder lightly with his.

"You look pretty great," Celeste agreed. "Both of you."

They sat in peaceful silence a few minutes until someone else joined them. Celeste's heart gave a little flop, but when she turned she saw Cameron Ridge. "Celeste, could I talk with you before we leave?"

"Yes, sir," she agreed. Neither of them was in the military anymore, but old habits died hard. She stood and dusted her backside, following him down the short rise to the steps of her house. There was no sign of Sam. Celeste didn't know if that was a good or bad thing.

"Sorry we missed the party. Thanks for letting us crash for a bit," Ridge said.

"It's no problem. You're welcome to stay, if that's easier."

"Thank you, but I need to get back, both to work and to my wife and son." He picked up a pine needle and twirled it between his thumb and finger. "You probably don't remember, it was so long ago, but we met once before."

"I do remember. It was sort of momentous," Celeste said.

"For us, too. I didn't realize it was you at first, with the name change and all. I didn't know you'd changed your name. All this time, you've been the famed Celeste The Colonel kept talking about."

"The Colonel talks about me?"

"A lot. You're one of his favorites, and with good reason. I knew you had something special that night long ago. That's why I called him."

She blinked at him, unable to translate what she was hearing. "You. You called The Colonel about me? I thought my commanding officer called him because I was in trouble. I thought you were mad at me."

"I was mad at myself. There we were, an elite SEAL unit, and an eighteen-year-old kid fresh out of basic snagged our haul. And took down the insurgent. It was humiliating, and also kind of awesome. All my men fell a little bit in love with you that night. I had to put the kibosh on any interest before it could take root or they would have ended in a fistfight."

"I thought you wanted to get rid of me because you were mad, because I was such a pest." She had run away with her tail between her legs, filled with shame as usual, certain he had been able to see her for the nothing she was.

"Are you joking? If my men hadn't had their tongues lolling, I probably would have hit on you myself. I'm a happily married man now, but you're a legend, girl. In fact I can't believe I'm sitting here with you, making casual conversation. Ethan's going to flip."

Celeste stared straight ahead, dazed. She had worn her shame like a shield, certain the first thing people saw about her was that unwanted, untrained, unskilled little girl. But what if that wasn't true? What if it had never been true? And what if the thing people saw in her was the truth? What if she was actually worthwhile, warts and all? What if she was working so hard to become perfect for nothing because she already had value as she was?

"Anyway, I wanted to touch base and thank you for the help all those years ago. You saved us a heap of work."

She shook her head to clear it, making herself focus on the moment. "No, sir, thank you. I don't think it's hyperbolic to say you changed my life that night. If not for your intervention in contacting The Colonel...well, things likely would have turned out much different."

"I tend to think things turn out exactly as they're meant to, so you never know. If he hadn't heard about you through me, I'm certain someone else would have mentioned. The Colonel has an eye for talent and potential, and you had it in spades. And from what I've heard over the years, you lived up to and then exceeded every estimate."

"Thank you, sir. That's very kind."

He stood and glanced uncertainly toward the house with a slight nod of his head. "Do me a favor and keep an eye on that one. Like it or not, I have a vested interest in his wellbeing."

"Me, too," she said, and he laughed.

"Good day, Sergeant Major."

"Good day, sir," she said, standing. She waved to Leo and Esther as they headed to join Ridge at the helicopter, waiting on the porch until they were gone, and then she turned and went inside her house.

CHAPTER 33

Sam sat on the couch staring into space. Celeste perched beside him with more space between them than she usually gave.

"How are you holding up?" she asked.

"Not great," he said. When he faced her, his eyes looked hollow. He'd been hit with the one-two punch of learning the truth of her past, followed by a run in with the current husband of the onetime love of his life. Not to mention the racist oaf who demanded his head on a platter for the sole sin of being the wrong color, from the wrong country. All in all not a great day to be Din Chatti. "How about you?"

"Same," she said. She took a breath. "It's been a long, sort of terrible day. Maybe we should call it a night and try again tomorrow." They needed to have a long conversation, the sort that went better after rest.

Sam swallowed hard and faced forward again with a little nod.

He can't even look at me anymore, she thought but quickly pushed it away. She wasn't exactly rational at the moment. It was possible exhaustion was clouding her emotions. Tomorrow she was certain things would look brighter. Probably not everything, but some things. And she'd have more energy to deal with them.

She went upstairs, took a long, hot shower, crawled between the sheets, and fell immediately asleep.

Sometime later she woke with a start, certain someone was in her room. And before she could reach for her gun or talk herself down, he spoke.

"How can you sleep at a time like this?" Sam demanded.

Squinting, Celeste snapped on the light. Sam stood beside her bed, frowning. "How long have you been there?" she croaked.

"I don't know. I poked my head in to assure myself you were still there and okay and got sort of lost staring at you while you slept."

"Creepy but okay," she said.

"Seriously, Celeste, how can you sleep?" he demanded tossing his hands in the air in frustration.

"Not well when you're yelling at me. Why are you yelling at me?"

"Because I'm so mad."

"What did I do?" she asked, voice going small and quiet. How had she messed up so badly without even knowing?

He sank to the bed beside her and gripped her shoulders. "I'm not mad at you. How could I be mad at you? So brave and kind and amazing. I'm mad at those idiot men who ruined your orchard. All your big plans to bring it back to life, and it's gone. Gone because of me. I swear. Everything I touch falls to ruin." He shoved his hands in his hair, dislodging it at his temples in the universal *I've lost my mind* gesture.

"What are you talking about? None of this is your fault."

"Of course it's my fault. If I hadn't come here, they wouldn't have bothered you. You wouldn't have had to fight someone almost twice your size, wouldn't have lost your orchard. This is all my fault, everything is my fault. I've been avoiding you all day because I didn't want to see that look in your eyes when you realized. I'm like King Midas except instead of gold it all turns to…charcoal." He gestured helplessly toward the orchard.

She laid a hand on his shoulder. "You are amazingly good at being astoundingly wrong," she said.

Slowly, he pulled his head out of his hands and swiveled to look at her. "What?"

"Why on earth would I blame you for any of that today? Nothing was your fault. You didn't make those men supernaturally stupid, didn't provoke them to attack. Bad things happen and we move on."

"But your orchard…"

"Bad things happen and we move on," she insisted, interrupting him. She dropped her eyes. "I thought you were avoiding me because of the things I told you."

"What things?" he asked, sounding so innocent she glanced up sharply again.

"What things? All the things, about my life, about my past."

"*Ya eazizaa*, why would I care anything about that? I'm sorry it hurt you, sorry for the ways you struggled. But it doesn't change who you are, nor how much I love you. Did you think it would? Or that it could?"

She nodded, eyes brimming with tears.

He nudged her aside and lay down, snuggling her tight against him. "What nonsense. You are my beloved, and I am the last person in the world to judge someone on her past. Didn't we agree too many things came before that have nothing to do with us?"

"But you kept pressuring me to tell you," she said. "I thought it was because it mattered."

"It does matter," he said, petting her head in that soothing way he had that made all her stress drain away. "It matters that you trust me with your secrets. I've given you all of mine, and you've kept them safe. I wanted to do the same for yours."

"What about Maggie?" she asked.

"What about her?"

"It must have been painful to see Ridge today."

"Must it? I thought it would, and I suppose it was a bit, if I'm being honest. But not the way I thought, not as much. Maggie is safe and loved and happy, I could wish for nothing better. And they have a baby, that's certainly something she and I never shared. I used to think of her as mine, but she's not and she hasn't been for a long time. She's his, and that's okay. As much as I used to resent him, I now appreciate him. He's good, he loves her, and he makes her happy. And you are good, and I love you, and you make me happy. We're all where we should be, I think."

She nestled closer, pressing her face into him and inhaling. *Home.* "I do love you," she said voice muffled.

"And are you happy?"

She paused. Was she? "Yes," she said slowly. Somehow, though she didn't believe it would ever be possible, she had created a life, one where she was beginning to reconcile her past, present, and future. One where she felt no need to run away from the truth of who she had been or try to perfect who she was becoming. She was flawed, incredibly, but so was Sam. Maybe so was everybody and they were merely better at hiding it.

Sam took her hand, threading their fingers together. "Are we going to stay in Paradise, even without the orchard?"

"Where else but this crazy town? I don't think anyone else would have us," she said.

Sam stared at their hands, a little sadly, she thought. "I'm not certain they want me."

"No, I don't believe that. Those men are not representative of Paradise, not the Paradise I've come to know and love. There are good people here, Sam. Don't let the bad ones push you away. Besides, I think you're wonderful and that's enough. Anyone who says otherwise can deal with me."

"Can't you tell me this last thing? Can't you tell me what you did for The Colonel?" he begged.

She shook her head. "I really can't. It's classified. But I've dropped a lot of clues, and so did Leo."

He squinted, trying to remember. "No, I would have remembered. All you said, all Leo said, was that if you told me you'd have to ki..." He broke off, his eyes doing the shocked blinky thing. "But, no." He glanced down at her, expecting confirmation or denial.

She remained mute.

"You are joking. You did not kill people for a living."

Again she said nothing.

"Celeste, no. I refuse to believe it. This is some quirk of your humor, of Leo's humor. You're in on it together. You are too tiny and adorable to be a killer. It's like a squirrel stumbled from the forest and started walking upright everywhere and wearing pants. And you expect me to believe that little squirrel is capable of killing people?"

"A few years ago a squirrel bit through a transformer and took out the power to the entire eastern seaboard for a week. Don't underestimate squirrels because they're small."

He stared at her, unblinking now. She sat up and kissed him. "Turn off the light. I'm so tired."

"I may never sleep again," he said, but he obligingly turned off the light, nestling close against her back. "Good night my little spoon. I love you so."

She gripped his arm where it lay on her stomach. "Sam."

"Hmm."

"I think our life is about to get very, very good."

"We'll make it so," he agreed, bestowing a sleepy kiss on the back of her ear.

Smiling, warm, safe, and happy, Celeste drifted to sleep.

CHAPTER 34

The next morning they woke to the sound of trucks barreling down the driveway. Lots and lots and lots of trucks. Celeste sat up, wild haired and confused. "It's a convoy." Her first thought was to warn everyone of IED's, proving army life would die a hard and slow death over the years to come.

"I don't know what it is," Sam said, yawning as he sat up beside her.

"I've got to get my gun," she said, hopping out of bed.

"You mean you weren't wearing it last night while we slept? That is progress," he said happily, slipping out of bed and padding down the hall behind her.

Someone knocked on the door and they froze.

"Terrorists with retribution on their minds probably don't knock," he whispered. "I think it's safe to skip the gun, just this once."

With a little nod, Celeste opened the door, blinking in surprise when she saw Maybe and Tony on the other side.

"Good morning," Maybe said cheerfully, doing the frantic wave thing once more, as if they were a great distance away and not right next to each other.

"Morning," Celeste said, giving her a few halfhearted hand flaps in return.

"We came to apologize," Tony said.

Maybe nudged him. "That wasn't how we practiced it. You were supposed to be smooth."

"I'm smooth by virtue of my existence," he returned and she retched loudly. They elbowed each other a couple of times, looking more like teenage siblings than grown friends, before coming to some kind of unspoken resolution.

"Anyway, we came to apologize," Maybe began again. "Because we feel bad."

"You do?" Celeste said. "But why?"

"Because we've put so much pressure on you about the orchard. It's not fair. All of us want it, true. But it's not a condition of all of us wanting you. Whether or not we ever have an orchard again doesn't matter. We're so happy you're here, Sam and Celeste, and we don't want you to go away."

"There were a couple of bad apples, orchard pun intended," Tony said when Maybe paused to dash at her brimming eyes. "We wanted you to know they have nothing to do with Paradise. They were a couple of drifters who became ranch hands and lingered. They're not from here, and they don't represent us."

"I appreciate that," Sam said, nodding.

"So do I," Celeste said. "You've made us feel so welcome. You've become…friends. As for the orchard, I think it's a loss."

"Well," Maybe drawled. "We were thinking about that, too. It was too much, expecting someone new and inexperienced to do all that work by yourself. So we had this idea…"

"A wonderful awful idea," Tony interjected. Maybe nudged him again, annoyed at the interruption.

"That maybe we should all help," Maybe blurted, anxious to get it out before Tony interrupted again.

"That's so sweet, but help with what? The trees are almost all gone," Celeste said.

"They're not, actually," Baird said, poking his head around the corner where he'd apparently been hiding during Tony and Maybe's *Laurel and Hardy* routine.

"Ta-da!" Fletcher announced, poking his head out from the opposite side, breathless and panting. "Sorry, I just got here and hopped over the porch railing. Firing trainer, not working well at all."

"What?" Celeste said, wary at the sight of Fletcher. If he was involved, it could be anything. And it was. Maybe took her hand and gave it a tug, urging her outside. They made space as she stepped onto the porch, followed by Sam. And then she saw them, practically all of Paradise, lined in a parade of trucks. And in those trucks were hundreds upon hundreds of trees, *fruit* trees.

"We thought we'd have a planting party," Maybe said, clapping her hands together excitedly.

"I thought that was supposed to be my line," Tony said resentfully.

"No, you were supposed to say… Oh, hush. You're teasing me," Maybe said, shoving his arm.

"From the moment we met," Tony agreed, turning his gleaming smile on Celeste. "What do you think?"

"I…I…I…" That was all she could utter. She tossed Sam an SOS, eyes brimming.

"We're so happy," he said, easing his arm around Celeste. "We already knew we loved it here and wanted to stay. This kindness is confirmation of that."

"Should we get started planting?" Fletcher asked. He glanced down at his hand. "I brought gloves. Got to protect the merchandise."

"It's okay, Fletcher. The television only cares about your pretty face," Tony told him.

Wow, Celeste mouthed to Sam. Apparently the entire town was in on the delusion of Fletcher's supposed fame.

People began unloading trees, asking Celeste where she'd like them. She had no idea. No one did. It turned out no one in Paradise had any idea what to do with fruit trees, besides plant them and hope for the best.

After the trees were unloaded and arranged, Elliot pulled Celeste aside. "I wanted to ask you something." He darted a look over her head, to make certain they weren't overheard. "I couldn't help notice that you seem well equipped to handle emergencies. Lately I've been feeling a bit overwhelmed, working two jobs, and I wondered if you might consider becoming a deputy, on a part time basis."

"Wow," Celeste said slowly. It came so naturally to say yes, she had to make herself pause to think about it. Being a deputy would be a natural fit, an easy transition from her last job. However… "Thank you so much for thinking of me, but I think I'm going to say no. I kind of want to explore a new path and figure out a life that doesn't involve keeping the peace. But I do know someone who is handy with a weapon and has a hero complex." Her eyes swiveled to Sam, at this moment holding one of Fletcher and Chloe's children on his hip and making her laugh.

"Do you think he'd be interested?" Elliot asked.

"I'll talk to him. I have some pull."

"He's so…*happy*," Elliot said with a grimace. "It would be like having my wife, but at work."

"Don't fall in love with him," Celeste warned. "He's taken."

Elliot snorted and gave her shoulder a light shove. They didn't talk about it again, but she noticed him watching Sam with a mixture of speculation and approval and was fairly certain an offer would be forthcoming.

Hours later, after Avery and her husband delivered food for the entire crowd, the planting was done, and everyone left, only Sam and Celeste remained. They lay on their backs hand in hand, staring up at the fading sunlight.

"You know this means we can never leave here," Sam mused.

"Spoiler alert: I never intended to."

"Me neither," he said happily.

A breeze drifted by. It was that sweet spot in late spring where any amount of sun or warmth brought swift giddiness and a promise of better things to come.

"Sam," she said softly.

"Mm," he returned, giving her hand an affectionate squeeze.

"This seems like a good time to tell you one more thing I left off my list. Another secret, a big one. Maybe the worst one."

"What's that?" he asked. To his credit he didn't sound tense or trepidatious at all, merely curious.

She took a deep breath and made herself say the words. "I really hate apples. So much. You have no idea."

He paused, then, "Good thing we didn't just plant two hundred of their trees."

She snorted a laugh and then couldn't stop. They laughed until they were spent, then crawled together, seeking warmth and each other.

Celeste sat up and smoothed the hair at his temple. "Are you hungry?"

"Always," he replied, smiling up at her, warm brown eyes brimming with affection.

"Come on." She stood and tugged him with her. They held hands on the way to the house. He planned to follow her to the kitchen and help prepare supper, but she led him to the couch, bade him sit down, and retrieved one of her journals, the first one in the series.

"Are you sure?" he asked, sounding a little awed. His tone made her feel humbled and more than a little loved. These were only her memories, and yet he was treating them like they were a precious treasure, merely because he wanted to know her.

"I'm positive," she said, trying to sound braver than she felt. She couldn't stick around and watch him read, though. It was too much. "I'll make supper." She could do that now that she'd learned to make an entire week's rotation of meals. *I can cook and love and open myself to the world around me; I am bent but not broken, well on my way to wholeness one baby step at a time.*

She whirled and immersed herself in preparing food. Tonight they would have chicken salad. As the first thing Celeste learned to make, it was now her go-to comfort food. She was nearly finished when she realized Sam stood in the doorway, watching her.

"Come here a moment," he said when he had her attention. He held out his hand to her. She took it and allowed him to lead her to the couch. He lay down and pulled her with him, encapsulating her in a full body hug, squeezing tightly.

"What's this about?" she asked, not that she was complaining. She enjoyed hugging, and she especially enjoyed hugging Sam, who was almost as deficient on his hug quota as she was.

"The common theme I'm reading in your journal is that you wanted to know you were safe and loved, and though it's a little late, I thought it seemed appropriate to pause and tell you that you are safe and loved. I am so proud of you. You are precious and worthwhile, and you always have been, even when no one else realized."

She squirmed a little, nestling closer as she hugged him back. "Thank you."

"Also, I think we should get a dog."

"What does that have to do with anything?" she asked.

"Every girl needs a dog. They're good therapy."

"Is this an elaborate way of making it seem about me, when you really want a puppy?" she guessed.

"Mitch and Caldwell's dog had a litter. They said we could have one. I told them I'd have to check with you. Please, pretty please can we get one?"

"I've never had a dog before," she said.

"Then it's well past time," Sam said.

"I'm nervous, but okay," she said. "Also, supper is ready."

"I'm hungry, but…"

"But…" she prompted.

"But I think maybe I like and need this more than food right now," Sam said, smoothing his hand on her neck, beneath her hair. He always seemed to know exactly how to touch her to make all her stress disappear, to bestow maximum affection, sort of like magic.

"Same," Celeste agreed.

They lay cuddled on the couch, feeling safe and warm and *content*, their supper forgotten until they eventually fell asleep. When they woke a few hours later, they ate their forgotten chicken salad and talked about their dog, attempting to preemptively find a name. It was all so ordinary, maybe even mundane, but Celeste had never been happier, and she knew Sam felt the same. And she realized, as they sat on the floor making a list of puppy names, that perhaps they had stumbled on some grand truth, that love made the ordinary extraordinary.

She rested her head on his shoulder and closed her eyes, a vision of their future dancing before her, so clear she could almost touch it. They would get their dog, and they would get married. Eventually they would have children, and those children would spend their days running barefoot on the orchard, greeting customers who came to pick fruit and buy apples. They would grow old together; Sam would shrink and his belly would round, Celeste would become a brittle wisp, but they would remain happy and in love, forever in Paradise.

ABOUT THE AUTHOR

Vanessa is a foodie who also loves to write. When she is not trying to find new ways to use sourdough, she likes to troll bakeries and taste test chocolate chip cookies. She lives in rural Ohio with her husband, children, and sheepadoodle. Her life's goal is to fill her books with enough coziness and sunshine to make someone smile. She would love to hear from you, drop her a line on email or facebook.

9 781953 339423